for better or for worse

diann hunt

THOMAS NELSON
Since 1798

NASHVILLE   DALLAS   MEXICO CITY   RIO DE JANEIRO   BEIJING

Published in Nashville, Tennessee, by Thomas Nelson. Thomas Nelson is a registered trademark of Thomas Nelson, Inc.

Thomas Nelson, Inc. titles may be purchased in bulk for educational, business, fund-raising, or sales promotional use. For information, please e-mail SpecialMarkets@ThomasNelson.com.

Unless otherwise noted, Scripture quotes and references are from HOLY BIBLE, NEW INTERNATIONAL VERSION®. © 1973, 1978, 1984 by International Bible Society. Used by permission of Zondervan Publishing House. All rights reserved.

Publisher's Note: This novel is a work of fiction. Names, characters, places, and incidents are either products of the author's imagination or used fictitiously. All characters are fictional, and any similarity to people living or dead is purely coincidental.

Library of Congress Cataloging-in-Publication Data

Hunt, Diann.
    For better or for worse / Diann Hunt.
      p. cm.
    ISBN: 978-1-59554-195-6 (pbk.)
    1. Middle-aged women--Fiction. I. Title.
PS3608.U573F67 2008
813'.6--dc22

Printed in the United States of America

08 09 10 11 RRD 6 5 4 3 2

To Jim, the man of my dreams,
who has loved me "For Better or For Worse"
for thirty-two years and counting.
Thank you for the awesome journey, honey.
I love you!

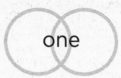

one

As the morning sun peeks over chilly mountaintops, warming frost from grassy tips and shaking loose the musky scent of bark and soil, I'm inspired to break into my own rendition of "the hills are alive with the sound of music," punctuated by a couple of twirls. But I don't share the talent of Julie Andrews, and the fact that I am jogging in Craggy Park at a mountainous altitude makes twirling—and singing—out of the question.

Barren trees stand cold and shivering in the late January breeze, but it's only a matter of weeks before spring comes calling in Smoky Heights, Tennessee—and with it, hope. That's what I have these days. After a rough season of grief, I've finally settled into the single life, and things are looking up . . .

Until I see Marco Amorini jogging my way with his dog.

Lean and muscular, Marco has a comfortable stride. Confidence looks good on him. Wish I could wear it. The morning breeze ruffles his dark, wavy hair, reminding me of how my own must look, since I only whipped it up into a scrunchie before leaving the house.

Before I have time to worry about it, a black cat dashes across my path. For the record, I'm not superstitious. But any colored cat crossing my path is not a good thing—for me or the cat.

Marco's boxer peels into a cheetah-like run, heading straight for me, leash straggling behind, slobber splashing the air, ears pointed and reared back, eyes focused on the cat.

"Brutus, get back here."

Before you can say *Lassie*, the boxer darts in front of me, causing me to fall in a heap at Marco's feet.

"Are you all right?" He bends over me, places one strong arm around me, his other hand warm and reassuring on mine, lifting me to my feet as though I were the size of Tinker Bell.

Oh, why didn't I put on makeup this morning?

After dusting myself off, I look straight into eyes the color of cocoa beans and try not to gulp. I will myself to breathe while shamelessly taking in his sculpted cheekbones, the firm set of his jaw, his straight nose. He blinks, causing Logan's words to shake loose in my mind.

Amorini victimizes women and laughs himself all the way to the bank.

"Are you sure you're all right?" Marco's voice is gentle and kind, not at all what I would have expected. Though something about him seems guarded. He's not smiling—although that could be because I'm standing on his foot.

"Are you all right?" he asks again.

I'm fine. Thank you, Mr. Amorini."

"Do I know you?" Dark, neatly trimmed eyebrows lift in a quizzical fashion. "Represent your husband in a divorce action?"

"My husband died three years ago."

"I'm sorry."

"Our kids went to school together," I continue. "Well, my son and your daughter, anyway."

He nods, but I can tell by the look in his eyes he has no idea who my kids are.

"I'm Wendy Hartline." I extend my hand. "My daughter, Brooke, is older, though, so you wouldn't have known her. But Colin was in Sophia's grade. He's away at college now."

Strong, rough fingers—calloused by years of paperwork, no doubt—curl around my palm, making me feel petite.

Still no noticeable spark of recognition. He thinks a minute and shakes his head. "Sorry, doesn't ring a bell. But I do recognize your name. We're going to be neighbors soon."

His teeth are white and dazzling. I can almost picture him in a top hat and dancing shoes. My heart skitters with the speed of hummingbird wings.

"Neighbors? You're moving into Mountain View Addition?"

"No, actually, I'm moving onto Appalachia Boulevard, right next to your chapel."

A hesitating breath hovers in my chest, refusing to release.

"The lodge that's been standing empty. You probably know the guy who built it filed bankruptcy. He had hoped to build a resort out of that area. I suspect he wanted to buy your place eventually."

The close flap of bird wings causes us both to look up briefly.

"The construction is pretty much finished, just a few tweaks needed, furniture set in place."

He stops and studies me while I try, in vain, to speak.

"Anyway, I bought the lodge and plan to open just after Valentine's Day. Which reminds me, I'd like to talk to you about co-owning the pond area. That would give my guests the opportunity to sit out there or walk the path around it."

This man is moving into my corner of the world, threatening my business, wants to co-own my pond, and I'm supposed to be okay with this?

"I'll have to think about it," I manage to speak out.

"It could benefit us both, you know. I'd help you with the maintenance of it, give you some extra cash."

Before I can respond, he glances at the gathering clouds.

"Yes, ma'am, the lodge is going to be first class all the way. Restaurant on the main floor. Heated pool, exercise room, honeymoon suites with heart-shaped tubs. For now, you can get them married. I'll take care of the honeymoon."

Hot adrenaline rumbles in my ears. *And when things don't work out, they can come to you to handle the divorce?*

I keep the thought to myself, as usual. I always thought by the time I reached middle age I'd be able to speak my mind, but I've never figured out a way to quell my constant need for approval.

"There's nothing worse than a job unfinished," he says.

"And how nice for you to profit from the other businessman's misfortune."

He shrugs. "Last time I checked the law books there was no crime in making money. I'm not the one who made him go bankrupt."

Whatever.

Not that I would wish bankruptcy on anyone, but once I had heard the lodge was no longer a threat, I was sleeping better at night. Now this. What would it mean for my wedding chapel and cozy cabins?

Marco is still defending himself. "What's the harm if I help myself in the process?"

Something tells me I hit a nerve.

His penetrating gaze causes me to shift on my feet.

"Besides, I don't know why you're complaining. For now, it should bring in more business for you."

"I'm not complaining, Mr.—"

"Marco."

"Amorini," I finish stubbornly. "I'm merely interested in how it will affect my business. Being a business owner yourself, I'm sure you can understand that."

So much for liking the man.

"So you're afraid I'll be competition?"

"I'm not *afraid* of anything," I say, carefully measuring my words to hide my annoyance.

This guy is a piece of work. I don't care if he does have good legs. Actually, now that I've gotten a better look, his knees are knobby.

Amusement lights his eyes. "Let's be candid, shall we? No doubt your little cabins have their place. Let's see . . . Snow White, Cinderella, Sleeping Beauty, and . . ."

"The Little Mermaid," I say dryly.

He snaps his fingers. "Yeah, that's it. A little cheesy, but to each his own."

My mouth dangles like a broken door hinge while my voice hides in some dark corner of my esophagus.

He hesitates momentarily. "We'll be catering to different wallets."

Pete's Dragon has nothing on me. With the least bit of encouragement, I could scorch Marco Amorini in one breath.

Brutus tugs on his chain, causing Marco to sidestep. "Guess he's ready to go. No doubt I'll run into you again soon, Wendy."

Not if I can help it. I don't care in the least that the way he says my name takes my breath away. Once I get it back, he'd better run.

Marco Amorini has met his match.

On my way to work, I spot vultures circling roadkill. That pretty much sums up my morning. Well, if Marco thinks I'm going to roll over and play dead while he takes away my business, he's got another thing coming.

"Wow, Antonio Banderas moving to our neck of the woods," Roseanne Raynor, my assistant and best friend, says in reverent awe while her nails clatter through her office desk drawer in search of something.

"Good morning to you too," I say, closing the door behind me and shrugging off my jacket.

Though we met about ten years ago when Roseanne and Gill started attending our church, I feel as though I've known her all my life. She stood by me through the dark days of losing my husband, held my hand when I struggled to breathe, and spoiled me with chocolate when I needed it.

"Oh, good morning." Whatever it was she needed from her desk, she didn't find. She gets up and walks over to peek out the blinds. "I still can't believe how much that man looks like Antonio," she says with a sigh.

"You think everybody looks like Antonio Banderas." Should I point out Marco's knobby knees?

Our office in the chapel smells of coffee and sweet perfume lifting from the potpourri—or Roseanne, I'm not sure which. With two desks, several filing cabinets, a table and chairs for conference purposes, and a couple of extra chairs for waiting, it's small but adequate. Our walls are a mixture of wedding white, burgundy wine, and rosebud pink. Wine-colored accents splash about the room in pictures and accessories. Warm and romantic, and just right for a wedding chapel office.

"I do not. Logan doesn't." Roseanne walks back to her desk, plops in her chair, adjusts the zirconia-studded turquoise bifocals perched atop her strong nose, and clicks on the small desk fan in front of her, causing her dangling earrings to jangle with abandon. Some days I worry that they'll get caught in the fan and suck her right in.

"Logan has blond hair and blue eyes. He could hardly look like Antonio Banderas."

"Exactly." She straightens the gold chain attached to her glasses. Something in her tone tells me I should be offended, but I ignore her.

"And Gill?" I ask, referring to her husband of twenty-two years.

She gets all dreamy-eyed. "Gill doesn't have to look like Antonio. He's, well, Gill."

"You are profound beyond words." I dig in my purse for my hand lotion.

She gives a slight nod. "It's a gift." With her back to me, Roseanne thumbs through the green hanging folders in the filing cabinet, charm bracelet tinkling.

"There's no reason you can't be friends with Marco, Wendy. Just give him a chance." Roseanne shoves the filing drawer back into place, causing it to close with a bang. "So he's a divorce attorney. There's no law against divorce, you know."

I glare her way, but she doesn't notice. "This coming from the woman who recites the consequences of divorce like a schoolgirl quoting the Pledge of Allegiance?"

"Hey, I just want to spare others from going through what I did." She gets a whiff of the lotion I've just rubbed into my hands. "Oh, that smells delicious, like a mixture of citrus and mint."

"Good nose. Want some?"

"Sure."

I put a swirl in her hand. "Besides, Mr. Amorini took almost everything Logan owned in the divorce settlement and gave it to his adulterous wife. That's just wrong."

Roseanne pulls out an emery board and begins to saw on her fingernails, which, by the way, look lethal. "Logan's a nice guy, but I'm not sure he's the one for you."

"No one said I'm ready to meet him at the altar. But he's nice to have around."

Just then the front door swishes open. A young man's smiling face peers over the top of a dozen red roses. He looks at Roseanne. "Are you"—his gaze flits to the card on the vase—"Wendy Hartline?"

She sighs and points in my direction.

"For me?" I bury my face in the abundance of fragrant petals and take a deep whiff. "Thank you."

He smiles and walks out the door.

Roseanne crosses her arms at her chest and stares at me while tapping her toe. She's a multitasker, that one.

I glance at the card from Logan. "See what I mean? Nice to have around," I say, drugged by the flowers' sweet perfume.

She sighs. "He's romantic—I'll say that for him." She fingers a petal. "But I thought you preferred daisies."

"I do, but Logan always forgets that. Hey, who am I to complain? Nobody's perfect." I look up at her. "Did I tell you we both love coffee shops?"

"On this you would base a lifetime commitment?"

"I told you—I'm not ready for the altar." After I find a spot on my desk for the vase of flowers, my fingers work through the arrangement, moving a sliver of baby's breath to the front of the vase, plucking one rose and putting it behind another.

"Well, that's what you're all about, right? Surely that has to be where this is headed, or you wouldn't still be with him after, what, a year?"

"Seven months." Her comment sucks the joy right out of me. I jot a note on a slip of paper to call the photographer to finalize plans for the Nelson wedding next month. "We're comfortable with things the way they are. Besides, I'm not sure I want to get married again. I'm just beginning to enjoy the single life. I can do what I want, when I want, with no one to answer to."

I can't imagine another man coming close to Dennis. We had a great marriage. Before I can allow myself to sag into a blue funk, I walk over to the coffeepot and pour myself a cup.

"Hey, how come you're limping?"

I turn around. "Was I?"

She nods.

"Wonder if I should sue Marco's dog?" I say with a vindictive laugh, then tell her what happened this morning.

Roseanne shoves her chin onto the edge of her palm and gazes dreamily into the distance. "Two lovers find each other in the misty dawn . . ."

I'd better hide the wedding books.

"Stop talking that way right this minute, Roseanne. Logan could walk in."

She rolls her eyes. "Logan Schmogan."

My face must show my distress, because she begins to babble. "I'm sorry. I know Logan is a good guy. He's handsome, romantic, all the things a woman wants in a man, but Antonio, er, uh, Marco—"

Holding up my palm, I say, "Let's not go there. The Anglin wedding is this weekend, and we have plenty to do." I flip through my wedding schedule to the appropriate page, pause, then look up at Roseanne. "And, just for the record, I plan to stay as far away from Marco Amorini as I possibly can."

9

Just after dinner, I step into my workroom in the basement. I figure I have a little time to do some work before Logan comes over.

This inner room blocks out all distractions, and I'm free to let my creative side soar. The smell of fabric tinges the air. Large industrial machines hug the cream walls. Bolts of cotton, polyester, and silk line a shelf. A variety of laces bulges from another.

Settling into my padded chair, I lift the gauzy material that will go in my dining room. Out of one piece of material I plan to make a throw swag that will fall to the floor; then I will bunch it into bishop sleeves with decorative ties to give it a more elegant appearance. Without a man in the house, I figure I can do frilly.

The serger hums along the material, wrapping the thread around the edge, giving it a nice, finished look. Snipping off the excess thread, I pull it out and look it over. "Perfect."

After Dennis died, some of our out-of-town friends came for a visit. Our guest room was in need of redecorating, so I created curtains, bed pillows, a duvet, and comforter. A couple of my church friends saw them and wanted me to make some for them. So now I usually have a project of draperies, pillow shams, or bed covers going.

Roseanne joked once that I should sell the chapel and start a new business, but I could never do that. The chapel was Dennis's life.

It just wouldn't be right.

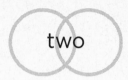

two

"Here we go." Handing Logan his iced soda, I reach for mine, along with a deep bowl of popcorn, and settle in beside him on the plump, blue-and-yellow-patterned sofa in my living room, tucking my feet beneath me.

Smoke curls from a flickering candle nearby, lifting the scent of freshly scrubbed apples. Logs simmer and hot twigs snap and crackle from my stone hearth. Before long, it will be too warm to enjoy the fireplace.

"This is nice." Logan smiles, gives my lips a quick brush with his own, then shoves another handful of popcorn into his mouth.

I give him a sideways glance. His shirt puffs at belt level, threatening to spill over and run amuck. His jeans have seen better days. Logan is no clotheshorse, but I'm okay with that. He's at home in flannel and jeans, and when the weather is too warm, he'll happily don an oversized T-shirt, no matter if it boasts the latest college team or a Shakespeare quote. He wouldn't wear a suit if you paid him, though he does wear a sport jacket and jeans to class.

"Thank you for the beautiful roses, Logan. What was the occasion?"

"As I said on the card, just wanted you to know I was thinking about you." He gives my hand a quick squeeze, leaving behind a smattering of salt, which I discreetly brush with a napkin.

"Well, it was very thoughtful. They're beautiful." Not daisies, but still beautiful.

We munch quietly on our popcorn, mesmerized by the bluish-gold flames in the fireplace.

"How did classes go today?" I ask.

He stretches out his legs and plops them on the coffee table. "Oh, you know Mountain View; it's pretty much same old, same old. Not like UT or the big college campuses."

"I thought you liked the charm of a small community college."

"I do. It just doesn't have a lot happening. Teaching literature doesn't exactly get the students' pulses thumping. They figure what's the use in studying writings by dead people?"

It seems to me they have a point. "Surely, some kids are into it?"

He shrugs. "Sure, some students are motivated, but some are just occupying space. Guess it depends on who's paying the bill." Another handful of popcorn.

Making sure he swallows most of his popcorn first, I say, "Did I tell you that I ran into Marco Amorini today? Literally?"

Logan's feet drop to the floor. He sits up and turns a Barnabas Collins-*Dark Shadows* expression my way. "Oh?"

I explain about my run, the cat and dog, all that. The calming little munch thing he was doing on his popcorn earlier has been replaced by fierce chomping.

"I shouldn't have mentioned it. The man obviously upsets you."

"He's a jerk," Logan says, surprising me.

That's not the way he usually talks. But when it comes to Marco Amorini, Logan is just not himself.

"There's something else."

He stops midchomp and looks at me.

"You might want to swallow that first," I say, and pause. "He's taken over that lodge next to my chapel. Going to finish it and run, well, a lodge."

At this Logan's eyes grow wide, and his face turns a frightening shade of red, as though he's tried—and failed—to swallow a chicken whole. I whack him on the back and mentally run through everything I know about the Heimlich maneuver. The first thing that comes to mind? Rule number one, never pound a choking victim on the back.

"Get up!" I shout, already crawling behind his back, whacking him upside the head with my left leg as I struggle to wedge myself between him and the sofa cushions. It's hard to tell where his navel is with all the commotion, but I try to position my fist just above his belly button, below the ribcage, at the point of his upper abdomen, and push. Fear brings out strength I didn't know I had. After a couple of thrusts that could pull up his spleen, his airway clears, and he gulps in air like a nervous groom. The gasping finally dies—for lack of a better word—and Logan credits me with saving his life.

"It's nice to know I can count on you in a crisis, Wendy." There is a sort of sexy 007 ring to Logan's thick, raspy voice, but knowing he almost died to imitate James Bond takes the thrill out of it.

"Drink some more tea." I hand his glass to him, praying he doesn't choke again. I haven't got the strength.

Just then someone shoves through the front door, and since I can't see who it is from the living room, I head into the entryway—but not before grabbing the popcorn bowl. Since they apparently have a key, they're most likely friendly visitors, but if not, I'll greet them with food.

"Hi, Mom."

"And how are the Waynes tonight?" I ask my daughter and her husband.

Brooke's voice sounds cheerful enough, but the look on her face tells me something's up. I give her and Kevin hugs, which they return with all the warmth of a mountain thistle. I know what that means. They're fighting. Again.

"Come on in. Logan and I were just having some popcorn. You want some?"

Brooke flips her silky-blonde hair behind her shoulders, shrugs off her jacket, and hands it to me. I give her the popcorn bowl in return and wonder if we've made a fair trade. Grabbing Kevin's coat, I hang the jackets in the hall closet.

They head for the living room, and I study them. Brooke has always been our confident one. At five-eight, curves in all the right places, and not an ounce of fat, it's easy to see why she walks as though she owns the world. She didn't get her confidence from me. I have to ask the advice of at least five people before I change dish-washing liquids.

Brooke and Kevin have only been married a year—not long enough to work up any real problems, in my book. 'Course, they say the hardest part of a marriage is the first five years. Maybe that's true. These days it seems they're always arguing.

I'm heading for the living room when Kevin steps around the corner, causing me to jump.

"Oh, sorry, Mom."

I like it that he calls me that.

He leans in and whispers, "Listen, I need to talk to you. Could you meet me tomorrow, say around five o'clock?"

The secrecy sends a shock of alarm through me. "Sure, Kevin. Come by the office. We can talk there."

"Thanks."

I smile and nod, trying to hide my fear.

After I serve the kids sodas, I return to Logan's side. "So what have you been doing tonight?"

Brooke lifts her chin. "We went to dinner." Her voice lacks luster.

A mother notices these things. I also notice a hippo could sit comfortably in the space between them. "Well, that sounds nice," I say, plumping a pillow and trying to think of a good joke to lift the dark cloud from the room.

"It wasn't," she says sharply.

Our eyes lock. Tension spreads around my heart, threatening to choke off my happy self. There's always been a sharp edge to Brooke that could slice my parental self-confidence to ribbons. Maybe she has the same effect on Kevin.

The clueless one, Logan, jumps in the ring. "Bad server?" He digs through the popcorn bowl in search of the last remaining kernels.

Brooke's hard gaze flits to Kevin. "Something like that."

His jaw clenches.

This type of tension steals the air from my lungs. I suck in just enough oxygen to keep myself conscious and offer an apologetic, "I'm sorry."

Brooke rolls her eyes, and I almost snap my fingers. She hates it when I say that. She says I'm always apologizing for the world. And I guess I am. But I truly am sorry they're having an off night. Why can't I say so?

Kevin ignores her. "Hey, Mom, we drove by the chapel and saw some guy walking around the lodge. Somebody gonna get that place up and running?"

Thankful for the change in conversation, my air passage balloons and I breathe deeply.

Logan makes a face. "Tall guy, dark hair?"

Airflow halts and retreats in the opposite direction.

"That's the one," Kevin says.

"His name is Marco Amorini. Thinks he's Robin Hood. Only he steals from the poor and makes the rich, richer."

I half expect Logan to spit after saying that.

"Wonder if that's Sophia Amorini's dad? She went to our high school. I think she was in the same class as Colin," Brooke says, leaning forward. Her legs are crossed, hands cupped around one knee, leg swinging violently. With a little more effort she could break into a Jackie Chan routine and chop my coffee table in half with one thwack of her high-heeled foot.

"That's the one." I refrain from saying more. Logan and I both have finally settled into a normal breathing pattern, and I kind of hate to spoil that.

"Do you think he'll take business from you?" Brooke asks matter-of-factly. Not a smidgen of concern in her voice.

My daughter and I have always struggled with our relationship. I tried to learn from my own upbringing—to provide our kids with a little more breathing room than I had, not to get overly involved. I've also tried to be there when they wanted me. Brooke has always favored her dad, and I suppose that's just the way it is with girls— me seemingly the only exception to the rule.

"You bet he'll take her business. That's the kind of jerk he is," Logan says.

My hand reaches over and touches his arm. "I'll be fine. I'm not worried about it."

The conversation then moves to the skyrocketing housing prices. Before long the evening is spent, and I'm not at all sure why Kevin and Brooke stopped by, unless it was so Kevin could set up a time to meet with me.

Maybe he's going to do something special for Brooke. A party or something, and he doesn't want her to know. That thought makes me feel tons better and lifts the boulder from my chest.

By the time I slip in between my bedsheets, I'm feeling much better about my meeting with Kevin. Of course, I'm ignoring completely the expression I saw on his face. He was probably just in a bad mood because of their argument. Or heartburn from their dinner. Probably had something with garlic in it.

Yeah, that's what it was. He ate garlic. I'm sure of it.

"Oh, my goodness, there he is! There he is!" Standing at the office window that overlooks Marco's parking lot next door, Roseanne screeches like a teenager at a Beatles sighting. She claps her hands, causing her multicolored bracelets to clang together and her jasmine perfume to waft through the room.

"Roseanne, don't let him see you." I step up behind her and peer over her shoulder.

Marco is standing in the late afternoon sun talking to some men just as a plumber's truck pulls around the corner and into his parking lot. Great. That's just great. I pour myself a mug of coffee.

Roseanne abruptly turns, causing her dangling earrings to sway like a willow branch on a breezy day. "I don't see what you're getting so stirred up about."

"Who says I'm stirred up?" I rub my fingers across my forehead where pain has begun to spike.

"It's four-thirty and you're drinking coffee."

She stares at me too long, and I want to tell her to take a picture—it lasts longer.

"Okay, spill it," she says, fists perched on her ample hips.

"Spill what?" I reach into my top drawer and pull out a bottle of Advil.

"You get headaches when you're stressed. What are you stressed about?"

"Nothing." Shaking two pills loose from the bottle and into my palm, I down the tablets with a swallow of coffee.

Roseanne sighs and sashays back to her desk. "It's your business, I guess." Her tone tells me she's hurt that I'm keeping something from her.

Before I can apologize, the front door swooshes open, allowing a gust of winter's chill to burst inside. Marco Amorini steps in, rubbing his hands together briskly. He locks eyes with me, and I swallow my voice with the Advil.

"Would it be all right if I used your phone? My cell is acting up again, and of course we don't have phone lines installed yet at the lodge."

So the little weasel comes crawling to me. I should tell him he can find a public phone booth in town. That thought shocks me. I'm never mean like this. Well, almost never.

"Sure. You can use mine." I step away from my desk to allow him my seat.

Again I get that whiff of sage and cedar that appears to be his registered trademark—though I think a wolf scent would better suit him.

He punches in a couple of numbers while Roseanne and I exchange a glance.

"Hey, Doug, I was wondering when the floor guys were coming out." Pause. "Yeah, uh-huh. Well, I can't stick around tonight. They will have to come in the morning now."

Embarrassment rushes over me when Marco turns my way, making me aware that I'm hovering. A slight smile plays on his lips, and I frantically rustle through the cabinet behind my desk, knocking a file over in the process, scattering papers about on the floor. Once again, I am at his feet.

Trying desperately to ignore him, I sweep my hands across the floor to gather the papers. After I stuff them back into the file, I turn around just as Marco stands up. We're so close we could rub noses. His handsome face doubles to two, or maybe that's just wishful thinking on my part.

I blink. They're still there. Both of them. Staring at me. My knees begin to crumple. *Please, not now!* I can't have an episode in front of Marco. But my muscles continue to slacken, and I reach out to grasp empty air.

"She's going down!" Roseanne shouts.

Sheer horror shadows Marco's face, and the next thing I know, he scoops me up with his strong arms and pulls me so tight against his warm chest that I can feel his heartbeat. Under different circumstances, I might enjoy this.

My face tingles with warmth. My legs are limp and dangling. If they would work for me right now, I might get down. Then again, maybe not.

"You all right?" His breath brushes against my face, causing my skin to tingle.

Before I can answer, the front door bangs open again. This time, Logan steps into view.

For the span of a heartbeat no one says anything.

Logan glowers at Marco.

Marco looks from Logan to me, shifts me in his arms, then shoots back a triumphant grin to Logan.

I share a glance with Roseanne, whose eyes absolutely, positively refuse to blink.

"Don't let me down," I whisper to Marco, knowing that my leg muscles aren't quite back just yet. It usually takes a couple of minutes, which right now feels like an eternity—in heaven, mind you, but eternity nonetheless.

"Wasn't going to," he whispers back, pearly whites dazzling me so that I may not see for days.

"So, Logan, um, how are you?" I ask pleasantly.

There's nothing wrong here, why should I feel guilty? Okay, so I'm in the arms of another man. I'm not married to Logan. Though I suppose Friday night dinners entitle him to some sort of explanation.

He gapes and takes a step toward us. Marco tightens his grip and shifts me in his arms once again. I can't help wondering if his arms are in danger of falling off, what with no circulation coming through and all.

"Listen, Logan, I'm having trouble with this letter, and I wonder if you could help me," Roseanne says, grabbing Logan by the arm and practically dragging him over to her desk.

This all could have been easily settled had I told Logan somewhere along the way that I have a problem with cataplexy—a medical condition associated with narcolepsy that can cause varying degrees of temporary muscle loss. In my case, my legs fold for a few minutes.

But I hadn't told him. I mean, it just never came up. "Pass the peas, please. Oh, by the way, have I mentioned that I have cataplexy? Yep, those doggone legs just fold on me without a moment's notice." Besides, it hadn't bothered me in so long the doctor took me off my meds. I thought it was in my past. Obviously, if Marco stays around, I'll have to call for another prescription.

A few minutes later a tingling sensation comes back to my legs, and I start to feel normal.

"You can put me down now," I say with as much dignity as I can muster.

"Why?" Marco asks, his mouth split open wide. The man is a walking dental advertisement.

Much as I'd love to snuggle further into his chest, my arms wouldn't let me if I wanted to. They're starting to tingle. Hopefully, they won't go limp on me too. Nothing like having my arms droop to the floor like a chimpanzee on muscle relaxants.

I glance at Logan, who is bending an ear toward Roseanne but obviously wanting to look my way.

"Did you hear me? I said, 'Put me down, please,'" I whisper firmly, as loudly as I dare. Wiggling free might be a good idea if I weren't afraid of making a loud thud on the floor.

"I heard you. I've just never been one to go by the rules."

Something about the way he says that makes my pulse jump. Think pole vault.

Logan turns our way. Marco shrugs and puts me down. I wobble for a few minutes while I try to catch my breath.

Marco takes a few steps, then stops beside Logan. "Don't I know you from somewhere?"

"Yes, you do." Logan doesn't bother to hide his scowl. "You represented my wife, Frieda, in our divorce."

"Ah, yes, Frieda Carter." Marco smiles again, then walks toward the door. He turns back to Logan. "If I remember right, she made out rather well for herself." His gaze flits to me. "Hey, Wendy, if you need me to rescue you in the future, I'll be right next door."

His impish grin puts a twist in my heart, and I make a slightly audible gasp.

"Thanks for the use of your phone." He taps his forehead in a half salute, and he's gone.

One look at Logan's face tells me it's a good thing.

"You want to tell me what that was all about?" He snaps the words with the sting of a rubber band.

"Listen, Wendy, I've got to get going," Roseanne says, gathering up her jacket and purse. "See you tomorrow."

You know who your friends are at a time like this.

As soon as she steps out the door, Logan whips around to me. "Well, what was that all about?" he asks again.

"I'm not enjoying your tone all that much, Logan. Besides, what are you doing here?"

"I went to my dentist down the road and thought I'd stop by. But this isn't about me. It's about you."

"Please don't use that tone with me." I've had about all the stress I can handle for one day. If my knees give way now, I have a feeling Logan will leave me in a puddle on the floor.

He sucks in a deep breath. "We've been dating for seven months, Wendy. I have a right to know why you were in the arms of another man."

He has a point. "Let's sit down at the table."

He follows me over to the round oak table where I sit with clients to pick out flower arrangements and cake designs.

"I should have told you a long time ago, but, well, it never came up."

Disbelief flits across his eyes. "Are you seeing Amorini?"

"Of course not. I hardly know the man."

"Well, you looked pretty cozy a few minutes ago."

My back stiffens. "Please stop talking and listen, Logan."

"I have a right to know what's going on, Wendy. You know how

I feel about that jerk, and then I come over here to surprise you, only to find you wrapped in his arms."

That *jerk* word is getting on my nerves. I rub my forehead. "You know, I really do have a headache. Can we talk about this later?"

"I don't want to talk about it later. I want to talk about it now." He actually slams his fist on the table, and that just does it for me.

"Logan, we're not married. We're not even engaged." The hurt that flickers across his eyes gives me a twinge of regret. But how dare he thump his fist on the table!

He rises from his chair. "That works both ways, you know."

"Are you threatening me?" I rise from my chair.

"I'm just saying two can play that game. If you want no ties, we'll have no ties."

A lump swells in my throat, blocking all words. I merely stand there and watch as Logan storms across the room to the door. He yanks on the knob to give a dramatic exit and runs straight into Marco.

"Your boyfriend's back!" Logan shouts over his shoulder, shoving his way past Marco.

I'm embarrassed beyond words, but the fight has gone out of me.

Marco watches Logan stamp off, then turns back to me. "Guess I came at a bad time. Just wondered if I could use your phone once more?"

I sink into the chair before my knees give way.

Sure, why not? In case you haven't noticed, I have no control over anything in my life.

three

I'm still crouched in the chair when Kevin enters the office.

"Sorry I'm late."

Straightening, I try to appear happier than I feel. "No problem. I had some last-minute things to finish up."

Thankfully, Marco left before Kevin arrived.

"Come over and join me at the table."

Kevin walks over and slinks into a chair. I wait for him to speak first.

"You're probably wondering what this is about."

"The thought had crossed my mind," I say with a smile.

He smiles too.

We'll work this out. Some little glitch in their family finances. I've got a few dollars saved back. And there's always Marco's offer of co-owning the pond.

Kevin cracks his knuckles, looks at his bulky hands for a minute, then looks at me. "I'm not sure how to say this."

"Look, Kevin, if you and Brooke are in some financial trouble, I'll be happy to help."

He holds up his hand. "It's not that, Mom."

"Well, whatever it is, I'm sure it's not as bad as all that." Conflict has never been my forte.

"I think Brooke is having an affair."

Well, I didn't see that one coming. The idea is so absurd, I almost laugh, but Kevin's expression stops me. "I'm sure you're mistaken, Kevin. I know my daughter, and I don't—"

"It's a guy at work. She's been meeting him for lunch, going out for coffee after work."

"Well, that's certainly something the two of you should talk over, but I don't for a minute think it's anything more than a friendship."

My mind is racing. Brooke, who rarely shares anything with me, mentioned recently that she was annoyed by Kevin's overspending and constant nights out with his "buddies." Maybe she was lonely. Maybe that just drove her to befriend someone. That wouldn't make it right, but it might explain what was happening. I couldn't believe she would do anything immoral.

I search for words that won't pry, yet might be of some help. "Do you feel you and Brooke need some help with your marriage?"

He lets out a sharp whistle. "There's the understatement of the year."

"Well, Kevin, whatever issues the two of you are having, surely you don't think it's all her fault."

He gives me a deadpan stare. "I'm just asking that you talk to her—whether you believe me or not. Because there's one thing I do know—I won't stay with a wife who's cheating on me." With that he gets up and walks out the door, slamming it behind him.

I can hardly believe it's Saturday already," I say to Brooke as we make our way on the walking path through Craggy Park. Was it only Monday when I ran into Marco—or should I say his dog ran into me?

"I know. The seasons pass so quickly. Wildflowers will soon sprout," she says with a sigh. Her steps are a little sluggish, which motivates me to put more zip in my walk. Not bad for forty-something.

"Kevin working today?"

"Unfortunately. It would be nice to see him once in a while." Her voice holds the slightest hint of discouragement, though she quickly hides it. "But I guess there's no avoiding it when you're starting out, right? Besides, overtime pays the bills."

Her smile attempts to hide her true feelings from me, as usual. If only I could get her to open up.

I think about Kevin's concerns but brush them away. How can I possibly talk to her about something so ridiculous—not to mention personal? If she *is* having an affair—which I don't believe for a minute—of course it would be wrong, but she's not exactly under my authority anymore, so what right do I have to say anything? But I'm her mother. I need to say something, don't I?

Her cell phone pierces the air with a fast tune.

"Hi, Kevin . . . Just walking with my mom . . . Huh? Sure, I'll be home by then, yeah . . . Okay, bye." She clicks her phone closed. "He's getting off earlier than he thought."

"Want to go back?" I ask.

"No, it's not that far to go around the path."

She seems happy enough that he's coming home early. I think the affair thing is all in Kevin's head. No need to talk to her about it. We're having such a pleasant time together, no need to start anything.

A cardinal calls from a nearby tree, and I remember how Dennis loved birds. He built a bird feeder outside our home and behind the chapel so he could watch them.

"Do you still miss Dad, Mom?" Brooke asks. Her gaze is on the tree with the cardinal.

"Yeah. How about you?"

"Every day. So many things I'd like to talk to him about."

"Listen, Brooke, I know you shared with your dad more than me, but, well, I want you to know, if you need me, I'm here."

"Thanks, Mom."

She changes the subject to a shoe sale at the mall, and my heart dips. I would love nothing more than a deeper relationship with my daughter, but how do I get there when I don't know what holds her back in the first place?

Wednesdays are usually fairly quiet, but not today. Couples are gearing up for spring weddings, and it seems this was the day everyone wanted to talk details. I'm exhausted by the time I get to bed.

After saying my prayers, I climb onto the foam mattress that Dennis really wanted. I prefer a traditional mattress. Maybe one day I'll get one. This one leaves my form in the bed when I get up. The word *crater* comes to mind.

The house is wonderfully quiet. When Colin first left for college, I didn't think I could handle the solitude. Dennis was gone, and so were the kids. The house felt like a tomb. Now I've not only grown accustomed to it, but it's become my haven. Though I'd much rather have Dennis here with me, I'm settling in to this solitary life. When things get crazy, the way they did today, I rush home to my quiet refuge, and all is well again.

Turning off the lamp beside my bed, I snuggle further into my comforter. My mind wanders to Brooke. We haven't talked since our walk in the park. I know Kevin hopes I can perform some kind of miracle, but if they're having marital problems, they need to talk it out, not have me meddling in their affairs. Sleep calls to me as I whisper another prayer for them.

A ringing doorbell pierces through my subconscious state. My mind hovers momentarily somewhere between a dream world and reality. Finally, several more rings pull my reluctant self back into an awakened state, and my eyes blink open.

Throwing back the covers, I shrug into my robe and slippers and head down the stairs. I can't imagine who would be calling this late. Stopping at my dining room, I peek through the blinds. Brooke's red Camaro is in my drive.

Walking over to the door, I throw up a prayer for wisdom.

One glance at Brooke, and fear ices over my veins.

"I tried to call you, but I kept getting a wrong number." Her whole body is trembling. Red blotches stain her cheeks. Smudges of mascara smear beneath her eyes.

My heart kicks into high gear, and I grab her and pull her into the house. "Honey, what is it?"

"I had to talk to someone." Her head falls against my shoulder. "Mama, what am I gonna do?" she wails in my ear.

When was the last time she called me *Mama?* We fall onto the sofa in the living room, and Brooke leans against me again, tucking her head just under my chin. I brush her hair away from her face and wait for her to tell me what's wrong.

"Honey, whatever it is, you'll get through it. You and Kevin just need time."

Her trembling body seems so vulnerable, childlike. Nothing like the confident woman she is.

She pulls away, wipes her nose with a tissue, and says, "He left me, Mom. Kevin walked out on me."

A ball of nausea starts in the pit of my stomach and rises up the back of my throat. He said he would leave if she was having an affair, but Brooke is not acting like someone who is having an affair. Was he just looking for an excuse?

She rocks back and forth. "He said he wasn't the husband type. He felt trapped and needed to get out." She turns to me. "I thought he loved me."

So he was looking for an excuse. All that affair business was just a cover-up. Instinctively, my arms clamp around my daughter and pull her close. If only I could fix this, make it go away.

"It will be all right, honey. We'll figure it out."

More rocking and tears. I wipe the wet hair from her face. Why does life have to be so hard?

The lights dim around me as the scene I've tried desperately to forget comes back in a heartbeat.

"Mrs. Hartline?"

"Yes."

"Your husband Dennis Hartline?"

"Yes."

"I'm Sheriff Haas." He nervously twirls his hat between his fingers. "I'm sorry to inform you that your husband fell while on his mountain climbing expedition." Hesitation. "He was pronounced dead at the scene."

In the fraction of a second, I'm back there. In that dark place. All moisture leaves my mouth. My lips feel cracked, brittle. My tongue is limp. My brain seems suspended in time. Numb. No emotion, thought, or flicker of life.

Stop this, I tell myself. You have to be strong for Brooke. This isn't about you. This is about Brooke and Kevin, and you have to get them through this.

"Can I stay here for a while? I don't want to be in that house alone."

"Of course you can, honey."

Brooke covers her face with her hands and gives in to violent sobs while I continue to rock her the way I did when she was little, back when she let me help her through life's pain. Rock her the way my mother rocked me after Dad's harsh words. Rock her the way every mother rocks her child to smooth away the pain. Only this time, I'm not sure the pain will go away.

Somehow, Brooke and I muddle through the next week together, and by Tuesday morning when I pull into the chapel parking lot, I have to admit it's good to see Marco's BMW ease in beside me.

"Hi," he says.

"Hi yourself."

Leaning on one foot, then the other, he stuffs his hand in his pocket, then takes it out again. "I was thinking, before either of us starts the day, how about I take you down to the coffee shop for a few minutes?"

He probably wants to try to talk me into selling half of the pond to him. I mentally go over my schedule. "Sure. Let me tell Roseanne, and I'll be right back."

This unexpected meeting offers a hiccup of relief from dealing with Brooke. After I let Roseanne know what's going on, I rejoin Marco.

"Thanks for meeting me this morning. I'm going to be at the lodge all day today, and coffee suddenly sounded good to me." He opens the car door on the passenger's side.

"How are things coming with the lodge?"

"We're getting there. Still have last-minute details to take care of, but we should hit our target date of opening the weekend after Valentine's Day."

"That's great." Though I'm not eager for him to take my business away, I haven't given it any thought in the last week. Some things are just more important than others.

He closes the door and walks around the car while I settle into the rich smell of leather and comfort. Once we enter the coffee shop, my nose twitches at the dark scent of coffee. We get our drinks and scoot into our seats.

He takes a sip. "Great coffee here."

"Guess you'd better get it while you can. Once your restaurant is up and running people will wonder about *your* coffee if you don't drink it there," I tease, trying desperately to shake off the gloom, if only for a little while.

He nods and cradles his cup between his big hands. "How's Brooke getting along?"

The day after Brooke had told me about Kevin, Marco caught me in a vulnerable moment and I shared the news with him. I feel stupid now that I was so emotional about it, but it had never occurred to me that a divorce would touch our family. I hoped Marco wouldn't be so crass as to offer his services.

"As well as can be expected, I guess. Right now, I'm just trying to help her put one foot in front of the other."

"These things are never easy." He looks up at me.

The fact that he's a divorce attorney makes me resent him at the moment, but the compassion in his eyes and voice causes a shimmer of warmth to stir in my heart.

"With God's help, we'll get through it."

He takes a drink from his cup. "Must be hard to see your kid go through something like that. I couldn't bear to see my little girl hurt that way." His glazed eyes look as though he's remembering days of pigtails and bare feet, pockets filled with frogs and old raisins.

What do you know . . . the gruff attorney is having a tender moment.

"There's nothing worse than seeing your child go through pain." I fidget with my cup. "So I take it you and your daughter are close?"

"Don't know what I'd do without her."

"And then one day we have to let them go."

My comment causes his faraway gaze to snap to the present.

"Not if I can help it."

I blink. "What, you don't think some suave, sophisticated young man will come along and sweep her off her feet?"

"Oh, I'm sure of it, but I'd better not catch some little twirp hanging around her. She's too young. She has to get through law school."

"It's hard to let go," I say.

"I can let go when it's time. It's just not time." At this point, his expression grows dark. Very dark.

"I understand," I say softly, hoping to calm him down.

His shoulders relax. "You know, when my wife walked out, I felt I could have forgiven her for dying, but not for abandoning us. I feel for your daughter."

"Thank you. Life can be unfair at times."

"Yeah."

It suddenly occurs to me that we're having an actual in-depth conversation here—baring our souls, almost. He fusses with his shirt collar and scratches his neck, so I figure he notices it too.

"So, how long have you been running the chapel?"

Oh, here we go. The real reason for this little meeting.

"Ten years." I wait for him to say something, but he doesn't. If he's not going to bring up the pond, I'm not either. "The chapel was my husband's dream." Taking the lid off my cup, I swirl the stirrer around in it a couple of times, then replace the lid. "As a chaplain, he loved to perform weddings. He had a passion for couples and the institution of marriage. We didn't just have weddings there. We also held marriage enrichment retreats."

"Was it your dream too?"

The question surprises me. "Uh, well, sure. Of course."

"I mean, obviously it was, or you wouldn't have given ten years of your life to running it and keeping it running after your husband died."

"Well, exactly."

"You still do the marriage enrichment retreats?"

"Not since Dennis died." It feels a little warm in here.

"That's had to cut down some on the income."

He's fishing for something, and I'm not sure I like it. "We get by."

"Didn't mean to get personal."

"No problem." Just don't do it again. "Listen, I'd better get back to work. I don't want to leave Roseanne to handle things alone for too long."

He helps me put on my jacket; we toss our empty cups in the trash and walk to the car.

"Thanks for the coffee, Marco," I say, when we arrive at the chapel. "That was really nice." If he had an ulterior motive, I hope the compliment makes him feel guilty.

"You're welcome. Maybe we can do it again sometime."

I'm thinking no.

"Maybe." I get out and walk back to the chapel with as much confidence as I can muster. I don't know what he's up to, but after all I've been through, I think I can handle the likes of Marco Amorini.

four

I'm dead tired by the time I get home that evening, but a sandwich for dinner won't cut it. Every day is a struggle to get Brooke to eat, so I've been trying to fix meals I think she'll want. In the meantime, I'm gaining weight.

"Hi, honey. You doing okay?" I say when I step into the living room.

She's still in her pajamas. Her normally flawless hair hangs in ratty strings over her shoulders. Her blue eyes are dull, vacant. I remember those days. When sleep was my only friend. When drinking a few ounces of water was the biggest accomplishment of the day. When no one seemed to realize life had stopped for me. Colors. Smells. Taste. All gone.

This is not a woman having an affair.

She clicks off the television with the remote control. "I'm pretty tired. I was just thinking about going to bed."

Before she can get up, I sit down beside her, carefully pulling my words together. "Brooke, I'm concerned about your health."

"I'm fine." Short, clipped words.

"I'm fixing lasagna tonight." For the briefest of moments a flicker of interest flashes across her eyes. "I'd sure love to have you join me."

"I don't know."

"All I ask is that you don't go to bed until dinner is ready. See how you feel then, okay?"

"All right," she says reluctantly.

"Come talk to me while I work in the kitchen." I attempt to keep my voice light and cheerful, but not overly so. When I was grieving over Dennis, I didn't enjoy people who bubbled on and on.

She slogs her way out of the chair and into the kitchen while I boil the noodles, layer them in the pan with the sauce, meat, and cheeses, then slip the pan into the oven. Pulling the garlic bread from the freezer, I set it out to thaw while I grab a head of lettuce and begin to whack off pieces for a salad.

We talk a while about her day, how she called the Realtor to get the house listed. I had hoped things wouldn't go this far, but evidently Brooke and Kevin agreed this was the best thing to do. Though she would rather keep it, she can't afford the payments on her own. She's going to stay here with me until she gets on her feet financially. She's accumulated four weeks' vacation and decided to use it now to get her life back in order.

I've decided to take Marco up on the pond proposal. It will help us financially, and besides, it will be nice to have someone help me maintain it. As for Brooke's needs, I'll help her with expenses until the house sells. If I have to, I'll dip into my savings. Family comes first.

As we discuss everything that has to get done, a somber mood settles on the room.

"You know, when your dad died, I couldn't believe everyone

went on with business as usual. I wanted to scream, 'Doesn't anybody realize I've lost my husband?'"

"At least your husband didn't choose to leave you."

My heart constricts. *How do I get my daughter through this, Lord? This wasn't supposed to happen.*

"I'm so sorry, Brooke." As soon as I say that, I remember she doesn't want me to "apologize for the world." But one look on her face tells me the comment didn't register. "Only time will ease the pain."

She puts her hand down. "I don't think so." She hesitates. "There's more to it than you know, Mom."

Fear clutches my heart. Surely Kevin's accusations can't be true.

"You know, Brooke, sometimes it helps to talk—"

"I don't want to talk to a shrink," she snaps.

"You don't have to talk to a psychologist. Just someone."

"Mom, why do you always have to tell me what to do?"

I place the covered bowl of salad in the refrigerator and turn to her. "Brooke, I'm just trying to help you."

She takes a deep breath, stares at her fingers, and whispers. "I know." Pause. "I've been having the weirdest dreams lately."

"Oh?"

"About plane crashes. I'm looking out our kitchen window, watching a plane streak across the sky, when suddenly it dips and zooms nose-first toward the ground." She looks at me. "Wonder what that means."

"I have no idea," I say, sliding into the seat across from her at the table. Though maybe that's how she sees her marriage—careening out of control.

"Well, until we figure it out, don't go on a plane trip," she says with the first half-smile I've seen on her since it all happened. She stares at a freckle on her arm. "Kevin and I have been struggling for a while."

I'm not sure where to go from here. "You mentioned his ten-dency to overspend."

"It was more than that."

I scarcely allow myself to take a breath for fear she'll stop talk-ing. How can I help her without her thinking I'm trying to control her? "Whatever it is, Brooke, I'm here for you."

Just then the buzzer goes off on the oven, removing whatever chance I had of her opening up to me. Shrugging on my oven mitts, I pull the pan from the oven. The cheese and sauce bubble and sput-ter, sending whiffs of garlic and oregano into the air. Brooke says no more as she walks to the cupboard, retrieves the plates, glasses, and silverware, then places them on the table.

After I say the prayer for our meal, the doorbell rings. Brooke groans. Maybe she had hoped for more time to talk together, alone.

I give her a quick squeeze. "No matter what, I love you. Remember that."

When I open the front door, I'm surprised to see Logan stand-ing on the other side. We haven't really talked since that whole thing with Marco.

"Logan, come on in."

He steps inside. "Is this a bad time?"

"Well, um, we were just sitting down to dinner." I hate to ruin my chance to talk with Brooke. But undoubtedly, the moment of clearing the air is over anyway. "Would you like to join us? We're having lasagna."

"I don't want to intrude." He pulls off his coat before I can com-ment, and I hang it in the closet.

Too late.

Since Logan is the first man I've dated since her father's death, Brooke isn't crazy about him. Our conversation over dinner seems stilted at best, and she finally excuses herself and slips off to her bedroom.

"Look, Wendy, we hit a rough patch before everything sort of broke loose for you. Roseanne told me about Brooke and Kevin. I stopped by to tell you I don't want our relationship to end. You've got a lot on you right now, and I'm not trying to pressure you. Just wanted you to know."

He plants a kiss on my forehead and grabs his jacket from the closet. "Call me when you're ready to talk."

It was good to see Logan again. I've missed him. But honestly, I've got my hands full just getting my daughter through this without worrying about my own love life—or lack thereof.

Shoving the last bit of lemon into the garbage disposal, I spot a smudge of oatmeal on the countertop and use a kitchen washcloth to wipe it off. The phone rings and causes me to jump. It's never a good sign when I get a call before I leave for work.

"Hello?"

"Well, it's about time."

My body goes into a Pavlovian response when I hear my dad's voice. Rapid heartbeat, tightness in my chest, constricted throat. I stand at attention. The tart smell of lemons rises from the garbage disposal.

"Hi, Dad. Just getting ready to leave for work," I say, hoping he'll take the hint.

"Oh, it won't hurt you to be late. You're the owner."

Never mind that I want to be a responsible person, someone who can be counted on to be there when needed. Martin Blume just wouldn't understand that, because that line of thinking would get in the way of what he wants. And right now, he wants to talk. It never does any good to argue. I learned that long ago.

"So, what's up?" I ask.

"Well, it looks as though I'm going to have to move."

It could be my imagination, but I think he's just dropped a bomb.

"Why is that?" I can still make it to work on time if we cut this short.

"Been down on my luck lately. Seems they don't want to give construction jobs to an old man."

His words cause a chill to scurry up my spine and plunk smack dab in my stomach with a thud.

"So you need money, Dad?"

He's never asked me for money before, but he sounds a little desperate.

"I'm not asking for money, Wendy."

He grows quiet a moment, and I watch the second hand inch forward on the clock, ticking against the white-and-green checkered wallpaper.

"Just a place to stay."

I'm not sure, but I think the second hand stops with my heartbeat. *Please, oh, please, take the money.* "What?"

"I thought this might be a good time to come back to Tennessee. I reckoned you could put me up until I find a job and a place of my own."

Deep breaths, Wendy. Not *Will you put me up?* mind you, but *I reckoned you could put me up.*

"I'm starting fresh, so I'll be coming with the clothes on my back and that's pretty much it. Well, I'll let you get to work. See you soon."

He clicks off before I can say *Mi casa es su casa.*

I sit down on a white wooden chair. Dad is coming here. In the same house. Eating the same food. Watching my TV. He'll be involved in my life. Again.

I can't breathe.

My mom died when I was thirteen. When Dennis and I met in high school and fell in love, I couldn't leave home fast enough—and as soon as I did, Dad moved out of our Tennessee home and headed for the sunny state of Florida.

We found as long as there was distance between us, we got along fine. Occasional talks on the phone kept us connected but far enough away that we didn't hurt each other. But now?

I walk back to the sink, squirt some lotion onto my hands, and take a deep breath. My family needs me. This is only temporary. I'm a grown woman, not a cowering teenager. This is my house, and I can take charge.

Dad and I under one roof.

I squeeze another dollop of lotion onto my hands and rub fiercely.

Mentally going over my schedule, I realize it's a light day at work. I pick up the phone again and call Roseanne, tell her I have a headache and I'll be in after lunch.

After swallowing a couple of Advil, I slip downstairs into my workroom. I turn on the iron and pick up the cut pieces of flowered chintz fabric for the pillow shams I'm making. Placing the right sides together, I run the warm iron over the crisp material, marking the seams as I go. At the machine, I complete the seams, allowing the serger to finish off the edges, leaving a slight opening for slipping the pillow form in and out. With the cording attached, my pillow is done, and I am much calmer.

By the time I arrive at the office, I'm feeling almost cheerful.

"Well, look who decided to show up," Roseanne says.

I pull off my jacket and grab a cup of coffee. "I'm sorry, Roseanne. It's been a rough morning."

"Oh, honey, I was only teasing you. You're the boss. You can take all the time you want." She stares at me a little too long. "Want to talk about it?"

"It's just everything," I say, settling into the chair behind my desk. "Dealing with Brooke's situation, Logan, and Marco. And this morning I had a phone call."

She looks at me expectantly.

"Dad's moving in with me."

"You are kidding me." She thumps a stack of paper into her in-box and shakes her head. "You have to tell him *no*, Wendy. You don't need this on top of everything else."

"He's down on his luck with no job. What could I say? 'Sorry, Dad—you can't come'?"

"Well, you should have said something. You'll go to pieces with him and Brooke there. Either that or Brooke will kill him, and your troubles will be over."

"That's not funny."

"I know." She turns on her desk fan. "So, when is he coming?"

"In a few days." It occurs to me that I may lose those ten pounds without even trying.

"Well, we'll just pray about it. You're committed for now, but that doesn't mean he has to stay forever." Her words vibrate into the fan, and her bangs flutter with abandon.

"Thank you for the silver lining," I say sincerely. She has no idea how that is a lifeline for me right now. I'll take whatever positive strokes I can get.

"Hey, Gill's taking me to the Comedy Barn Theater in Pigeon Forge Friday night. You want to come along? It could get you out of the house." She flips off her fan and smoothes her hair back into place.

"Thanks, Roseanne, but I don't want to be the third wheel. Sounds like a special date night."

"Oh, please. You know you're always welcome. We're not newly-weds, for heaven's sake."

Just then the front door swishes open, and we look up to see Logan, hair disheveled, shirt a tad wrinkled and slightly stretched across his belly. "Wendy, can I talk to you a minute over coffee?"

So much for no pressure and waiting on me to call him. I glance at Roseanne, and she smiles.

"Y'all go ahead."

It's a good thing I own my business. A boss would fire me.

I shrug my jacket back on and follow Logan out the door. Stepping into the parking lot, I glance next door and spot Marco, who sees us and waves. Logan mutters something under his breath, but in as discreet a manner as possible, I wave back.

Climbing into Logan's Chevy Malibu, I pull on my seat belt and hope Dad won't ever see Logan's car. He doesn't trust anyone who doesn't drive a Ford.

Logan gets behind the wheel and straps on his belt.

"What are you doing out of classes?" I ask.

"I have an assistant teaching, so it's an easy day for me." He runs his hand through his hair. "Which as you can see is a good thing. I haven't been sleeping well lately."

And this, he thinks, will make me feel sorry for him? Hello? My son-in-law has gone AWOL.

Once we arrive at the coffee shop, Logan turns to look at me. "Listen, Wendy, I know I told you I'd wait for you to call me, but I have to clear things up between us. I let jealousy get in the way of my good sense, and that's not like me."

It's true. I'd never seen Logan act jealous before that day with

Marco. Suddenly I feel a smidgen of pride. Pride in all its puffed-up glory.

"So, do you want to tell me what that business with Marco was all about?"

I explain about the cataplexy, and Logan visibly softens.

"I shouldn't have jumped to conclusions. I'm sorry."

"Apology accepted," I say cheerfully.

"But you need to let Marco know you don't want him coming over all the time and using your stuff."

Well, that didn't last long. We both know Logan's saying that more for his protection than for mine. The memory of Marco's strong arms and warm brown eyes flickers to my mind. I shake it off.

Instead of answering, I unhook my seat belt and hurry into the coffee shop. I can feel Logan eyeing me as I order a peppermint mocha. Drinks in hand, we slide into our seats.

"Thanks for coming with me today. I'm not trying to pressure you. I just was too impatient to wait on you to call me."

His eyes search mine for understanding, and I smile.

"It's all right, Logan. I wouldn't toss our friendship away over a small argument."

"Friendship? Is that what this is?"

We've never really defined things between us. I care a lot about Logan, but I just feel a little confused right now. His penetrating gaze makes me shift in my seat.

"Well, whatever it is." I give a nervous chuckle, tuck my hair behind my ear, and take a drink from my cup. The caffeine bolsters my courage.

"I like to think it's more than that." He reaches his hand over and covers mine in a smothering, possessive way.

Is seven months synonymous with serious? I'm not ready for an exclusive relationship, and I get the feeling that's where Logan is headed. I ease my hand away and reach for my drink.

"Let's just take it one day at a time, okay?"

When he looks at me, he no doubt sees that's all I can promise right now, so he agrees.

I take a deep breath. "I have more news."

"Oh?" He lifts a worried glance.

I tell him about Dad's phone call.

"He's the controlling one, right? You need to tell him he can't stay with you."

For a moment I stare at him, wondering if he sees the irony in that statement. "It's not that easy."

"Wendy, you're a big girl. Surely he's noticed you're over forty?"

"I'm trying to look for the good in that comment, but I'm struggling. Help me out here."

"No offense, but, well, you are of age. You don't have to let him stay with you."

I feel my mood plunging. "I know, but I guess he thinks he's entitled since he's my father."

Logan frowns. "I don't like this, Wendy. You need to handle it."

I seriously consider pointing out that it's not about him, but I let it drop. I just don't have the strength to fight him right now.

"Guess it's time for both of us to get back to work," he says, slurping the last bit from his cup.

We scoot out of our chairs and head for the car. Since we've patched things up, I should be feeling better, I guess. But for some reason, I'm just, well, not.

five

Brooke manages to put on jeans and an oversized sweatshirt for dinner, but no makeup and no plans for leaving the house. I try to talk her into a movie, but she's just not ready to meet the public yet. I'm wondering if she might be better off going to work. It would at least keep her mind occupied.

She sets out the plates and silverware on our farm table with its oak top and white legs—not the one I wanted, but Dennis said we had to make do—while I put together a salad. A colorful floral centerpiece adds some cheer to the less-than-fancy table setting.

She watches me scoop up the fried hamburgers and says, "Mom, I can't eat a whole burger."

With everything in me I try not to give her the "mother look."

"Just do your best, honey."

She's lost some weight since Kevin left. I'm trying not to panic over it, but she's eating barely enough to survive. Sorrow can do that to you. I keep trying to tempt her with cookies and cake.

Once the table is set, the doorbell rings. With a sigh, I wipe my hands on a towel. "Be right back."

I'm really tired, and the idea of company doesn't appeal to me. I hope it isn't Logan again. With any luck, it will be a Girl Scout selling cookies. She could make enough off me tonight to put herself through college.

One yank on the doorknob, and I'm not seeing Girl Scout cookies in my future.

"Well, it's about time you opened the door," Dad says, stepping inside. His white hair has thinned slightly, but his bushy mustache takes up the slack. He's wearing a torn jacket with a broken zipper.

"Dad. I wasn't expecting you for a couple of days yet."

He scratches his jaw. "I thought I told you I was staying with a friend in Atlanta. Didn't take long to get here."

No, you failed to mention that little fact.

He steps inside. We stand there for an awkward moment, and I reach over to hug him. His frame feels frail and small beneath my arms, surprising me, but the familiar smell of mint surrounds him. For as long as I can remember, Dad has always smelled of breath mints. Wintergreen is his favorite.

I hope it's not there to cover the scent of alcohol. In the years after Mom died, he turned to booze while I turned to Dennis. But he told me he'd quit over a year ago.

Wait. What if he's come back to tell me he's sick? *Please, God, I can't handle one more thing.*

With a loose touch, Dad's arms wrap around me, then quickly drop. Awkward moment.

"We're just sitting down to eat if you want to join us," I say over my shoulder, leading the way to the kitchen.

"Great. I haven't eaten yet."

"Hamburger and salad."

"Anything else?"

"Well, that's all we fixed. Brooke's appetite isn't that great—"

We step into the kitchen, and Dad sees Brooke. "Don't tell me this is my granddaughter?"

Brooke lifts a slight smile. "Hi, Granddad." She gets up and gives him a hug. He's no friendlier to her than he was to me.

"You've sure grown since last time I saw you."

I just refuse to comment on that.

"So, where's that husband of yours?"

Brooke looks at me, then back at her granddad. "We're separated." The expression on her face says he'd better not hassle her.

Taking a long look at Brooke, he finally just shakes his head and slips into his chair at the table.

Evidently that's the extent of his compassion. Surprise flickers in Brooke's eyes, and I want to bop my dad on the head. He can be mean to me, but he'd better be nice to Brooke or I'll throw him out on his skinny tailbone with only his mustache to keep him warm.

On that note, I say a prayer for our meal with a teensy bit of uncertainty as to whether God heard it, what with my attitude and all.

"You go ahead and eat my hamburger, Dad. I'll make some more," I say sweetly, pulling the meat from the refrigerator.

He doesn't hesitate. In fact, he's halfway through the sandwich before I can get the meat to the stove.

He talks about his drive here and the perils of working in construction at sixty-five years of age. Brooke says very little. The way she's moving her fork around in her salad, I'd say she was checking for bugs.

I prepare two more hamburgers, and before the plate can settle on the table, Dad lifts both sandwiches onto his plate, leaving none for me.

"You're going to eat both of those?" I ask, wondering if I should feel sorry for him or smack his hands.

"Well, that was the plan," he says, as in, *What else am I going to do with them?*

Brooke looks at me, and for the flash of an instant I see the hint of a smile tug on her lips. I roll my eyes—Dad's too busy eating to notice—and get up to make yet one more sandwich.

"Thanks for the meal, Mom," Brooke says.

The fact that she's eaten only two bites of her hamburger keeps my pride from getting the better of me. I try not to show my disappointment. At least she ate something. Unless Dad ate them when we weren't looking.

After my hamburger is done, I put it on the bun and take a bite before I get to the table. I don't want to risk Dad getting to it first.

"How old are you now, Wendy?" Dad plops the last bite of his third hamburger into his mouth and licks the catsup from his fingers.

"Forty-four."

He had started to get up, and now he stops in a half-bent position. For a second I consider going to the garage and grabbing the WD-40.

"Are you that old?" he asks.

I don't know whether to be offended or to apologize. "Yes."

He shakes his head and straightens. "My, my, where does the time go?"

This would be a perfect time to let him know we were here. Where was he? But once again, I swallow the words. Maybe one of these days I'll manage to actually tell him how he's hurt me.

Dad stretches and pats his stomach. "Good food, Wendy. Could have cooked the meat a tad longer, but it was good." He throws a wink. "Got any cake?"

I'll give him cake.

"No, I'm sorry, Dad, we're fresh out of cake."

"What you got in those cupboards?" he asks, rummaging through them before I can say *Sara Lee.*

My throat constricts. If he touches my chocolate popcorn, so help me . . .

Get a grip, Wendy. You can buy more popcorn.

"Help yourself to whatever you want. I'll be right back."

I practically run to my bedroom and close the door behind me. My face feels hot right to the very tips of my ears. It's best if I lock myself in here until I've prayed away my bad attitude. And right now, I'm thinking I could be here till I rot.

While I'm in my bedroom, the phone rings. Thankful for the reprieve, I snatch it up. "Hello?"

"Uh-oh, I don't like the sound of that," Roseanne-the-ever-intu-itive-one says.

"Nothing gets past you."

"Why are you whispering?"

"Am I?"

"I thought I called a 900 number by mistake."

"Sorry. I'm in my bedroom, trying to grab a moment of peace. Dad's here."

"Already?"

"Yeah, seems he called me from Atlanta and forgot to tell me that little fact."

"Uh-oh. And already you're hiding out in the bedroom?"

"Yes. And he hasn't even been here an hour."

"This calls for chocolate popcorn."

"Exactly what I was thinking."

We laugh together.

"You poor thing. I'm praying for you."

"Thanks." We pause a moment. "So, what are you doing tonight?"

"Gill is installing a new toilet in our bathroom. Do I have the life or what?"

Just then I hear a flush and a yell.

"Uh-oh. Got to go. Talk to you later."

As much as I would love to just hole up in my room, I figure I'd better get back out there. I need to spend some time with my dad, set an example for Brooke. Taking a deep breath, I look in the mirror and tell myself, "You can do this."

Grabbing the lotion on my dresser, I squeeze the linen scent onto my palm and rub vigorously. It smells clean, like fresh-washed garments that have been drying on a clothesline. My mother smelled like that. When I was little, I used to sit beside her on the piano bench and watch her slender, porcelain fingers glide effortlessly across the keys while she played the tunes of Mozart, Beethoven, and so many others. Those notes would comfort me like nothing else could. How many nights had I fallen asleep to her music?

She used to say you can tell a lot about a person by their hands. Calloused hands might show strength of character, people who work hard. Well-manicured hands could reveal a happy, organized person. Neglected hands might give insight into a deeper problem. "And some hands," she once told me, "are scarred."

"Like Jesus' hands?" I had asked with my five-year-old reasoning.

"Yes, honey, like Jesus' hands."

Tears prick my eyes, chasing away Mom's image. I glance down at my own hands, starting to show signs of age. Lotion softens the rough places. If only life were that easy.

A knock sounds on my bedroom door.

"Wendy, you coming back out here?"

Dad's scratchy voice rubs against me like a straggly tree branch. He probably wants something else to eat.

"Yeah, I'll be out in a sec," I say lightheartedly. One more squeeze of lotion, another deep breath, and I reach for the door.

I can do this.

My fingers slide off the knob. No, I can't. Too much lotion. Once more I rub the lotion from my hands on up to my elbows and reach for the door. Another deep breath.

May as well get used to this. It looks as though Dad is here to stay.

The next morning Roseanne and I work feverishly on the small wedding scheduled for this weekend. Last-minute calls to the caterer, photographer, and florist make sure everything is on schedule. Our pianist contacts us to say she has the flu, so we have to get a backup.

The morning is over before I can blink, and Dad shows up at lunchtime. He's wearing yesterday's clothes.

"Hey, I was bored and thought maybe you could take me to lunch at the diner down the road," he says.

I didn't miss the "you can take me" part. Wonder if I can beef up my window treatment business? Something's gotta give.

"Sure," I say. "You remember Roseanne?"

"Good to see you again." Roseanne gets up to shake Dad's hand, stirring loose the sweet scent of her perfume. She chats with him while I get my things.

"Hey, you've sure got a nice neighbor there," Dad says while I shrug on my coat.

I stop shrugging.

"What nice neighbor?" I ask with fear and trepidation.

"That Italian fellow." Dad strokes his jaw thoughtfully. "Marco somebody."

"You talked to Marco Amorini?" I ask, trying to hide my shock.

"Yeah, that's it. Now, there's a man with potential. He's not married. You oughta date him." His mustache twitches slightly, an idiosyncrasy that tells me he thinks he's on to something.

My jaw comes unhinged. I'm forty-four years old, and my dad is still trying to control who I date. I let him know in no uncertain terms am I interested in Marco.

"Well, you kids have a great lunch," Roseanne says, offering me a smile of encouragement.

"Oh, you're going to lunch?" It's Marco, meeting us at the door. If he keeps showing up at work, I'll have to add him to the payroll.

"Yeah, want to come?" Dad asks. "Wendy's buying."

"Now there's an offer I can't refuse," Marco says, flashing a smile so brilliant he's giving me a headache.

Anyone notice I'm not exactly rolling in dough here?

"Great." Dad rubs his hands together and starts talking to Marco about Florida and the construction business.

I turn and shoot a pray-for-me look to Roseanne.

With a groan, I turn to walk out the door. Something tells me this day couldn't get any worse. When I look up at the car coming down the road, I realize I'm wrong. It's a Chevy Malibu.

Logan's.

We scoot into the blue upholstered cushions at our booth, my side noticeably protesting—more like screaming—in response.

"So, here we are," Marco says, flipping his napkin across his lap while Dad, Logan, and I all follow suit.

"Yep, here we are," Logan says, his narrowed gaze fixed on Marco, who doesn't seem to mind at all.

"So, you two fellas know each other?" Dad asks, while I try not to slink down into my seat.

"Yes, we do," Logan says, with all the talent of a ventriloquist. I swear I did not see the man's lips move once.

Marco tosses back a grin and with a twinkle in his eyes says, "I represented Logan's ex-wife in their divorce."

"You a lawyer?" Dad asks.

Marco turns to him. "Guilty as charged."

"Well, can't say as I've had many dealings with lawyers, but I suppose they're good to have around if you need one."

"That's my hope." Marco lifts his ice water in the gesture of a toast before taking a drink.

"He's known around here as a ruthless divorce attorney," Logan says, with nary the hint of a smile on his face. In fact, granite comes to mind.

"What was that?" Dad asks.

"He said I'm known for being a ruthless divorce attorney," Marco repeats. If he were wearing suspenders right now, I'm sure his thumbs would give them a crisp little snap.

"Is that a fact," Dad says.

"That's what I deal with. Facts. Plain facts," Marco says.

"Yeah, everything is black-and-white with you, right? I thought you guys were supposed to take into account that pain-and-suffering business." Logan is almost whining.

"We take that into consideration—if it's our client experiencing the pain and suffering. Fortunately, if we're good"—he turns to Logan and flashes a grin—"and we are"—he turns back to Dad—"we're able to get them by with minimal suffering."

"You ought to help Brooke with that scoundrel husband of hers," Dad says in no uncertain terms.

I gasp. "Dad, there's been no mention of divorce. They may still work things out. Besides, I'd rather not talk about it here."

Dad looks at the guys. "That's Wendy for you. Believes all of life ends on a happy note."

Has he not noticed that my husband is gone?

"Well, Brooke had better get crackin'," Dad says, "so he won't cash in whatever money they have together and skip town. She needs to take the initiative."

He's been home less than twenty-four hours and already he's the expert on what my daughter needs. Never mind that he has never met Kevin. Though I can't remember now why he didn't make it to the wedding.

"So, tell me about your resort," Dad says to Marco.

"Well, it's going to be a state-of-the-art lodge: forty rooms, restaurant, swimming pool, hot tubs on the balconies of four honeymoon suites. Heart-shaped Jacuzzis in four other rooms."

They continue on in conversation while my mind drifts to Brooke and Kevin. My heart squeezes as I remember their happier days of dating. They seemed made for each other right from the start. There is no way I believe Brooke is having an affair, but what could have gone wrong?

Did Kevin mention his suspicions to Brooke? Did they have words before he walked out? Does she have regrets? Worries swirl around in my mind. I don't have time to think about my own problems when my daughter's life seems to be spiraling out of control.

"I'm really doing law more on a part-time basis now," Marco is saying when I jump back into focus. "I've been weaning away, buying up investments here and there to sustain me once I retire from the practice."

"Smart thinking, boy," Dad says before sipping the coffee from his cup. "I should have done that. Wasted too much money on booze."

I'm surprised at his candor.

"But I'm done with that now. Haven't had a drink in sixteen months." Dad looks up. "One day at a time."

"We all have things in our past we're not proud of," Marco says with equal candor.

Logan grunts and gives Marco a judgmental look.

As I watch the two of them, I realize they're as different as night and day, and I wonder how I could be drawn to both of them. Well, not exactly drawn to. I definitely don't want a relationship with Marco, but there's no denying the man has a certain charm about him—especially when he shows his soft side. Logan, on the other hand, is driving me crazy right now, but he's a good man, and he has helped me start a new life without Dennis.

"Now, there's a good retirement job, working at a lodge," Dad says, looking in the distance, rubbing his chin thoughtfully.

"Got any experience in maintenance?"

Dad brightens. "Sure do."

"I could give you some work. We'll be plenty busy, and we could use extra help. Probably could give you a little work even before we open over Valentine's weekend. Will you be around a while?"

"Yep. I've moved back. Just staying with Wendy till I get on my feet."

"You gonna let him get away with that? Your own dad will be competing with you," Logan says in a not-so-quiet voice.

Marco looks at me. "Is that what you think, Wendy?"

The way he looks at me and the way my name rolls off the tip of his tongue makes my mouth go dry. I try to swallow, but it's not happening.

"Well, it does kind of seem that way," I finally say.

"I don't think so. You're in the marrying business. I'm in the—"

"Divorce business," Logan says.

"—hotel business."

A rare moment of assertiveness comes over me. "What about my four cabins?"

"We've discussed that, remember? How I'll handle your over-flow? More than four couples get married on any given weekend. I'll take the excess honeymooners. We'll have hot tubs and a few more amenities for the happy couples."

Marco winks, and my face grows hot. I don't know if it's because he gets my ire up or because we're talking about honeymoons. Maybe I'm being too hard on him. He can't know the extent of what I'm going through with Brooke's situation, Dad's appearance, and now the business. He's just trying to look out after himself, same as me. I rub the back of my neck, trying to ease the taut muscles.

"You okay?" Logan asks.

I nod as a young waitress walks up to our table. She looks a little familiar.

"Oh, hi, Wendy," she says. "Do you remember me? I'm Polly Ward—well, it's Ray now. You handled my wedding to Rick a couple of years ago."

"Polly, so good to see you." I shake her hand and note the shadow in her eyes. Her gaze drifts across the table.

"Oh, hi, Mr. Amorini." She shakes his hand. "You remember me? You handled my divorce."

I gasp.

Logan grunts.

Marco clears his throat and shifts in his seat. "How are you, Polly?"

She shrugs. "I've been better, but I'll make it."

"That's the spirit," he says, while our table comes to an awkward silence.

She takes our order and walks away.

"Ah, another satisfied customer of Marco Amorini," Logan says, stretching back into his seat, looking rather victorious.

"Hey, she was the one who wanted out of the marriage. I just helped her get there."

"It's a sad, sad world these days." Dad clucks his tongue. "So many couples give up on each other at the first sign of imperfection. Whatever happened to that 'for better or for worse' part of the vow? Do people even say that at weddings anymore?"

For some reason, Dad's reaction surprises me.

"Sometimes," I say. "Sometimes not."

"Isn't the fact you're a divorce attorney and offering honeymoon suites at your lodge a conflict of interest?" Logan asks.

"I don't force people into divorces. I help them if that's the way they choose to go. Legally, they're entitled to representation. I give it to them."

"But do you have to help them make a mess of their lives?" I ask. Wow, where is this sudden burst of boldness coming from?

"The world is not black-and-white, Wendy. Sometimes physical safety is involved."

"I understand that not all marriages can be saved. I'm merely saying that maybe *some* could be salvaged if society didn't make it so easy to get out of a troubled marriage."

"The spouse doesn't always have a choice in the matter."

It's obvious this discussion has hit a nerve with him. It's best we move on. If only life were that easy.

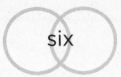

six

Leaving my car behind, I click the remote to lock it up and begin my steady run in Craggy Park. Bright orange-yellow rays shoot from the mountaintop, causing it to glisten and sparkle against a sapphire sky scrubbed clean by yesterday's wind. The scent of pine perfumes the air. Nothing improves my spirits like a run through the park at this time of day, before the actual work begins and Tennessee is just waking up.

A barn swallow flutters overhead, revealing its rust-colored belly.

There is no time to give in to the luxury of self-pity. My pain for Brooke goes deep, but there's a deeper pain I've been afraid to take out and examine. Missed opportunities. Kevin came to me before he left. Could I have said or done anything that might have helped him to tough it out? I still don't know what happened between them, but I have this nagging feeling in the pit of my stomach.

My thoughts scatter as I head into my usual turn, which represents my half-mile mark. Dennis used to tell me I refuse to see things as they really are, and when I finally do see the problems, when they can no longer be avoided, I want to fix them immediately.

"Some things just can't be fixed, Wendy," he would say.

At the time, I didn't believe him. Seemed to me there was a solution to everything, if you looked hard enough. I mean, when the kids were little, I could fix their childhood problems. We somehow even managed to get them through the teen years.

But my husband's death wasn't part of the plan. I couldn't fix that. Nothing I can ever do will bring him back. Tears fill my eyes. Did I tell Dennis enough that I loved him, or did we get caught up in the daily hum of life and just do the work? Does my son-in-law know that I care about what he and Brooke are going through? Does he know that I love him like a son and pray for him?

As my legs carry me around the bend, tears spill down my cheeks, and I brush them away. We'll get through this.

I round the curve and see Marco Amorini.

He slows his pace. "Well, we meet again."

"Hi, Marco," I say, embarrassed that he's caught me in an emotional moment.

"You okay?"

"Yeah, I'm fine."

"Mind if I join you?"

What am I going to say? *Why no, you stay on your side of the park, and I'll stay on mine?*

He falls into step with me. "Listen, I probably spoke out of turn yesterday when I offered your dad a job. If you would rather he not work for me, I'll tell him I've made other arrangements."

"He's really counting on it, so please don't drop him now." Besides, the sooner he gets a job, the sooner I get him out of my cupboards.

"Well, I'm sorry if it made things harder on you."

I give him a sideways glance. The great Marco Amorini is apologizing? Wow. This is a good day.

He clears his throat. "You sure you're okay?"

My heart trips a moment, and it has nothing to do with the exercise. His concern touches me in a real way. "I'm fine." For a moment, neither of us says anything while our shoes scuff the path with every footfall. "Thanks for asking."

He turns his head to look at me. "You're welcome."

An involuntary shiver races through me. I hate it when that happens.

Wonder what Logan would say if he knew I was running in the park with Marco? Not that it matters. I'm a grown woman. I certainly can run in the park with whomever I want.

A new day is dawning.

Adding more sunflower seeds to the bird feeder outside our backyard, I slip back into the house and look out the window. I don't mind sharing my sunflower seeds when it draws in the likes of cardinals, blue jays, goldfinches. It's such a gentle sport, bird watching. Guess it's another thing my mother passed on to me.

Mom used to make up this concoction of suet or bacon grease, peanut butter, and a variety of birdseed. The birds came in droves to the feeder when Mom put that out.

The phone rings, interrupting my thoughts.

"Hello?"

"Hi, Mom."

"Colin. You're not one to call so early. Everything all right?"

He laughs. "Everything is fine. Just thought I'd call and see if it's all right if I come home tonight for the weekend."

"Well, of course, you can come home. You can come home anytime you want, you know that."

"I know, but I wanted to make sure you didn't have a busy weekend planned at the chapel."

Okay, that perks my interest. "Well, I do have a wedding tomorrow, but it's early in the day. I'll be free after three o'clock. What's up?"

"Nothing really. Just wanted to spend some time with you and Brooke. How's she doing?"

"She's getting by. It will be good for her to see you. I think she needs some younger company. Oh, speaking of which, I should warn you that your Granddad Blume is staying here."

"What's he doing there?"

I explain what's going on, and Colin gets quiet. "Boy, that's the last thing you and Brooke need right now."

"We're doing fine so far. I could use another job to pay the grocery bills, but we're okay."

"Oh, man, don't tell me my food stash is being threatened," he says.

"Are you kidding? *My* food stash is being threatened."

"Okay, I get it. I'll bring my own grub."

"Oh, you. That's not necessary. It will be great having you here. Thanks for making the effort."

"Uh, Mom? There is one more thing."

"Yes?"

"Is it all right if I bring someone with me?"

"Of course. Your friends are always welcome here."

"How about we take you to dinner? Do you think Brooke would come along?"

"Don't count on it. She hasn't gone out much—and she hasn't had much of an appetite."

"Okay. Well, you plan on it. We'll see you tonight around dinnertime."

With that, he's gone.

I always like it when Colin brings his friends home. There's something about a house full of boys—the laughter, the empty pizza boxes, the video games.

Hmm, good thing it's only for the weekend.

So what did Colin tell you when he called the second time? Brooke's dressed in the same wrinkled sweats. I'm wondering when she'll let me wash those. She's twirling a strand of hair between her fingers while she sits Indian-style on the sofa.

"Just that he and his friend would be here in about five minutes and that they were taking me to dinner."

Thankfully, Dad is working at the lodge tonight, so I didn't have to cook for him. He looked pretty nice, too, when he left, if I do say so myself. The department store sale helped matters, or I could never have afforded those clothes for him.

"Are you sure you won't come with us? Colin's coming home to see you, too, you know. Besides, that salad will not hold you."

"I told you, Mom, I don't have much of an appetite."

I sigh, but bite my tongue. Something I should have perfected over my lifetime.

"I'm looking forward to seeing Colin. I kind of wish he didn't have someone coming with him. I'd like to spend some time alone with him," she says.

"Maybe you'll get time together before he leaves."

Just then tires crush pebbles on the driveway. We look at each other.

"I'd better get to my bedroom," Brooke says. "I'll be cleaned up before you get back. Tell Colin I'll see him later."

"Will do." I grab my pocketbook and head for the door. Before I can get there, Colin walks inside.

"Hi, Mom." He pulls me into an enormous hug. "Great to see you."

He's all smiles, and I'm thinking he's either had a great week at school or he's greatly relieved the week is over.

"Great to see you, honey." Though I've had a long, stressful day, just seeing him so happy makes me feel better instantly.

"I have someone I want you to meet."

He turns, and I see the figure behind him. One glance at the dark-eyed beauty with ebony ringlets and perfect skin, and my breath catches.

"Mom, you remember Sophia Amorini?"

Oh, boy, do I remember. Marco's words come back to me. He will not be happy about this. Not that I'm thrilled either, but there's no need to overreact. After all, we can't keep them locked up in their dorm rooms from now until graduation. Still, knowing that the hypothetical "little twirp" Marco referred to is my son does little to ease my mind.

"Certainly, I do. Sophia, how good to see you again." I reach over and give her a hug.

"Nice to see you, Mrs. Hartline."

"Please, call me Wendy."

"Wendy," she says with a shy smile.

We stand there for an awkward moment.

"Listen, we thought it would be fun for you and Sophia's dad to join us for dinner. I hope you don't mind."

My hand absently reaches for a nearby stand to steady myself.

"You don't mind, do you?" Sophia asks, almond-shaped eyes filled with worry.

"Oh, no, of course not. I'd be happy to go with you. You kids go ahead and get in the car. I need something from my bedroom . . . " I'm thinking smelling salts. "I'll be right out."

Colin turns back to me. "Is Brooke coming?"

"Not this time."

"She in her room?"

I nod.

He looks at Sophia. "Go ahead and get in the car, babe, and I'll be right back. I'm going to go say hi to my sister."

Babe? He called her *babe*? Cutie, sweetie, honey, I could handle those. But babe? No. *Babe* is serious.

Could he have gotten over Emily, his high school girlfriend, so soon? I admit that I still hoped that they would get back together one day. I was just sure they were meant for each other.

And I thought the toddler stage was hard.

Some days I fantasize about the kids living at home, playing in the backyard while Dennis and I sit on a wooden swing nearby beneath the canopy of a maple on a lazy Sunday afternoon. I thought those days would last forever.

Inside my bedroom, I pause to catch my breath. I can do this. Marco can't blame me, after all. So why do I feel guilty? I dab on a little more perfume, touch up my lipstick, take one more swipe at my hair with a comb. Then I walk down the hall and out the front door, wondering what the night will hold.

At the restaurant, Sophia runs into the ladies' room and Colin walks over to talk to the hostess about our table, leaving Marco and me standing in the waiting area.

"Well, this isn't exactly how I had planned to spend the

evening," Marco grouses. He glares at me. "Did you know they were dating? Is this what that lecture was all about the other day when you talked about letting go?"

"Lecture? If I remember correctly, I merely mentioned that we have to let them go. And no, I didn't know they were dating."

His eyes flash with distrust.

"What's the matter? Are we cutting into your social life?" I ask.

He stares at me. "What's Logan doing tonight, playing solitaire on the computer?"

"Wake up too early from your nap?"

"Ssh. Here they come. Try and be civil."

My mouth drops. He starts the whole thing, and suddenly *I'm* supposed to be civil? Why, I have half a mind to . . .

"Our table is ready," Colin says sweetly, ushering Sophia into the room with his hand at the small of her back.

Much as I hate to admit it, that little gesture makes me nervous. They're only in their second year of college. It's way too soon for serious. But I'm not about to tell Marco I agree with him on anything at the moment.

I notice a bowl of business cards near the cash register for winning a free lunch and drop my card inside. The card staring back at me has Marco's name and address on it. What kind of man advertises to get divorce business? How could I have ever thought him attractive? Logan is right, the man is a jerk.

The kids sit beside one another and thereby force Marco and me to sit together. We order our drinks and finally our meals, making small talk.

Once the server brings our dinners, Colin offers to pray, which is a good thing. I'm certain my prayers would bounce like e-mail gone haywire.

Sophia smiles and squeezes Colin's hand. Marco resembles a six-year-old on his first visit to church. His eyes glance around, and he reluctantly bows his head.

Halfway through the meal, the discussion turns to high school days.

"You know, I always thought you were beautiful in high school, but—"

"But you had a serious girlfriend."

"Something like that," Colin says with a melting grin.

"I thought you were cute, too, but you were already taken," Sophia says with a laugh so delicate, it reminds me of ice tinkling against glass. I've always admired women with dainty laughs.

"Okay, we get it. You didn't talk in high school. So how did it happen in college?" Marco asks, sawing on his T-bone so hard, I'm afraid he'll cut through the plate.

"You tell him." Colin nudges Sophia's arm.

"Okay." She puts down her napkin. "It's like this. We were both in the library. All the computers were taken, and I was using one. Colin came up to me and said, 'When you're finished with that, would you let me know? I really need to use one, and I have to be at work in a half hour.'" She laughs.

Marco and I look at her as though she has a screw loose. Then I look at Marco, figuring the apple doesn't fall far from the tree.

"And then?" Marco asks, trying but failing not to show his impatience.

"I offered him my computer, since I had all evening. He used it for fifteen minutes, then told me to come to the coffee shop when I was finished, and he'd buy me a latte. I did, and he did. He walked me back to my dorm. The rest is history." She smiles at Colin and puts her hand on his arm.

"The rest is history?" Marco visibly stiffens. His jaw is set, and he suddenly appears ten years older. "What does that mean?"

"Dad—" Sophia says.

"Mom—" Colin says.

They clasp hands and take a deep breath while Marco and I hold ours.

"We're engaged," they say together.

We let out our breath with a force that could send them into the next county, but they hold their own. Marco drops his fork onto his plate, and it makes a loud, ringing sound before dropping to the carpet with a *kerplunk*.

The kids are not deterred. Their determined jaws, unblinking eyes, all say they're not backing down.

"Daddy, I know how you feel, but Colin and I have talked about it at length. We'll finish school, of course. Go on to law school together, as husband and wife." Their fingers are still laced together, and I notice Colin gives her a hard squeeze.

Marco's unwavering gaze on his daughter has a *Pit and the Pendulum* Vincent Price-ish quality about it. It's just that scary.

"Sophia, remember, before you went off to school we talked about this."

Marco's words are measured, controlled, but I think I see smoke seeping from his ears.

Don't I have enough on me right now without adding this, too, Lord? I'm so tired.

Her dark eyes flash, her teeth grind. This girl is so ready to take him on.

"Daddy, we're getting married with or without your approval."

Marco turns to Colin. His eyes shrink to mere cracks. "Young man, can you even afford a ring? Or a honeymoon?"

"Well, I—"

"How do you plan to support yourself and your wife while you're going to school?"

"I—"

"In other words, how will you eat?" His eyes spark like hot coals.

"I—"

Just as I'm about to step in, Marco cuts me off.

"Then there's law school. Who's going to pay for that?"

"If you'd give him a chance to answer, he might be able to tell you," Sophia says.

Marco stops mid-rant, his dark gaze fixed on my son, chest heaving.

"I work at the coffee house—"

Marco rolls his eyes and shakes his head.

"—and I plan to get a second job."

"Where? McDonald's?" Marco waves his hands. "I don't believe this."

"I've got some money saved from landscaping work I did in high school. We can use some of that for an apartment deposit and things like that."

A smidgen of respect flickers in Marco's eyes. He has to be impressed that Colin has saved money from his high school earnings.

"I have a job offer to work maintenance on campus. The pay isn't bad."

"And I can get a job," Sophia says enthusiastically.

"You two can't be serious."

"We have no debts accumulated, and we set up a budget. Things will be tight, but we can do it."

At least they've given money some thought. I'm proud that they've worked on a budget together. Colin must have gotten that from Dennis.

Sophia's lips form into a thin line, making her look very much like her father. "We most certainly are serious, Dad." There's no doubt her mind is made up.

She turns to me and in a most professional tone says, "Mrs. Hartline, if you will help us, we'd like to have a small wedding. We thought we could get married in your chapel. Since we're trying to use our money wisely"—she shoots her dad a dirty look—"we thought it would be best to keep things simple." Her hand covers her mouth. "Oh, I didn't mean that your chapel was simple, I—"

"It's all right, honey. I understand."

"No, she will not help you," Marco snaps.

Okay, now he's gone too far.

"Thank you, but I think I can speak for myself."

All eyes turn to me, and I lose my resolve. "If you'll excuse me, I'm going to the ladies' room." With that, I scoot out of my chair and head for the restroom, praying I don't hurt that man when I get back.

seven

I didn't have time to pray long, but I was hoping the Lord would give me a burst of wisdom by the time I returned to the table.

He didn't.

"Well, Mom?" Colin demands. "Can we get married in the chapel?"

"And Daddy, we were thinking we could spend the first night of our honeymoon at your lodge before we head to the Cayman Islands."

"Cayman Islands?" The color of blood shoots up Marco's ears.

"Like I said, I've saved some money," Colin says.

"But first, we'll stay in your lodge." Sophia's eyes are swimming with joy.

Judging by the look on his face, I'm not sure Marco appreciates the thought of his daughter spending the night in his lodge with my son. If the situation weren't so serious, his expression would be comical. He says nothing; he simply sits there, smoldering like a pine log in a forgotten fire pit.

"Daddy?"

"I can't talk about this right now, Sophia."

Before anyone can say anything else, the server comes and places our desserts before us. With a frown, Marco picks up his fork. In the mood he's in, I'm glad it's not a knife.

"Just when were you planning on this wedding?" he asks.

Sophia clears her throat. "We were thinking shortly after school is out. We're looking at July."

"July, as in this year, July?" he asks incredulously. He leans threateningly close to my son, fork prongs in attack mode. With eyes squinted, mouth pursed, he says, "What's the rush?"

"Daddy!" Sophia glares at Marco.

Colin leans back in his chair, palms up, eyes wide. "Nothing like that, I promise." With his finger, he crosses his heart. And I kind of wish he hadn't pointed out its exact location to Marco.

"Then you have plenty of time to think this over," Marco says, leaning back.

"So, how long have you been dating?" I want to know, trying to decide if things are as serious as they think they are. Obviously, both Marco and I want to talk these kids out of this silly notion, but we have to do it rationally, not allowing our emotions to get in the way.

And if Marco can't do that, I'll grab my own fork.

Colin and Sophia exchange a glance and a smile.

"We started dating in October," Colin says, to my surprise.

I wonder why he hadn't mentioned it. As if reading my mind, he turns to me. "I didn't tell you, because—" He shoots a quick glance at Marco. "Well, I just didn't."

I toss a self-conscious look Marco's way, and he coughs.

"Colin, I'm sure you're a nice kid, but I have to tell you both right now, I'm opposed to this marriage. I will not support it whatsoever."

Not exactly a news flash, but to hear Marco say it out loud causes the kids' shoulders to slump.

Sophia's eyes fill with tears, and they both look to me.

"Though you kids are of legal age, I have to agree that you should think this through a little longer. Getting through school will be difficult enough without trying to adjust to marriage. What will it hurt to wait? You can date through school and then get married once you've got college behind you," I say cheerfully.

One look at their young faces, and I can see they're not buying it. Actually, the scene looks familiar. Seems I remember Dennis and me having this same conversation with my parents.

Sophia looks glumly at her plate and says softly, "We hoped to have your blessing."

Colin jumps in. "But the truth is, we're getting married with or without it."

Stubborn, just like me. So many years ago. Maybe I should tell them.

Colin looks up at me. "Mom, if you don't want to handle the wedding, we can go through Roseanne, or we can get married at Sophia's church, or ours."

"So what are your goals, Colin?" Marco asks in an even voice, as though trying to calm the kids down—now that he's got them all stirred up.

Colin explains that he hopes to concentrate his efforts in family law, specializing in adoptions and other matters concerning children.

"A noble cause," Marco says, in a degrading sort of way. "Not much money in it, but noble."

"Daddy," Sophia says with a sharp edge.

"There are more things in life than gathering money," I say, coming to the defense of my son.

"True, but you have to admit money makes life easier." Marco's eyes dare me to argue.

Has he surmised that my business is down and I'm struggling? Well, he certainly can't care, since he's about to add to my financial problems.

"Where do you plan to live?" Marco presses.

"Well, for a while, of course, we'll live in married student housing—if we can get in. Otherwise, an apartment off campus," Colin says, clearly unruffled by Marco's intimidation.

"What is your academic status?"

Sophia gasps. "Daddy, how dare you question him this way. You're being totally unreasonable." She throws her napkin onto her plate and stands up. "Let's go, Colin."

Colin looks confused. "We don't have a car here."

"We'll call one of our friends."

It's easy to see Sophia has her father's temperament. I'm not sure that's such a great thing for Colin. I had hoped he might marry a woman with a gentler nature. Someone like Emily.

"Sophia, don't go." Marco grabs her hand as she brushes by him.

"I just can't talk right now." She pulls her hand free and turns to Colin. "You ready?"

He looks at me. "I'll be home later, Mom."

With that, they walk off hand in hand, obviously more determined than ever.

Marco shoves his fingers through his hair, then looks up at me. "That didn't go over so well."

"They're probably on their way to Vegas as we speak."

His expression grows so dark that I scoot away in case he goes for his fork.

"I didn't exactly see you fixing things, Dear Abby," he snaps.

"Who had a chance? You were off and running before I could say anything."

He holds up his palm and sighs. "Look, we've obviously got a situation on our hands. How about we declare a truce and help those kids to not make the mistake of their lives?"

I will not be so easily mollified. "It's not as though Colin is the worst mistake Sophia could make."

"That's not what I meant, and you know it. I don't know your son, but I know my daughter, and she's not ready for marriage. She's impulsive and headstrong like her mother."

My eyebrows spike. "Oh? Only her mother?"

He cracks his first smile of the evening. "I might play a small part in that."

"Can I get you anything else?" the server asks.

"I'd like another cup of coffee, please." Marco looks at me. "Would you like anything, Wendy?"

Considering he's my ride home, I don't have anywhere to go, so I order a cup of coffee.

"You do realize they're too young to get married, right?" he asks.

The thought of my own life rushes to mind. So young, so determined. "Yes, I realize that. But they are technically adults."

"They're too young." He tries to hold the edge from his voice, but I hear it just the same.

The dark cloud has returned tenfold.

He softens when he looks at me. "Listen, I'm sure Colin is a fine young man, but law school is draining. I also know what it is to be stuck in a bad marriage. I want better for my daughter."

"I don't know about law school, but I know what it is to be in a wonderful marriage, and that is what I want for my son."

Marco gives me an odd stare. "Do you always see the world this way?"

The server places my coffee cup in front of me, and I take a sip. "What way is that?"

"Through Doris Day eyes."

I'm not sure whether to laugh or get mad. "I've never heard it called that before."

He shrugs. "Sophia's mother always watched those movies. I think that's what made her so dissatisfied. They depicted a perfect life, perfect hero, all that. Life isn't that way. I leave my dirty socks on the floor." He shrugs. "So shoot me."

His wife has hurt him, no question about it. My fingers trace the weave of thread on the tablecloth.

"It doesn't mean you can't strive for that."

"And be beat down again? No, it's better to meet life head-on, eyes wide open, so you're not blindsided in the end."

We lock eyes. He coughs and shifts in his seat.

"I guess we need to come up with a plan of some kind," I say. "Something that will help them to see that it's better to wait awhile, make sure this is what they really want."

"So you'll help me?" he asks, eyes twinkling.

"Help you?"

"Help me come up with a plan to wake them up?"

"I don't know. My relationship with my son is first and foremost."

"I agree. And when we help them to see that we have their best interests at heart, our relationship with our kids will be stronger than ever."

"Okay," I say with some hesitation. "What can it hurt? I mean, we'll try to stall things, and if they decide to marry in the end, so be it. At least we can know that we did our best to help them."

He doesn't look so convinced. "We'll do more than try. We'll stop them." Marco speaks with such conviction it makes me nervous.

"Wendy?"

The familiar voice breaks through our conversation and causes me to jerk around so quickly, I almost fall off my chair.

"Logan? What are you doing here?"

"I could ask you the same thing." His gaze goes from me to Marco.

"Good to see you again, Carter." Marco grins, lifts his mug in a toast gesture, and takes a sip.

"Wish I could say the same." Logan turns to me. "Where's your dad?" He's giving me one of those teacher stares that puts me on the defensive.

"He went with some friends to the River Walk."

"It's hard to bond with him when you're here and he's there, huh?"

Okay, I don't necessarily want to discuss this in front of Marco, though by the look of amusement on Marco's face, I'd say he's enjoying the whole scene.

Marco puts down his empty coffee cup and looks at me. "Listen, I'll leave you two to hash this out. You'll take Wendy home, I presume?"

He gives me no say in the matter, making me feel as though I'm a burden to be dealt with. Heat starts at my neck and burns its way to my face.

Logan fumbles for words. "Well, uh, yes, of course."

Marco smiles. "Wendy, thank you for an interesting evening. I'll be in touch." With a quick salute, he turns and walks away, leaving Logan and me to gape after him.

By the time I stumble into the front door of my home, I could kiss the foyer floor. Logan's cold shoulder tonight, Marco's reaction to the kids' news, everything makes me want to run to my workroom and make enough drapes to furnish every home in the county.

"Hi, Mom."

To say Brooke looks like death-warmed-over is putting it mildly. Still dressed in Kevin's oversized T-shirt, hair in complete disarray, and wearing the familiar downtrodden expression are nothing new. But the fact that her skin tone could rival white milkweed gives me room for pause.

"How are you?" I ask, trying to hide my concern so she won't clam up.

"I've been better."

"Can I get you something to eat?"

Her hand immediately goes to her stomach, and she moans. "The last thing I want is food."

"Brooke, I know you hate for me to interfere, but won't you listen to me just this once and go see a doctor?" I follow her into the living room. "I think a checkup would be a good idea."

She sags into the sofa and pulls a red-and-white crocheted throw around her legs. The one Dennis bought me on our last Valentine's Day together.

"Okay."

Her immediate compliance almost makes me miss my chair.

Wouldn't you know it's Friday night. She'll probably change her mind by Monday. While studying a ruffle on a throw pillow, I say nonchalantly, "How about I just schedule an appointment with my doctor and see if we can get you in next week?"

She nods. And before she can respond further, I make a beeline for the phone book and pick up the receiver in the kitchen for privacy. The doctor's answering service tells me to call back Monday. Oh well. I'll just avoid the subject with Brooke until after I've made an appointment for her.

"So, how did it go with Colin?" she asks when I return to the room. "Are he and his friend coming back?"

I explain about Sophia, Marco, the whole disastrous affair.

Brooke leans her head back on a couch pillow. "Well, there's not a whole lot you can do about it if they want to get married, Mom."

"Yeah, I know. I just want him to think it through. It doesn't seem to be his smartest choice at this time."

"According to you."

"Well, you should give me a little credit for having been around the block," I say, feeling frustration ball up in my stomach.

"You? Around the block?" She gives a rebellious laugh. "Mom, please. You don't know the first thing about how it is today."

"And you do?"

"Well, I'd say I have a little better handle since I've been out there more recently. Things have changed some since you were there."

"I don't live with my head under a rock, Brooke."

"I'll bet the most daring thing you've ever done in your life is leave the crust on your peanut butter sandwich even after your mother told you about the hungry children around the world."

"That's just mean, Brooke."

She rolls her eyes.

"Besides, I would never do that."

"What?"

"Leave the crust when there are starving children." Which would probably explain the extra weight I've been carrying around lately.

She goes for a different tactic. "Please don't tell me that you and Marco are going to try to put a stop to it."

"Okay, I won't tell you."

"That's a sure way to get them to the altar in a hurry," she says, studying her nails. "But then, what would I know?"

"Well, it might not work, but at least we'll know that we tried."

Memories of Mom and Dad trying to talk Dennis and me out of getting married come to mind. Actually, Mom just stood beside Dad while he forbade it with a loud rant about rebellious teenagers. Brooke was right. It made us all the more determined to get married. Though we loved each other, we went about it all wrong.

"Where's Granddad?"

"Supposedly down at the River Walk with some friends."

"So, who brought you home?"

"Logan."

She looks confused. "Logan? I thought you were with Marco and Colin."

I reach for the hand cream on the stand. The scent of coconut soon perfumes the air.

The front door squeaks open.

"We're in here, honey," I call out. Hopefully, it's Colin. A robber might think me overly friendly.

"Hey, there's my favorite sister," Colin says, scooping Brooke into an enormous hug.

It thrills my soul to see them treat each other so well. Makes me feel as though we did a good job raising them.

He turns to me. "Thanks for your support tonight, Mom," he says sarcastically.

So much for the good job raising them thing.

"Listen, Colin—"

He turns to Brooke. "Did you know I'm engaged? Or did Mom already complain to you about it?"

Before I can defend myself, Colin turns to me. "Sophia is everything I've ever wanted in a woman. She's beautiful, smart, sweet, and more than that, I love her. I'm sorry, Mom, but my mind is made up."

He looks back to Brooke. "We missed you tonight, sis. I'll visit more tomorrow, but at the moment I'm pretty beat. Good night." With that, he walks out of the room.

I stare after him as though he's just announced the total annihilation of chocolate popcorn from the universe.

Though I can't pinpoint why, I feel Brooke's gaze on me, and I'm almost sure it's an I-told-you-so type of gaze.

"I can't remember when I've seen Colin more determined," I say with a heavy chest.

"Don't you like Marco's daughter?"

"I hardly know her. She seems nice enough. But the thing is they have a lot of school ahead of them. And, well, this is the first I've even heard of him caring about her, and now they want to get married? It's too sudden."

"If I remember correctly, you and Dad planned things in a hurry too. The word *elopement* springs to mind."

"I've told you kids before, your dad and I didn't have a lot of money. We didn't want our parents to have to pay for a wedding. Besides, they were against it."

"And were they right in being against it?" Brooke asks.

Her question causes my heart to stumble. "It just doesn't matter anymore, Brooke. Good night." I kiss her on the forehead and walk out of the room.

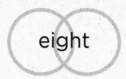

eight

"*Hey, Wendy, I just talked to Katy,*" Roseanne says over the phone.

"She called you at home?" Pouring a mug of coffee from my carafe, I manage to spill a couple of drops. I grab a paper towel and clean the countertop.

"Yeah. She couldn't find your number. She wanted us to know her laryngitis is better and she wants to sing for the wedding on Saturday. I told her we already hired someone else, but she wanted me to ask you. I guess she needs the money."

"Oh, dear. I want to help her, but it wouldn't be right to promise it to Candace and not let her have it. On the other hand, Katy is our regular singer. Still, Candy has put in the practice this week." Finding my place on the living room sofa, I say, "We'd better go with Candace."

"Yeah, that's what I thought, too, but since you're the boss, I thought I'd better run it by you. What time will you be at the chapel?"

"I'm heading there in another half hour." Glancing up at my

watch, I wonder if I have time to get the dirty dishes loaded before I go.

"Why so soon?"

"Just making sure everything is in place. Plus, I want to make sure the honeymoon cabins are in order."

"Are you still beating yourself up over the cake thing? Don't worry about it. Everyone makes mistakes," Roseanne says.

"Did you happen to notice the couple was middle-aged? Meaning lots of boomer women on the guest list. Menopausal women want their cake, Roseanne. I didn't give it to them. They wanted to hurt me. I could see it in their eyes."

"They were kind of scary, I'll have to admit. Buying the entire cake inventory at the bakery was sheer genius. That appeased them."

"I know, but *Congratulations on your Bar Mitzvah* scrawled across the cake did take something away from the wedding celebration."

Roseanne laughs. "The bride and groom were pretty calm about it all."

"I think the fact that I paid for the cake helped."

"Maybe."

Gill's voice calls out to Roseanne.

"Listen, I've gotta go. Gill needs my help."

"Did he get the toilet installed?"

"Yeah. Thankfully, once he installed a new shut-off valve, it worked. He's moved on to the shower now. He's putting in tile. Should be real nice when he's done."

Gill is like Tim the Toolman, but Roseanne seems okay with that. She loves him, strengths and weaknesses. Isn't that what life is all about—seeing the good in people instead of focusing on the negative stuff?

"Sounds great. Listen, you're busy with Gill. Let me call Katy about the music."

"Are you sure?"

"I'm sure. I'll see you at the chapel."

Staring at the phone, I feel a tinge of guilt tug at me. Have I been seeing the good in Marco Amorini? Maybe I haven't given the man a fair shake. He's worried about his daughter, and maybe he overreacted. Okay, he definitely overreacted. But maybe that's because he's a caring, if a little overprotective, father.

Still, I'm just as worried about my son, and you won't find me acting that way.

The wedding went off without a hitch—*well, aside from the* fact that we had two soloists. Trying, but failing, to get some quality time in with Colin, it totally slipped my mind to call Katy. She showed up late, and knowing she needs the money, I didn't have the heart to turn her away. So we had two people sing "We've Only Just Begun" (the bride and groom were in their fifties). I have to say Candace did the better job. Of course, Katy did just get over laryngitis.

"Was the couple okay with two versions of the same song?" Roseanne whispers at the reception hall a few miles from the chapel. The tables are dressed in linens and wedding color-coordinated centerpieces.

"What are they gonna say when I ended up paying for the vocalists?"

Roseanne's eyes grow wide. "You've got to stop that, Wendy. You're using up all your profits."

I shrug. "Don't I know it."

"Are we okay?"

"We've been better. Hey, hey, watch out!" I yell when a band member knocks over the ficus tree with his microphone stand. "You'd think these guys would be more careful."

"You've done a great job with the decorating, as always," Roseanne says.

"It's fun. It gives me a chance to be creative."

"Still keeping busy with the window treatments?"

"Yeah."

"I don't know how you do it all," she says, shaking her head before taking a sip from her punch cup.

"Well, obviously not all that well, or we wouldn't have scheduled two soloists. But with Brooke and Dad staying with me, I really can't afford to turn down work."

"Is Brooke feeling any better?"

"Not much. She did finally agree to see a doctor, though, so I plan to call first thing Monday, before she changes her mind."

"Sounds like a good idea. How's your dad?"

"Other than the fact that he's eating me out of house and home, he's the same old Dad."

"I can't imagine where he puts all that food," Roseanne says.

"He's always had a healthy metabolism. The man has ten cups of coffee before my eyes blink open in the morning."

"Is he helping to pay for the groceries?"

"Not so far," I say, feeling a little guilty about complaining. After all, he is my dad. My mom always defended him by saying, "That's just Dad." But what did that mean? Does that give him an excuse for being rude or inconsiderate?

"Well, hopefully, once he starts making money at Marco's lodge, he'll help out."

I smile and nod. With the way my business is going, he'll probably be making more than I am by summer's end.

We'll get through it. It's just the winter slump. Spring is just around the corner, and people like to get married in the spring. I just hope they choose my chapel for their ceremony.

"*Mom, I don't know what you have against Sophia, but it's* not going to stop me from making her my wife." Colin is sitting calmly across from me on the sofa, his eyes fixed on his folded hands.

"I understand." I've lived with Colin long enough to know that if I try to buck him on something, it will only make him dig his heels in further. "I'm sure Sophia is a lovely girl, Colin. It's just that I think if you give it some time, you'll know for sure if this is right for you."

He stares at his hands. "I know it's right."

"You thought the same thing when you were dating Emily—"

His head snaps toward me. "I knew that's what this was all about." He gets up and starts pacing. "You think I still care about Emily, and I don't. Emily and I are over. We've been over since last August. You have to let her go, just as I had to let her go."

"But so soon, Colin? I mean, can you fall in love so soon with another woman, when you told me you loved Emily all that time?"

"I not only can, I have."

His young mind is made up, so what can I do? "Has Emily met someone else, is that it?"

"I don't know. She made it clear she needed to move on, so I let her. I have no idea what she's doing these days."

"I'm sure the distance didn't help you two in your relationship."

"If you love someone, distance shouldn't matter. Those were your words."

"You're right."

Colin is right; it is hard to let go of Emily. I had come to think of her as family. With her parents moving to Florida and her transferring schools, there was just a lot of confusion in her life. I can't help thinking that if Colin gave it a little time, she'd come to her senses. But with Sophia in the picture, there's no hope.

He heads for the door. "Well, I'd better go. I'm taking Sophia to dinner and a movie tonight." He looks at my crisp white blouse, black pants, and silver jewelry. "You going somewhere?"

"Supposed to go out with Logan, but I have a bad headache. I think I'll have to cancel."

"Have you taken anything?"

"Yeah, but usually when I get one of these, I have to lie down awhile."

Colin walks over to me. "Look, Mom, I love you, and I'd really like your blessing on this. Just think about it." He kisses me on the cheek. "I hope you get feeling better."

"I want to give my blessing, Colin. Just give me a little time to get used to the idea, okay? All I want is what's best for you. Take it from the voice of experience, marrying young is not an easy way to start."

He nods and walks away.

Emily was so perfect for him. Wonderful Christian young lady, a Martha Stewart type, homemaker. Would have made a great attorney's wife. But Sophia wants to work alongside him.

I don't know. I don't consider myself a controlling mom, but things just aren't turning out the way I had thought they would.

"See you later," he says before going out the door.

The disappointment in his face breaks my heart, but I just can't think about it right now. My head hurts too much.

The doorbell sounds through the hazy fog of my dreams. My consciousness finally surfaces, my eyelids flutter open, and I realize I've fallen asleep on the sofa. I sit up slowly, feeling groggy from my migraine medicine.

Probaby Logan stopping over to check on me. I really wish he wouldn't. He's been suspicious ever since he caught me in Marco's arms. And in spite of everything, the mere vision of that day in my memory brings a smile to my lips.

I stop at the hallway mirror, finger my messy hair to make myself presentable, then walk to the door. At least my headache is gone. Hopefully, it left a few working brain cells behind.

I swing the door open. "Marco?"

"Sorry to bother you, but I knew the kids were out, and I wondered if I could talk to you a minute."

My feet are planted as I waver with whether or not I should let him into my house.

"Look, Wendy, I'm sorry about everything. I reacted badly to the thing with the kids, and I guess I took it out on you."

His apology makes me feel a little better. Though I don't know why, I look around outside and then step aside for him to come in. The truth be known, I wouldn't be at all surprised to see Logan lurking in my bushes.

I nod slightly, but not overly so, not wanting to give him the impression that I'm actually glad he's here. Because I'm not. I'm really not.

Marco follows me into the living room and sees my blanket strewn across the sofa. "I'm sorry . . . You were resting?"

Great. I'm resting on the sofa. On a Saturday night. I have no life, and now Marco knows it.

"Oh, no, no, that's fine. I had a migraine and just sat down a moment to wait it out. And next thing I know, the doorbell rings." I laugh. "Could I get you something to drink?" I instantly add, "Sweet or unsweetened tea, soda, coffee?"

He smiles. "Unsweetened tea would be great." Oh, of course, a manly man would never drink sweetened tea. He wants the kind that grows hair on his chest.

Once we settle in the living room with our drinks, Marco begins. "So, about the kids. What are we going to do?"

"Oh, no. This devious stuff is your department."

He shrugs, takes a sip from his iced tea, and looks at me. "I was thinking, who knows your son better than you, and who knows my daughter better than me?"

"I'm listening."

"We know they're not right for each other—or at least the timing isn't right—but they can't see it yet. So we'll just have to help them see the light."

"And how do you propose we do that?"

"I know what Sophia likes, and you know what Colin likes. Maybe we can make a list and compare notes. Find those things that are sure to annoy the other, and we'll focus on bringing those things to the surface so they can see what they're truly getting themselves into."

I stare at him. "You're serious."

"Yeah, why?"

"Marco. I want to help Colin make the right decisions, but I don't want to manipulate and control him."

His eyebrows slip into sharp sloping angles. "Then what do you propose?"

"I don't know."

Before we can talk any further, the doorbell rings again.

"Excuse me," I say, rising to answer it. With all the company I'm having these days, it's possible I could give up jogging. I get enough aerobic workout just answering the door.

One look at Logan's face tells me I'd better slam the door immediately or hightail it for the Smokies.

"Well, I see your headache is better," he says, stepping inside uninvited. He marches straight into the living room and stops smack dab in front of Marco with the stance of Gary Cooper in *High Noon*. "What are *you* doing here?"

Marco merely smiles and lifts his glass. "Just enjoying some iced tea with this fine lady," he says, making me want to bop him.

Logan swings around to me. "Wendy?"

I hesitate, half expecting him to add *Are you going to let him talk to me like this?* I'll bet anything Logan was a tattletale in school.

"Would you like a glass of tea, Logan?"

"No, I would not like a glass of tea."

"Then sit down," I say with a bit of a growl. I'm ashamed, really, at the power I feel when he immediately plops into a chair.

We explain the dilemma with the kids—that they're dating and how we hope to stop things before they turn too serious. By the time we finish, Logan is emphatically shaking his head.

"All you're going to do is alienate them," he says.

"That's what I think too," I say.

"Excuse me, Logan, but if memory serves me, you have no children." Marco sets his glass of tea back on the coaster.

Logan blinks. "Well, no, but—"

Marco raises both hands in the air, palms facing up, then lets them fall at his side. "Why is it people without children think they have all the answers for people who have children? It would be like me coming to your classroom and telling you how to teach."

For once, Logan is at a loss for words. Trust me, this doesn't happen often, what with him being an English professor and all.

"He's just trying to help, Marco," I defend, but he won't hear of it.

"We don't need his help. They're our children, not his, so I don't see how this affects him one way or the other." Marco stands and paces around the room.

Why do guys do that?

Logan stands up, cocks his head, and with a lift of his chin says, "Well, it affects me a great deal, as a matter of fact, because Wendy and I are—are—"

This would be where all the air is sucked out of the room. Whatever he's about to say, I don't think I'm ready to hear it.

I stand and put my hand on Logan's arm, attempting to calm him—or shut him up, I'm not sure which. "Concerned," I finish. "Logan is also concerned."

The expression he turns my way is one of confusion and . . . disappointment. The tiny throb at the back of my head returns and swiftly marches forward, gaining momentum.

"Listen, can we talk about this later?" I sag back into my chair and rub my head.

They both look at me.

"I'll call you," they say simultaneously.

Funny, when I've dreamed of men vying for my attention, this is not the way I had imagined it.

The pounding in my head increases tenfold.

The doorbell rings again, and I consider hiring a butler. I look up, hoping one of them will offer to get the door, but they have this obvious distrust thing going on. Marco won't give Logan the satisfaction of leaving the room, and Logan doesn't trust Marco enough to leave him alone with me. I start to get up.

"I'll get it for you," Marco finally says, making his way for the door.

"Oh, hi, Mr. Amorini," I hear Brooke say. "Sorry, Mom, I forgot my key."

"Help me up," I say to Logan. The fact that he grits his teeth when he hauls me out of the chair is not lost on me. When my headache gets better, I plan to sit on him.

"Brooke, I thought you were in your bedroom asleep." I look at her swollen eyes. "Are you all right?"

She looks at the men. "I'll talk to you about it later."

"No, no, we were just leaving," Marco says, giving Logan a sharp look that says it's time to go. "Thanks for the tea, Wendy. I'll be in touch." He gives the now-familiar salute and turns to go.

Logan drags his heels to the door, making it obvious he doesn't want to leave, and hoping that I will ask him to stay.

"Good night, Marco. Logan," I say.

They step through the door, and I breathe a sigh of relief—until I turn around and look once again at Brooke.

"Now what's this about?" I ask, settling onto the living room sofa across from her.

"Kevin has carried his spending too far, Mom." She wipes her nose on a Kleenex. "It seems we have quite a few debts."

A sick feeling swirls in my stomach when I think of where this might be going. "Oh?" I try my best to keep alarm from my voice.

She stares at her Kleenex and nods.

"How do you know?"

"I picked up my mail today and found that we're two months behind on our house payment and some other bills."

"Could he have overlooked the bills?"

"No. He used the mortgage payment to buy the big-screen

television. He told me he made some extra money on eBay, but he didn't. His spending is out of control." She looks up at me. "Are you okay, Mom?"

No doubt the empty look in my eyes tells her I'm coming up short on the wisdom thing tonight. "Just a headache."

"I don't know where he's staying, so I haven't been able to reach him. When I call his work, he doesn't return my calls. I'm afraid to bother his parents with this in case he hasn't told them yet. What am I going to do?" Brooke dabs at the tears in her eyes. "What if we lose the house before we can get it sold?"

"Don't worry, honey. Since I sold half ownership of the pond, I've got some extra cash. We'll be fine." I reach over and wrap my arms around her frail body, pulling her into a reassuring hug. The amazing thing is, she doesn't pull away.

"The whole thing makes me sick to my stomach," she says when we part. "Now I wonder if I even know my own husband." Her face looks clammy; her T-shirt that used to hug her more than I wanted it to now looks a little loose.

I'm worried about Brooke. Really worried.

When I feel inadequate like this, I long to talk to my mother. If she were here, she'd know just what to say.

On the other hand, Dad would tell Brooke to get a grip and get her body back to work, showing nary a smidgen of compassion. That's how he handled me after Mom died. "You've got to get over it, Wendy," he'd say. "Life goes on." Then he'd take a swig from his brown bottle.

I'll call the credit union in the morning and see how much I have in savings. If I have to cash in some of my investments, I'll do it. Whatever it takes to help my daughter through this.

Things will get better. They have to.

nine

Straightening the kitchen before I go to bed, I place the last glass in the dishwasher and crank it on. Dad steps in with another dirty glass. I stop the washer and shove the glass inside, then start it again.

"Think you'll like working at the lodge, Dad?" I ask.

"Yeah, I do. That Marco is an all-right guy."

That's quite a compliment, coming from my dad.

"He's sure got a way with the ladies." He scratches the whiskers on his jaw. "One worker told me once or twice a week he brings the staff a dessert that different women have made for him. He goes dancing at least once a week. Yep, that boy is a regular Casanova." Dad chuckles.

"I don't see what's so funny about it."

There's too much snap in my voice, and Dad's raised eyebrows tell me he's picked up on that.

"Well, what kind of man takes advantage of so many women?" I ask.

"Who says he's taking advantage? He's spreading himself around and making everyone happy."

I fiercely scrub the countertop.

"If you're not careful, you'll rub a hole in that," Dad teases. "'Night, Wendy." He turns and walks out of the kitchen.

I don't know why I let what he said bother me. Marco can have however many women he wants. Makes no difference to me. The—the—Casanova!

By the time the kitchen is clean, Dad and Brooke have already gone to their rooms. I pluck a photo album from the bookshelf in the living room and take it to my room.

What a way to spend a Saturday evening.

I settle into bed, my back propped on pillows. The pain in my head has finally subsided, allowing me a quick jaunt down memory lane as I flip through the pages of my childhood. I linger over pictures of my mom. We never got to share the usual mother-daughter things. My wedding, the kids' births, and now the current disintegration of my life.

And then there's Dad. He changed after her death. He shut himself up in his room with his booze, and I isolated myself in my room with my records. He wasn't there for me. It felt as though I lost my mom and my dad at the same time. To the world around us, our neighbors, friends, everything looked just fine. "My, see how well they're handling their grief," they would say. Only Dad and I knew we hid our pain well.

And now he expects me to be there for him.

Though I know he was working through his own grief at the time, I still can't seem to get past the bitterness. I'm working two jobs to help put food on my table at a time when I should be carefree, enjoying the single life that was forced upon me. Instead, I'm taking care of my grown daughter, my homeless father, and a son who is about to make the mistake of a lifetime.

My thoughts make me feel guilty. Shouldn't I be happy to help my family when they are in need? If only I had more time. If only I could work less at the chapel and more on my curtains. If only . . .

Life can be so unfair.

I flip the page, and my gaze falls on a photo. My mother's golden hair is pulled into a French twist. Dressed in a light yellow suit, she's sitting at the piano bench with me at her side in my Sunday best. My first piano recital. I was so nervous. Now that I'm a mother, I can't help wondering if she was nervous for me.

Every time Brooke or Colin had a solo or speaking part in a play, I was a nervous wreck. Gained five pounds every time because I would binge on chocolate. If my mother was nervous, she never showed it. She was always the picture of calm. No chocolate wrappers anywhere. Wonder if I was adopted?

The only time I ever saw her ruffled was the day I came home from school and found her wrapped in Dad's arms, her eyes swollen and red. I don't know if it affected me because she had been crying or because Dad was holding her. I had never really seen a tender side of him. After her death, I rarely saw him express any emotion—other than anger. He had plenty of that. Cancer changed our lives forever.

Every mother in town who wanted her child to be a piano star brought her son or daughter to my mother. Mom used to tell me I was her star pupil, but that we should keep that our little secret so the other kids didn't feel bad.

I trace the photograph with my finger. Dad never let me play after she died. My music teacher tried to encourage me to practice at school, but the few times I tried, it made my stomach hurt. Maybe I should start playing again someday. Mom would have liked that, I think.

What would she say about this mess I'm in? What would Dennis say? I wish I could talk to Dad.

Yeah, right. In my wildest imaginings I can't envision Dad and me having a real father-daughter talk. I'm sure he has no idea what his presence here is doing to me. Not that it would make a difference. He cares only that he has a place to stay.

Reaching over to the CD player, I put on Brahms's piano sonatas. Visions of Mom and Dad, Brooke, Colin, and Logan swirl around in my mind, causing sleep to elude me. Until Marco steps into my dreams and my heart calms to a steady rhythm, and I'm pulled into the warm embrace of slumber . . .

Since Kevin is currently out of the picture, and Sophia stayed with her dad, I had the kids all to myself in church this morning. A true rarity, and I enjoyed it.

After lunch, Colin gathers his belongings and prepares to head back to school.

"Listen, I'm sorry with how everything turned out this weekend, Colin." I give him a hug at the door, breathing in the scent of leather from his jacket.

He pulls away and looks me square in the face. "I'm going to marry her, Mom." His jaw is set, his eyes unblinking.

I nod but say nothing.

"We'll be in touch." He hauls his bag over his shoulder and walks toward his gold Escort.

I watch and wave good-bye, then close the door and walk into the living room. A streak of sunlight splays across the carpet, and I can't help but notice how the drapes are blocking off some of the light.

Maybe I should make something new to put up in the window. Instead of a heavy rod, I could give it a more tailored look, go with a smart cornice and complementary covering. I'm not sure how long I sit on the sofa just allowing myself to relax when the phone rings.

"Hello?"

"Colin just picked up Sophia."

The familiar voice makes my pulse quicken. No surprise there. Marco Amorini upsets me every time I see him or hear his voice.

"Want to meet for coffee?"

Everything in me tells me I'd better run. "Well, I don't know, Marco."

"What's the matter? You worried about your boyfriend?"

Why does he have to challenge me? "No, I'm not worried about my *boyfriend*." There's a sinister twist to my voice, but I don't care. "Logan doesn't own me."

In fact, right about now, living on a deserted island sounds appealing.

"Then, do you want to meet? We need to figure out how to bring those kids to their senses."

"Colin isn't such a bad catch, you know? Your daughter would do well to marry a man like him." Why I'm on the defensive, I'm not really sure. Marco just seems to bring that out in me.

"Well, no man could do better than to snag Sophia, but that's beside the point. They're not ready to get married, and we have to show them that."

"Marco, I told you, I don't want to be a controlling parent."

Okay, the truth is I don't want my son marrying this young, and when he does get married, I choose Emily. Still, I know I don't have the right to make that decision for him. And neither does Marco.

"Look, can I stop by your house? Just give me a half hour of your time. Hear me out. Then, if you don't agree, I'll leave you alone."

"No, I don't think you'd better come here." Logan would have a fit for sure, and I don't need any more confrontations right now. "But I haven't run my mile today, and I need to do that before choir practice."

"Choir practice?"

"Yeah, at my church. You might have noticed that it's Sunday?" Not that I should mention it. I'm not exactly showing Christian charity here. "We're having a special practice with a guest soloist for the evening service."

"Do you just want to meet at the park?"

"Yes. I'll be there in half an hour. Meet you in the parking lot."

I scribble out a note for Dad, who went out with some church guys to do who-knew-what. They'll probably climb a mountain or take on a bear or something. No use thinking about it. He's a grown man. Brooke went over to her house to go through more things in preparation for moving. I offered my help, but she said she needs to be alone right now. All I can do is pray and respect her wishes.

I rush to the bedroom to get my workout clothes on. Just then the phone rings.

"Hi, Mrs. Hartline. This is Emily."

"Emily, how are you?" How odd that she would be calling now. Is it a sign?

"I'm great. I just wondered how you were doing. Even though Colin and I aren't dating, I still want to keep in touch with you and Brooke. You've been like family to me."

My heart melts with her words. We talk about her family and school, and it's clear that she's not happy. In fact, she says she wants to come back for a while, stay with her grandparents, and think things through.

Hmm. This could be very timely. She hasn't made definite plans yet, so I decide not to tell Colin or Marco. No need to get anyone stirred up just yet.

After we say our good-byes, my heart is lighter. But that's the only thing that is. One glance in the mirror tells me if I don't get some of this weight off, I'll have to buy a jogging outfit the next size up.

I'm thankful for the drive over to the park. A blazing sun causes the city to shine, lifting my earlier gloom. My mother always said there was a silver lining to every cloud, and I couldn't agree more.

Climbing out of my car, I see that Marco is already here. His smile makes my stomach somersault, but I'm not about to fall for that charm act. He's right: we *do* need to stop Colin and Sophia from making a big mistake. I mean, do I want to attend family functions with this man for the rest of my life? I think not.

Marco is dressed in long pants and a T-shirt that's stretched tight across his broad shoulders. "Thanks for meeting me," he says, brushing his hand on my arm.

A chill ripples through me, no doubt from the slight Tennessee breeze rustling through the trees. I slip on my jacket and zip it up.

We do a couple of bends and stretches, then he stands and looks at me through those warm chocolate eyes. "Ready?"

My tongue feels laden with peanut butter. "Ready."

We start out at a light pace, falling into a steady rhythm, side by side.

"I thought it might be good to talk about things they don't like," he begins. "For instance, Sophia hates fish. Knowing that, you could encourage Colin to take her to the town fish fry or something."

I turn to him. "That's the best you can come up with? I mean, taking her to a fish fry is hardly enough to stop her from marrying him."

"It's a start. One event after another might make her question things, that's all. She also hates it when guys bite their fingernails. Does Colin do that?"

I shake my head. "He's practically a germophobic."

We jog a few steps in silence.

"What do you suppose brought them together in the first place?" Marco asks in short bursts of breath, his stride taut and steady.

"For one thing, I believe Colin is on the rebound. He dated another girl through high school, and I was sure they would get married. Her parents moved to Florida at the beginning of the school year, and she transferred to Florida State. She decided long-distance romances were too hard to pursue, so she broke it off with Colin. He was devastated."

Marco frowns. "He obviously got over it fast."

We jog past a mother pushing a stroller carrying a happy toddler whose golden hair lies on her head in a cloud of curls.

"That's just it. I'm not convinced he is over it. I just think he's lonely and—"

"Using Sophia?" There's an edge to Marco's voice.

"No, I didn't mean that. Colin would never *use* someone. But without realizing it, he could have fallen for her to fill the void Emily left."

"My daughter plays second fiddle to no one."

"Listen, don't get bent out of shape. You asked what got them together. I'm just giving you my opinion." It's hard to get mad and run at the same time.

A shapely woman of around thirty jogs past us with a noticeable slowing of pace when she spots Marco.

"Marco Amorini?" she says. "How are you? You probably don't remember me but I'm Courtney, Wilma Bradenton's niece. We met at her house a couple of weeks ago before you, um, went dancing." Her eyes shine.

I know I should just keep jogging and let them talk, but for the life of me, I can't get my feet to cooperate. I might miss something.

Marco coughs. "Yes, well, good to see you again," he says, his feet already starting to move.

She blinks. "Good to see you too." She glances at me and smiles, then jogs away.

How curious.

"So, what are some of Colin's quirks? Maybe we can play on those."

He obviously doesn't want to talk about our drop-in visitor, so I guess I'll play along.

"I don't know," I say between breaths. "He leaves his dirty dishes in the sink, just the way his dad used to do." I'm not sure what made me say that.

"Was that hard?"

"Oh, we had a few arguments over it when he was in high school, but he picked them up after a time."

"That's not what I meant. Was it hard when your husband . . . never mind. Dumb question."

I'm surprised he would ask me something so personal, but I don't mind answering it, really. "Yes, it was hard. Very hard. But you learn to move on, you know?"

"I guess some people do that."

"What do you mean?" A droplet of rain falls on my arm, then another.

He shrugs. "I'm not so good at it."

Wonder if that means he's still in love with his wife.

More rain begins to fall, and Marco points to a nearby shelter.

"We'd better go over there for a few minutes."

We jog over to the wooden structure covering a smattering of weatherworn picnic tables.

"That seemed to come up out of nowhere," I say, shivering into my jacket.

"Here, you're cold," he says, slipping off his jacket and putting it over mine.

"Oh, that's not necess—"

He tucks the front of his jacket just under my chin and stops, looking me square in the eyes. "Please, allow me to be a gentleman just this once."

Breath congregates in my throat and stays there. My brain freezes the same as it does when I eat ice cream too fast, while my heart attempts to pound its way through my chest.

Marco blinks, steps back, and looks out toward the sky. "Yeah, it just came up out of nowhere, all right."

Air eventually makes its way to my lungs. When I finally get moisture back into my mouth, I swallow past the knot in my throat. I'm not sure what just happened, but I know one thing: I can't let it happen again.

"Where is your dad today?"

I gasp. My hand flies to my mouth. "Dad."

"What's wrong?"

"He went out with his friends, and one of them mentioned white-water rafting. Surely, they didn't try that today."

"Your father is old enough to take care of himself. He'll be fine. Men are all about taking risks." His head shoots up. "I'm sorry."

"No, you're right. Dennis loved adventure."

"Not everyone gets hurt, Wendy," he says in a near whisper.

The way he says that causes my breath to stick in my throat. "I know." We stand just inside the shelter, watching as the steady rain soaks the Tennessee soil.

"What about you?"

I turn to him. "What about me?"

"Are you a risk taker?"

My stomach flips. Must be time for a snack. "Not really."

He keeps his gaze locked with mine. "That's too bad."

Right then one of us gulps out loud. I'm not sure if it was him or me, and I don't think I want to know. I turn back to the rain.

"So do you think we're going to be stuck in here all day?" As soon as the words leave my lips, I wish I could take them back.

"I can think of worse things."

Don't think about it, Wendy, or your legs will fold. Eyes on the rain. Eyes on the rain.

"So back to the kids," I say.

I can't help but notice the way his lips are lifting ever so slightly at the corners. He's clearly amused with my fumble to keep things moving. As Dad said, he's a regular Casanova, this one. Like Fred Astaire in a carefully choreographed dance routine, he never skips a beat.

He clears his throat. "Right. The kids."

Just then my cell phone rings. The tune to "Funny Face" comes out loud and clear. I told Logan not to put that on there, but he thought it would be, well, funny, which irritates me to no end. Now I have to stand in humiliation while the singer croons the embarrassing words and Logan's face flashes on the screen of my phone.

I laugh nervously. "Excuse me."

Marco nods, with a noticeable smile in place, and I turn away to answer the phone.

"Hello?"

"Where are you? I stopped by your house with a caramel latte and you were gone." Logan's voice is thick with disappointment.

I know I shouldn't complain, but why can't he remember that I prefer peppermint mocha?

"I'm sorry."

"So where are you? I could meet you."

With a quick glance at Marco, a panic ball—okay, boulder—forms in my stomach and threatens to take over my entire abdominal cavity.

"Well, I'm, uh, at the park for my run."

"Great, I'll come on over."

"Oh, well, I'm really just getting ready to leave. Why don't I meet you at my house? Save you the trip."

"That sounds good. See you there in a few minutes."

Closing my cell phone, I look over at Marco. "Sorry, but I need to go."

"So I heard. Guess we'll have to talk about the kids another time."

There's something in the way he says that that tugs at my heart-strings, though I'm not sure why.

"That would be fine." I head for my car with Marco close behind me.

"Listen, are you sure you're okay about your father working for me?"

I stop and look at him. "My dad's a grown man. He can do what he wants." I resume walking, and Marco grabs my arm.

"But I want to know if *you're* okay with it."

Another chill up my arm. If this keeps up, I'll have to start wearing long underwear.

"I'm okay with it," I say. I mean, the man needs to help with the groceries.

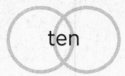

ten

"*Hi.*" *Logan gives me a quick kiss as we meet at my front* porch. I shove open the door and step inside. He places our drinks on the table while I hang up our jackets.

"Dad, are you home?" I call out. No sound. "Guess he's still gone."

"Hopefully, he's not out robbing a bank," Logan says with a laugh, handing me my drink.

"Worse. He was going white-water rafting."

"Well, that's one way to work out your frustrations," he says.

Maybe I should try it.

"What can he have to be frustrated about? He doesn't pay rent, he's eating my food, and all he has to do is play." Well, okay, he is working for Marco, but still, it's only parttime.

Logan studies me. "Someone getting a little bitter?"

"Forget it," I say with a wave of my hand. Confiding in Logan is like baring your soul to a rock.

He doesn't press the issue. "Did you get caught in the downpour?" he asks.

Must be why he's a college professor. Nothing gets past him.

"I got a little wet." My hand absently reaches to smooth down my damp hair. "Listen, Logan, I need to tell you something."

"If it has anything to do with Marco Amorini, save it for later. I just don't want him to ruin our afternoon together. Unless, of course, you plan to tell me there's something between the two of you. Then I should know."

The way he looks at me makes me want to squirm in my seat, but I hold firm. "Don't be ridiculous."

His eyes are still on me.

"What?"

Something flickers in his expression, but I can't quite make it out.

"Nothing." He stirs the whipped cream in his drink. "So do you think Colin and—what's Marco's daughter's name?"

"Sophia."

"That's right. So, do you think Colin and Sophia are really that serious?"

"Not if Marco and I can help it." It's enough that he knows they're dating. No need to tell him they're engaged. The news could send him into cardiac arrest. I take a quick sip from my drink until I see him watching me. "What's wrong?"

He shakes his head. "Nothing."

Logan's expression makes it clear he doesn't like me linking our names together.

"Listen, Logan, don't be so jealous. Marco doesn't want Sophia to get serious right now, and I think Colin is on the rebound from Emily, so we're trying to help them see what they're doing. That's all."

"He just wants to add you to his list of women conquered; you know that, right?"

"What are you talking about?" I plunk my cup down on the stand. "He is not trying to 'conquer' me. We're trying to help our kids through a hard place."

Logan shakes his head and gives a cynical laugh. "I don't know how he does it, but he manages to manipulate himself into women's lives this way all the time. Please tell me you're too smart for that, Wendy."

His condescending words prick at me like tiny needles.

"Stop treating me as though I'm a silly schoolgirl with a crush. How many times do I have to tell you there's nothing between us?"

If anyone is trying to manipulate, it's Logan.

"I'm sorry, but I just don't trust that man any farther than I can throw him."

"You've pretty much made that clear."

Before we can work up a full-blown discussion, the front door squeaks open.

"Anybody home?" Dad calls out.

"We're in here," I say.

I hear Dad kick off his boots, hang up his jacket, and tromp his way into the living room.

His face is red and vibrant, his eyes shining. "That was some kind of fun," he says. His face may look vibrant, but the rest of him needs a nap.

"Did you go white-water rafting?"

"Sure did," he says with a voice that sounds ten years younger.

"Dad, you need to be careful."

A muscle in his jaw twitches. "I guess I'm not too old to take care of myself."

So, you're living with me, why?

"Sounds like fun," Logan joins in.

Dad turns to him. "Yeah?" The funny expression on Dad's face tells me he can't imagine in his wildest dreams Logan doing such a thing.

"Yeah. Tell me the next time you go. I'd like to go along."

Logan isn't fooling me. He would hate every minute of it. He'd rather read about someone else doing it.

Dad eyes him carefully. "I'll let you know."

One last slurp on his drink, and Logan's cup is bone dry. "Well, that was good. Guess I'd better get going so you can get ready for choir practice. I'll call you tomorrow."

Logan goes to a different church, and that suits me. If we were together all the time, well, I don't know. I think we both need our space.

"Boy, this week has flown by," I say, locking the door to the chapel. A gust of February wind blows my hair into my face as Roseanne and I make our way to our cars.

She shivers. "I wish spring would hurry and show up."

"Me too." I click the remote to unlock my door while Roseanne fumbles through her purse for her car keys.

"Are you sure you don't mind coming in tomorrow? I hate to mess up your weekend." I'm giving her one last opportunity to bail.

"Of course I don't mind. I'd rather be here than at home working on toilets, showers, or whatever else Gill comes up with. By the way, wasn't Brooke's doctor's appointment today?" Roseanne thumbs through her keys and plunges the appropriate one into the hole.

"Yeah."

"Have you heard from her?"

"No. I'm sure she'll play it down. Doesn't want me to fuss over her. She's an adult, you know. She'll tell me tonight. At least selling Marco half the pond helped bail her out for now." The fat check was enough to pay off Kevin's debts with a little left over.

Roseanne chuckles. "She sure got a heavy dose of Dennis's stubborn side, didn't she?"

I stiffen a tad. Dennis, stubborn? Okay, I guess he was—a little. Most of the time his stubborn ways didn't bother me too much. Besides, I've been known to drag my heels from time to time myself. "I'm afraid we've both given her a hefty amount."

"Yeah, right," Roseanne counters. "I'll bet you've never bucked anything in your life."

Her comment rubs me wrong. Does that make me a peacemaker or a spineless dweeb?

"I want to hear all about it tomorrow," she says, waving wildly, causing her bracelets to tumble toward her elbow. She starts toward her seat, then pops back up again. "Hey, I forgot to tell you. The Masons who are scheduled for an April wedding will not be using the Snow White cabin after all. I made a note in the logbook."

"They were only staying one night, if I remember right. They must have decided to go on to Florida after the wedding."

One look at Roseanne, and I realize she purposely waited until now to tell me. She didn't want to face my reaction—for whatever reason. "Okay, spill it."

"No, they're staying here." She sighs, then looks at me. "They're taking a room at the lodge."

"Well, I knew it would start happening. What did I tell you?"

"It's still not time to close shop. It will all blow over."

I shrug. "Time will tell. Hey, see you tomorrow." I force as chipper a voice as possible.

By the time I arrive home, I'm surprised to see that Dad's car is gone. I didn't think he was working at the lodge so late today. If he starts working longer hours, we could carpool. Or maybe not.

I drop my keys on the kitchen counter and listen to the tick of the clock. Brooke's car was in the drive, so she must have gone to her room for a nap. Hopefully, she told the doctor about her need to sleep all the time.

A noise sounds behind me, and I swivel around to see Brooke, crumpled and pale, standing in the kitchen doorway.

I rush over and put my arms around her. "Brooke, what is it? Let's go in the living room." I grab her hand and practically drag her into the other room.

"Mom." She stops abruptly at the sofa. With a lift of her quivering chin she announces, "I'm pregnant."

The words hit me like a blow to the abdomen. I fall backward onto the sofa, thankful it was there.

"Are you all right?" she asks, sitting down beside me.

"Pregnant," I repeat out loud into the expanse of the universe. I swallow hard. "Are you sure?"

"There's no doubt." A hint of color lifts the pallor from her face. "I'm due the first of July."

"July? That means you're . . . about four and a half months along. Didn't you have a clue?"

"Not really. You know how emotions can throw your cycle off. My nausea I just chalked up to everything that's happened. I know I'm not all that big yet, but the doctor says it's because I'm not eating."

Well, duh.

"Now, I'll have to force myself to eat right—for the baby's sake."

The baby's sake. Acidic bile, strong and familiar, churns in my stomach and climbs my throat, causing it to sting and burn. I remember how I felt three years ago just trying to sort through how

I would parent our children alone—and Brooke was already out of the house with Colin not far behind.

"Mom?" Brooke's voice shakes me from my worry.

"A baby will be a wonderful blessing," I manage through a tight throat. Then I give her another hug that seems to erase the tension in her face.

She leans into the sofa. "If I tell Kevin, he's going to think I'm using this to get him back."

"You're over four months along, Brooke. He can hardly think that."

"He'll hate me."

"This is his baby as much as it is yours. He'll have to deal with it, same as you."

"A baby is such a huge responsibility—especially for a single mom. Everything will be all right, won't it?"

I pat her hand. "Yes, honey, everything will be all right."

Oh, sure. I mean, why not? So she's pregnant and the baby's father has left them. Another jolt. Oh my goodness, what if Kevin isn't the father? He thought Brooke was having an affair. If she was, had it gone that far? Had she been with the other man long enough to have conceived a child? More swirling emotions and tangled thoughts.

"Mom, did you hear me?"

She's shaking me now. No wonder my thoughts are scrambled.

"I'm in shock, Brooke, not deaf. And stop shaking me. You could knock my teeth loose."

She stops. "Those aren't your teeth?"

"Of course they are. And I want to keep them."

She shrugs.

"Okay, let's talk about this," I begin.

She shakes her head. "Not now. I haven't got the strength." With that, she gets up and heads for her room.

"I can hardly believe Marco's lodge is opening today." Roseanne folds a letter, stuffs it in an envelope, and attaches a stamp. Placing the envelope in our mail stack, she turns to me. "Three days after Valentine's Day, not bad. Maybe Gill and I will have to give it a try for a weekend getaway."

"Next door from where you work?" I ask, before standing to put away a file.

"You're right. No fun in that."

I walk over to the window and look at all the cars pulling into the lodge parking lot.

"Don't worry," Roseanne says, stepping up beside me. "It can only help us. Our little cabins aren't enough of a draw for some couples. This will help. You'll see."

"I hope you're right." I can't take something else right now.

Brooke and I have barely talked about the baby. I've lived around her long enough to know I can't push her. She'll talk when she's ready, so I'll have to leave it at that. Though Roseanne is my best friend, I haven't been able to tell her yet. She'll want to discuss it in detail, and there just hasn't been time.

"By the way, did the cleaning lady come out yet to do the cabins?" I ask.

"Yep. They're all done and ready for the next guests."

"Great."

"So how does your dad like doing the maintenance work at the lodge?" Roseanne thumbs through her Rolodex.

"He enjoys it, I think. Plus, it keeps him out of my cupboards, so I'm all for it—even though he is working for the competition."

"Do you think he'll be with you long?"

"Who knows? He's not exactly making big money, so I doubt he'll be moving out any time soon."

"You okay with that?"

I shrug. "It's not as though I have any choice. I mean, he's my dad, after all."

I'm a little irritated that she's questioning me. I'm letting him live in my house and eat my food, for crying out loud. That should count for something.

The phone rings, and Roseanne answers it while I check a couple of dates on my calendar.

"Roseanne, you don't need to stay here. It's Saturday. Go home and spend some time with your husband," I say, once she's off the phone. "I'll see that the Campbells get their cabin keys before I leave."

Her expression says she doesn't trust me. Can't say that I blame her.

"I promise." Scribbling myself a note on a nearby Post-It, I stick it on my computer screen. "There. I'll remember. Now, scoot."

"I'd rather stay a little while. Nothing to do at home but work anyway."

I edge my way over to the window and peek out. "He does have a lot of business over there."

"I think I'll get Gill to take me to the restaurant tonight. I want to check things out. You want to go with us?"

"No, thanks."

"Maybe you can get Logan to take you." Her comment almost makes me trip.

"Yeah, uh-huh. Logan taking me to a restaurant owned by Marco Amorini? Like that's gonna happen."

"Good point."

"Oh my goodness, Marco and Dad are coming this way." I flip the curtain back and run over to my desk.

"Do you think something is wrong?" Roseanne asks, straightening the paperwork on her desk.

"I have no idea. They didn't look upset that I could tell."

Just then the door swings open and Dad steps inside, grinning from ear to ear. "Opening day is a huge success," he says as though he owns the place.

I'm so happy for you.

Marco steps in right behind him. He's been so busy for the past week with the lodge and his legal practice that I've hardly seen him. The squeeze in my heart when he appears irritates me.

"Hi, Wendy," he says, closing the door behind him.

"Hi. Business seems to be going well," I say in an effort to be civil. I do want him to have a successful opening . . . I just don't want him to steal business from me.

"I wondered if I might treat you lovely ladies to dinner tonight." Marco turns to Roseanne. "Why don't you call your husband and invite him to dinner? My treat."

Roseanne's eyes brighten. "Why, thank you. What time?"

"How about seven o'clock? I'll make sure they know at the restaurant that it's complimentary for my special guests." Marco turns to me. "I'll have a table set aside for you and Martin," he says. "And of course Brooke is welcome." He shrugs. "I guess your boyfriend can come too," he says without the hint of a smile.

"That's really nice. Thank you, Marco."

"Great. It's all set. I'll see you around seven."

Just then the phone rings, and Roseanne answers it while we talk about the things going on over at the lodge.

"Wendy, it's for you. Colin."

I lock eyes with Marco and make my way to the phone. "Hello?"

Dad and Marco talk with Roseanne while Colin proceeds to tell me Sophia wants to come home for her dad's grand opening. I let him know we're all planning to eat there, so we make plans to get together.

"Everything okay?" Marco asks when I get off the phone.

"Everything is fine, but we may need a bigger table. The kids will be joining us tonight."

I can't remember the last time I dressed up to go out. My dates with Logan normally consist of a movie or going to a nice family restaurant. Sometimes we even settle for bowling and pizza.

This place is much more elegant in a rustic sort of way, if that's possible. It has a lodge feel to it, but an upscale lodge, mind you. The room is a mixture of rough-hewn logs, mountain décor, and a stone fireplace, but with the elegant touch of fine linens. Thankfully, no bearskins are stretched across the walls. When my black pumps step onto the polished hardwood leading into the massive dining room, I breathe deeply of steak scents and spices.

A maître d' leads us to a table in the back of the room. We settle in to our places—Logan, Dad, Brooke, Colin, Sophia, an empty seat, and then me. A server steps forward and takes our drink orders—soda all the way around—then scurries off on his mission. The whole place is alive with well-dressed servers, flickering lanterns, patron chatter, and clinking of dishware. A healthy blaze dances in the stone hearth in the back of the room.

"Good evening, folks. I hope you're having a good time." Dressed in a sharp black suit, complete with tie, Marco lifts a grin that causes my heart to miss a beat.

Logan grunts loud enough for my ears only.

We all chat about how beautiful everything is—though I confess to myself I might have decorated the lobby a little differently. I should check out the room draperies. Maybe I could offer some suggestions.

Marco steps away and says he'll join us later. In no time at all we're enjoying great food and conversation in a beautiful environment.

Looking over at Colin and Sophia, I catch them staring into one another's eyes with a gaze reserved for the one you love. It may be harder to separate them than we think. If only Emily were around. Then Colin could know for sure.

Dad is laughing with an older couple the next table over, talking about how great Tennessee is and how he wonders why he ever moved away. I'm seeing empty cupboards in my future.

My gaze flits across the room where two attractive women are sitting at a table while Marco stands talking to them. He throws his head back and laughs. He gets along with the ladies, no doubt about it. He has an electric presence in the room. Two gentlemen join the ladies at the table. Marco greets them and moves on.

"My steak is tough," Logan whines, bringing my attention back to our table. Never mind that he only has two bites left.

Logan is dressed in khakis and a button-down shirt that has a slight stain on the left pocket. Sometimes I don't know if his clothes are a statement that he doesn't care or if his eyesight is going.

"I'm sorry. I would tell you to send it back, but . . . well, there's not much to send back, is there?"

He looks at me point-blank. "I didn't want to complain. Marco would think I was looking for something about which to complain."

I want so desperately to say, *Well, aren't you?* but I clench my teeth tightly.

"Must be nice to be able to afford a place like this. I might have been able to once—before my divorce." The familiar bitterness that shadows Logan's every step is with us tonight.

"So I've heard." *Did I say that out loud?*

"What do you mean by that?" He gives me a glare, and I'm wishing I were at home right now working on my drapes.

"Nothing."

"You meant something by that, Wendy, and I want to know what." His demanding tone puts me on the defensive.

Marco joins us at the table. "So, are you enjoying your dinner?"

"It's wonderful. Thank you, Marco."

Logan gives another grunt, and I hold my breath, hoping Marco didn't hear him.

"Everything is really nice, Dad. But the next time you introduce Colin, please let people know he is my fiancé, not just a friend from school." Sophia says this politely enough, but I note a tad bit of frustration in her voice.

My gaze shoots to Logan to see if he heard her.

"Could you get someone to refresh my coffee? The only thing that would make it colder is if I threw in an ice cube," Logan says.

No wonder he didn't hear Sophia's comment. He's too busy looking for things to complain about.

"I'm sorry." Marco waves at a server, who immediately comes our way, hears the request, and is back with hot coffee in two seconds flat.

Logan drinks his hot brew and never says a word.

"The food is delicious and the atmosphere beautiful," I say, trying to make up for Logan's rude behavior.

"Thank you, Wendy. I'm glad you could come." Marco's eyes hold mine two beats too long, and Logan belts out a cough that's sure to dredge up a hairball.

Marco agrees to have dessert with us. The server brings chocolate cake to everyone at the table and refills coffee cups.

"I wonder what happened to Roseanne and Gill," I say, looking toward the entrance.

"Oh, they called and said they couldn't make it," Marco says. "Seems they had a problem with the water heater."

"Poor Roseanne," I say.

"I don't know why Gill doesn't just hire someone to do all this remodeling and save himself a ton of money. The man is obviously not a carpenter," Logan grouses.

"I take it by that comment that you are?" Marco asks, causing alarm to burst through my veins.

Logan is not in a mood to be challenged. He drops his fork on the plate and it makes a pinging noise. "If one can follow instructions, one can do anything," Logan says with a superior attitude. "I doubt Gill bothers to read them."

Marco shrugs while cutting into his cake with a fork. "Some men have an innate ability to do carpentry things. It's in their blood. Like Wendy's dad." Marco grins at Dad, which only seems to aggravate Logan all the more.

"I never read instructions," Dad says with a mixture of pride and I-dare-you-to-challenge-me-you-little-twit attitude.

"And some men learn by trial and error. Maybe Gill is one of those. He's got my respect for not giving up," Marco says.

"You always have the answers, don't you, Romeo—er, uh, Marco? Too bad we're not all as wise as you."

"Logan, please," I say, grabbing the sleeve of his shirt.

He yanks away. "I'm ready to go home." He downs his last bite of cake, makes an unpleasant face, then says, "Let's go, Wendy."

I consider my options. In the mood he's in, I don't necessarily want to leave with him, but he is my ride. Unless Colin would take me home. I shoot a glance his way and see him smiling at Sophia, seemingly oblivious to any of the tension sparking around the table.

"If you're not ready to leave yet, Wendy, I would be happy to take you home," Marco says.

Logan's eyes could shoot fire right now. "You will not take her home."

Marco isn't ruffled in the least. "As much as I know you love to be in control, I think this is something Wendy can decide for herself, don't you think?"

Marco looks at me with a soft expression. Logan looks at me and basically says with his eyes that I'd better do what he says.

"Thank you, Marco." I turn to Logan. "If it's all the same to you, I'll have Dad take me home."

Dad nods and grins.

Logan's face turns to stone. Flaming stone. Volcanic rock comes to mind. "Fine. Good night." He scoots away from the table and stomps off without so much as a *Thank you for the dinner* to Marco.

I glance over at Brooke. She smiles and gives me a discreet thumbs-up. Let the heavens rejoice. I've made my daughter proud.

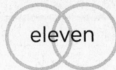

eleven

"*It can't be a good sign to have all those geese on the lawn on* a Monday morning." Breathless and shivering, Roseanne steps inside the office and bolts the door securely behind her. She turns around and leans hard against the door.

"What are you doing?" I ask.

"Have you never seen Alfred Hitchcock's movie *The Birds*?" she whispers, wide-eyed.

"No."

Her hand flies to her throat. "Oh, my goodness, I was in third grade when I saw it at the theater. I've never been so scared in all my life. All those birds. The pecking. The blood." An uncontrollable shiver overtakes her. "Gives me the willies just thinking about it."

She inches over to the window and peeks through a blind.

"Now what are you doing?"

"Looking to see if I was followed."

"By a goose?"

She flips the blind back in place, lifting her nose. "I'll have you know they can be mean. Your head is all caught up in that fairy-tale stuff, but let me tell you, they're not all Mother Goose."

"I suppose not. Some of them have to be dads."

"Make fun of me if you want, but I'm here to tell you, birds can be dangerous."

I shake my head and look back at the computer screen. "Speaking of birds, I'm going to add the option of releasing white doves at the end of a wedding."

"Huh?"

"There's a place in town that raises these doves, and they'll deliver them in wicker baskets. At the end of the ceremony, when the wedding party steps outside, they release the birds to flap their way into a beautiful blue sky, where they will then turn homeward." I look over at Roseanne. "That's the plan, anyway. I guess it's quite a spectacular thing to see."

"You can't be serious."

"Why not?"

"You're talking about setting a group of birds free all at once? What if they decide to attack someone? Are you insured for that?"

"Ever heard of the saying 'harmless as doves'? They're not vultures. Alfred Hitchcock has nothing to do with these birds. You don't have to be around for the display if you're afraid."

"I'm not afraid." Her voice is dark. Very dark.

She's opening yesterday's mail, and the way she's holding that letter opener and glaring at me makes me uncomfortable.

"So, what about the geese?" she asks, ripping open an envelope with such force my hand goes for my throat to make sure everything is still intact.

"What about them?" I look back at my screen, click to save the Web site for the doves into my favorites file, and click out.

"We can't let them congregate out by the pond. They could take over the place. That can't be"—she stops and looks up at me—

"*healthy* for anyone." She picks up the next piece of mail, shoves the sharp point of the letter opener through the envelope, gives it a nasty little twist, and rips it open with sadistic vengeance.

"You're taking that bird thing way too far, Roseanne. Tell the truth. Are you really worried about the health risk, or is it the fact that they have feathers and a beak? I have to know."

"You'll be sorry if they start to molt." She looks up, her face contorted in a silent scream.

"What's wrong?"

"Naked geese strutting around our pond, that's what's wrong."

"We'll buy them little goose outfits."

"Oh sure, go ahead and make fun. I'll have the last laugh when you have to clean up all those feathers—to say nothing of the other things they'll leave *behind*"—she clears her throat—"um, so to speak."

I think for a minute. "I'm not really sure what to do about the geese. We've never had them before. Maybe they'll just move on by this afternoon."

"From what I understand, you can't let them establish a feeding pattern, or we'll never get rid of them. Maybe Marco will help you out with this."

"I'd better not ask him. Logan thinks I'm spending too much time in close proximity to Marco as it is."

"Well, he does co-own the pond. It's his responsibility too. Besides, a twenty-five-mile radius is too close by Logan's way of thinking." She snorts. "I can't say that I blame him. If I were Logan, I'd be worried too."

I walk over to the table and thumb through the sample photo album, looking for the packages to offer the Hamilton couple when they come in this afternoon. "That's ridiculous, and you know it. Marco is not a threat to Logan. I'm not interested in him."

Okay, I admit the man is good-looking, but he certainly isn't husband material. Not that I'm looking for a husband, mind you, but if I were, I wouldn't choose Marco Amorini.

Roseanne doesn't say anything, which causes me to look up at her. The look on her face makes me want to hide a goose in the back-seat of her car.

"I don't care about him that way, Roseanne. Now, stop it!"

"Okay, fine. By the way, you never told me how things went Saturday night when you ate at the lodge together."

I tell her about Logan's complaining and how it merely escalated as the night went on and how he eventually left—alone.

"I have to admit, Marco was very kind in spite of it all."

Someone knocks hard on the front door, startling us both. Roseanne looks nervous.

"Geese can't knock. They have wings, remember?" When I whip open the door, one look into Marco's face tells me a goose would have been friendlier.

He brushes past me and steps inside. "What are we going to do about those geese?"

Roseanne and I exchange a glance.

"Don't tell me you haven't noticed." He's pacing the floor like a nervous, well, bird.

"I've noticed. Could you keep your voice down, please?"

He stops and stares at me. "Geese don't understand English." More pacing. "What are you doing to get rid of them?"

"What am *I* doing to get rid of them?"

"That's right."

My adrenaline rises to match the flash in his eyes. Still forcing myself to appear calm, I take my time, saunter over to my desk, and sit down ever so pleasantly. "Why, I'm not doing anything to get rid of them. I don't see them as a problem. In fact, I think they add a whimsical touch to our chapel."

Roseanne sucks in air.

"They'll add more than that to your chapel if you don't get rid of them." His voice is raised, hands slicing the air—not quite kung fu-style, but close. "The guests won't be able to stroll around the pond, sit on the benches, or anything, because of those stupid birds. Springtime is when they set up nests. Did you know that? We could have them here for nesting season, and then molting season will follow. We could be talking months. Shall we talk about what they'll do to the ground cover?" His voice is rising with every word. "Get rid of them."

With that he whips around, plows through the entrance, and slams the door behind him.

I turn to Roseanne. "Well, I guess Saturday night is over. It's back to reality."

"I'm going for a walk." I stomp out the door and walk around the back toward the pond, talking to myself all the while. "That man is a jerk, pure and simple. I have half a mind to—"

One sweeping glance at my surroundings stops me in my tracks. There must be seventy-five geese on my property. It's a beautiful sight, but admittedly alarming as well. Roseanne's paranoia is rubbing off on me.

Several geese saunter and strut nearby, a few honk and bite at a feather here and there, while others fluff about and glide along in the pond. The smell in the air puts me in mind of a musty bathroom. Speaking of bathroom, I won't even mention what's squishing beneath my feet.

I may be dumb, but I'm not stupid. There is no way I'm stepping any closer to that group. They might notice I'm lacking feathers and a beak.

"See what I mean?" Marco's voice makes me jump and let out a slight scream, causing more geese to turn my way.

"What are you doing?" I snap. "You might make them mad."

"We have to get rid of them. They could frighten off our customers."

"Well, I didn't invite them here." A few more geese turn my way, and I feel I should apologize. I whisper with attitude, "Why is everyone acting as though this is my fault?"

"No one said it's your fault. I just want it handled."

I spin around to face him. "And what would you suggest I do? I don't mean to be argumentative here, but we do co-own this pond. So maybe *you* could offer a solution?"

Marco releases a sigh and places his hand on my arm. "Look, I'm just tired. I know what havoc geese can cause. You might think they add to the romance of the landscape now, but trust me, it won't last."

Though I feel sorry over how much he's been working, no one told him to buy this lodge. I look at my arm where he's still holding it.

He follows my gaze. "Oh, sorry." His hand drops the hold.

To my mortification, a flash of disappointment shoots through me.

"So, what are we going to do?" I ask, looking back at the geese.

"I don't know. I'll ask around."

"And I'll check some Internet sites."

"Hopefully, it will prove to be easier than trying to keep our kids apart," he says with a lopsided grin. "I have to go to the law office for a while. Then I'll swing by the lodge to check on things. If you're still here, I'll come over, and we can discuss it."

"What time?"

"Probably won't be until around six o'clock—or you could just meet me at the lodge restaurant for dinner, and we could talk about it there."

A tiny gasp, and I'm praying he didn't notice, but the look on his face tells me he probably did.

"But if you think your boyfriend—"

"His name is Logan. Loooo-gan." I'm afraid my sarcastic mood is here to stay.

He gets it. "Logan. So what do you think? Will Loooo-gan mind if we go to dinner?"

"Of course not. He's not that way." A flat-out, bald-faced fib right there, as big as you please. What has gotten into me?

Marco lifts an eyebrow.

I hurry on. "But I have to fix dinner for Dad and Brooke."

"Oh, you can bring them along," he says.

For some odd reason that disappoints me. "Okay."

"I'll ask Martin when I go back to the lodge, and you can ask Brooke."

I nod.

We turn and walk back to our businesses, and Logan's angry face pops into my head. I'm thinking it will be best if Dad and Brooke come along.

"So if Granddad is not going to dinner with you, what's he doing tonight?"

Brooke is sitting on the edge of my bed, reminding me of the days when she was a teenager and would come into our room to tell us some tidbit that was going on in her life. The little blip on her stomach tells me time marches on.

It's hard to imagine Kevin hasn't contacted her yet. When Brooke finally got through to his boss, she was told that Kevin had taken another position. She finally contacted his parents and found they were on an extended trip to Europe.

"He said he was going out with some lodge buddies. Who knows what they're up to?" Brushing my hair, I continue to study her through my mirror. Watching her work through her pain has been like seeing myself only a few years ago. The sleepless nights, the lack of energy, the loss of appetite.

The news of the baby seems to have helped her, though. I don't think that bit of news would have done the same for me.

"You sure you won't come to dinner with me?"

She gives me a *well-duh* look. "Yeah, right, like I want to have dinner with you and Marco? I don't think so."

"You make it sound like a date. It's not that way."

She makes a face. "It isn't?"

"No, it isn't. So what are you going to do tonight?"

"I got a couple of baby books from the library, and I thought I would start reading one."

I turn around and look at her, concern crowding my heart. "What will you eat for dinner?"

She smiles. "Don't worry. I picked up a salad from Wendy's on the way home. I'm forcing myself to eat now—for the baby's sake."

"The least you could do is order French fries and a shake to put some meat on those bones of yours." I smile.

She gets up from the bed. "Well, you have a fun time tonight." She gives me a peck on the cheek and walks out of my room while I stare after her.

I can't remember the last time she's done something like that—if ever. Did we just have a mother-daughter moment?

With no time to linger, I take a final look at myself in the full-length mirror. Fortunately for me, Roseanne left work early today for a dental appointment, so I was able to sneak away early myself, come home, and change clothes.

A final swipe through my hair, touch up of lipstick, and I'm good to go. I'm thankful I still have my natural light brown hair, though I've spotted a few grays slipping through here and there. I pluck them, of course.

Just as I'm easing into the lodge parking lot, "Funny Face" croons from my cell phone. I bite my lip. Not wanting to discuss this with Logan, I've ignored his calls all day. Obviously, I'll have to face the music soon. Just not now. I turn off my phone and tuck it into my purse.

The air has turned chillier than usual for mid-February. The smell of burning wood lifts from the lodge chimney and curls into the night sky. I pull the warm collar up near my face as I head for the door. Inside, I look around and spot Marco.

He sees me at the same time, waves and heads straight for me. Why does he have to look so good?

"Glad you made it," he says, surprise on his face.

"Did you think I wouldn't come?"

"I was just hoping—um, I didn't know." He puts his hand on my back and ushers me toward the restaurant.

The slightest trace of guilt is edging its way around my heart. What if Logan came in right now? That's silly. It's not as though I'm doing anything wrong. Besides, why would Logan come here? Still, I glance around the room cautiously before stepping inside.

"Do you want a table near the fireplace?" Marco asks.

"Sure, that would be fine."

Amid smells of grilled steak, tangy sauces, and baked rolls, the host seats us near the fireplace. Warmth wraps around me the moment I sit down. The wood crackles and sputters, sending fragmented cinders fluttering into the air and falling in the ash heap on the floor of the hearth.

While reviewing our menus, Marco says, "Could I interest you in some ravioli? It's pretty good."

I scrunch up my nose. "Italian food doesn't agree with me." Right after I say that, I realize I may have offended him and look up. "Sorry."

Amusement flickers in his eyes. "No problem. But that's probably because you haven't tasted traditional Italian. One of these days I'll treat you to one of my pizzas. I've been told I could sell them. Just call me Papa Amorini." He grins.

"If you don't mind, I'll pass on Italian tonight." Number one, I don't need the calories; number two, the last thing my stomach needs right now is garlic.

In a matter of moments, orders are taken, menus returned, and drinks delivered. It pays to eat with the owner.

Elbows propped on the table, Marco asks, "So, did you find out anything on the Internet?"

"A little. For one thing, geese don't like tall grass. It's evidently not palatable."

"But that takes too long to remedy," Marco interrupts.

"I'm just telling you what I found."

He nods.

"There was also an advertisement for some kind of gadget with a light that you stick in the middle of the area where they congregate, and it supposedly makes them stay away."

Marco listens intently, saying nothing. He looks so serious it makes me nervous.

"The other thing they suggested was frightening the geese. Maybe setting out a scarecrow." I pause, then add, "I thought maybe you could stand out there."

A smile trickles from his eyes and spills onto his lips. "Not only beautiful but with a sense of humor."

His comment runs through me like warm sunshine on a chilly mountain peak.

The way he's watching me, it's all I can do not to knock over my drink. I hope my mascara isn't smeared. I'll check it as soon as I can make a break for the bathroom.

I take a drink from my soda, then pat my lips with the napkin. With a quick glance down, I see that the producers of my stay-on lipstick were right. The rest of me can be a mess, but my lips will be perfect.

Why does he keep staring at me that way?

Marco clears his throat, professional voice back in place. "Environmental Protection talks about building fences to deter them—but what are we supposed to do about our businesses in the meantime?"

"We'll come up with something."

The server places my plate of oak-grilled chicken marinated in a sharp barbecue sauce, baked potato with a dollop of sour cream, and a side of steamed broccoli in front of me. Marco in turn gets his Angus center-cut beefsteak with mashed potatoes, green beans, and a salad. Another server places a basket of hot buttered rolls on the table.

"Hi, Marco. Have you talked with Sadie today?" A beautiful brunette struts up to the table, all legs and smiles. She gives me a cursory glance, not a very friendly one at that, then turns back to Marco.

"No, I haven't."

"She won't be able to go dancing tomorrow. Something came up. Said she'll tell you about it later." She gives me another quick glance.

Marco coughs twice, his gaze darting from me back to this woman. I'm getting the feeling there's a whole lot more going on than meets the eye.

"That's fine." He extends his palm out toward me. "This is Wendy Hartline. She owns the chapel next door."

The brunette turns to me, offering her hand. "Dora Baden. Nice to meet you."

"You too."

She takes a breath to say something else, but Marco gives a mournful glance at his meal.

"Well, I'll let you two eat before everything gets cold. Good to see you again, Marco." Her eyes linger on him shamelessly, then she turns to me. "I'm sure I'll see you around when I come to the restaurant."

We smile, wave good-bye, and I can't help wondering if she's someone special to Marco. Her interest was obvious. The man has no problem putting women under his spell. As Roseanne would say, "It's a gift."

Humph. All that charm. Who does he think he's fooling? I'm not about to fall under his spell too. Marco Amorini is not my type. I don't need a ladies' man. I want a man I can trust. A man who doesn't need his ego stroked every five seconds.

A man like Dennis Hartline.

Marco turns his attention to his plate. Rubbing his hands together vigorously, he wiggles his eyebrows and says, "Let's eat. I'm famished."

I bow my head and close my eyes, quickly sending a prayer of thanks heavenward. Marco says something. Once I finish, I look up. "I'm sorry, what did you say?"

"No, I'm sorry. I didn't realize—I'm sorry."

The way he's floundering for words is kind of cute. I can almost picture him as a little boy realizing he's stumbled upon his Sunday school teacher while she was talking to God.

"So what were you saying?"

"Oh, just that it takes a lot more time to run this place than I had planned. I'm afraid my legal business will suffer."

"Which could be a good thing," I say with a teasing grin.

He looks at me.

"Divorce and all that."

He shakes his head. "Oh, that's right. You want to get them hitched and live happily-ever-after."

"Is that so wrong?"

"No, it's not wrong." He saws a bite from his steak and looks at me, fork hovering near his mouth. "It's just not real life."

"Maybe not. But I think we make it too easy for people to get out of marriage relationships, rather than helping them make things work. Call me old-fashioned."

He looks at me. "You are old-fashioned."

I stop chewing and look at him.

"But that's not necessarily a bad thing."

"Thanks."

"I just don't happen to agree with you." He scoops a bite of potatoes onto his fork.

"Well, of course not. That's how you make your living." Okay, that sounded a little nasty even to me, but I feel passionate about this issue, and I'm not backing down.

"So you're saying no one should be allowed to get a divorce?"

"Of course not. I know there are circumstances—"

He cuts me off. "And just who will represent the people in those circumstances?"

"Okay, I get it. But are you telling me every divorce case you've handled was the best thing for everyone involved?"

"No, but their minds were made up, and I believe everyone has a right to legal representation."

I spear a broccoli piece with my fork. "It's just too bad that more people can't find that one true love."

"Don't tell me you're one of those who believes there's someone for everyone out there?" He leans back in his chair and grins at me.

"Absolutely."

The way he's staring at me makes my cheeks feel hot. 'Course, it could be the heat from the fireplace.

"There's a happy-ever-ending waiting for those who will search for it with all their hearts." Okay, now I feel stupid. It sounds as though I've been reading too many romance novels.

"Is that what you had—with your husband, I mean?"

The broccoli catches in my throat, and I take a drink to wash it down. I'd hate to be the first choking victim in his restaurant.

"Yes, we had that."

"A knight in shining armor, huh?" He takes a bite of green beans and looks at me, waiting for my answer.

"Yes, he was."

"Most guys can't live up to that, you know."

The way he's tearing his meat away from the knife makes me glad I'm not a cow. Though with all I'm eating tonight, that could be debatable.

"That's why it doesn't pay to be in a hurry."

He shakes his head and chuckles.

"What?"

"I just think it's funny the way you look at life." He puts his fork down and looks me seriously in the face. "What happens if you search with all your heart and think you've found your soul mate, only to find out you were wrong? Dead wrong."

Remembering what he told me about his wife walking out on them, I'm not sure what to say. There's obvious pain in his voice, and anything I say will merely sound like a cliché. I offer a weak, "I don't know."

He shakes his head. "Life isn't black-and-white, Wendy. Not all things work out with a happy ending. You're a nice woman. I'd hate to see you get hurt."

"My husband died, Marco. I think I understand that things don't always turn out the way we want them to. I'm just saying it doesn't hurt to look for the happy ending."

"Yeah, and we fill young girls' heads with all that knight-in-shining-armor stuff, and they're quickly dissatisfied with real life."

"No one said it doesn't take hard work."

"You bet it takes hard work. But when you lose someone—when you have no choice in the matter, what do you do?"

"You move on," I say, feeling as though we're in a counseling session, and I'm underqualified to give advice.

He leans into the table and looks me in the eyes. "And just how do you do that, Wendy? Ignore it? Pretend it didn't happen?" His words hold accusation. The waiter comes and refills our glasses.

"Well, no, of course not—"

"Isn't it a fact that you haven't given up your husband?"

Air sticks in my chest, and he barrels forward.

"And isn't it a fact that you indeed still love him and have no plans of getting involved with anyone else, ever again?"

Anger shoots through my veins, and tears sting my eyes. "Last time I checked, I wasn't on the witness stand. Not that I owe you an explanation, Marco, but Dennis was my husband. I'm not going to blot him from my memory and pretend he didn't exist just because he's—he's dead."

People are looking our way. I lower my voice.

"If I had no plans of getting involved with someone, explain Logan," I challenge.

Marco leans back in his chair. "He's a mere decoy to make people think you've moved on."

Words bunch in my throat, and I clench my teeth to keep them there.

"Don't worry about it. Your secret is safe with me. I'm pretty good at observing people."

My blood pressure is at boiling point. "I thought we were here to discuss the geese and possibly our children."

"It just irritates me when you Pollyanna types think you can fix the world, make it a happier place if we'd all just choose to see it your way. A way that basically ignores the truth. Life isn't always a happy ending, Wendy. In fact, most times it stinks—" He stops himself short of saying something he shouldn't. "Well, it stinks. You need to deal with that and move on."

My stomach churns. "Who says I haven't dealt with it? You know, the bottom line is that my life is none of your business. I share a pond with you, Marco. Nothing more." Hot tears sting my eyes and plop down my cheeks before I can stop them. I slap the linen napkin on my still-full plate. "Let me know the cost of the meal, and I'll pay you later. Good night."

I stand up and walk toward the door as calmly as possible. My legs are holding me this time, though I'm praying my trembling isn't noticeable. I've never been so bold in my life. I actually said some things I wanted to say. But the thing is, I'm not sure if it makes me feel better or worse.

As I make my way to my car, the geese honk and rustle about near the pond. Yanking open my car door, I toss a fierce glance at them.

"You don't want to mess with me tonight."

twelve

"Have you talked to Marco since the restaurant incident?"
Roseanne asks while we walk in the park after work on Friday
evening. It's a strain for her to walk and talk, so we decided not to
try jogging.

"No, I haven't. But that's okay by me. Every time he comes
around he brings trouble."

There can't be any truth to what he said. It wasn't easy, but I've
moved on from Dennis. Well, moved on as much as possible. How
can you ever move on from a man like that? Besides, just because I
haven't found someone new doesn't mean I haven't moved on. These
things take time. And what he said about Logan being a decoy is
totally ridiculous.

Roseanne shrugs. "It's too bad, really. Marco has such potential."

"Not in my book. I'm just glad Logan understood everything
and didn't get mad when he found out about our dinner together. I
think he finally gets it that Marco is no threat to our friendship."

"Yeah, I guess."

We take a few steps in silence.

"Hey, I keep forgetting to ask you how Brooke's doctor visit went. Since you haven't said anything, I assume she's fine."

I knew I would have to get around to this sooner or later. "Yeah, I've been meaning to tell you about that."

She stops abruptly and turns to me. "What's wrong, Wendy? She's not sick, is she?"

I take a deep breath. "Nothing four or so months won't cure."

Roseanne's mouth drops. "Are you kidding me?"

"I wouldn't kid about that, believe me."

"Oh, my goodness," is all Roseanne says, and we pick up our walking again. "What is she going to do?"

"I honestly don't know. She has to get back to work before too long, and I just hope she's up to it by then."

"You said she got the thing with her house payments worked out, right?"

"Thankfully, yes."

"Pregnant. Wow. That never once entered my mind," she says. "What did Kevin say?"

"Nothing yet, 'cause he doesn't know. Seems he's fallen off the face of the earth."

"So weird. Well, the good news is you'll be a grandma," she says happily.

Her comment hits me between the eyes.

She giggles. "You hadn't thought of that until now, had you?"

I laugh. "You know, I hadn't. I've been so consumed with Brooke's health and everything else that has been going on, I didn't stop to think about becoming a grandma."

"So how does it feel?"

I think a moment. "Other than the fact it makes me feel a little

old, I have to say I like the idea of having a little one around."
Pausing a moment, I add, "Just wish the circumstances were
different."

"Yeah, me too."

"Guess I'll need to drench myself in a season of *The Waltons* to
see how it's done."

Roseanne laughs. "You're a great mother, so I have no doubt that
you'll be a wonderful grandma too." She gives me a friendly pat on
the back.

Oh, yeah, I'm wonderful all right. Complaining every step of the
way about Dad and Brooke's intrusion into my life.

A woman jogs past us and smiles. We say hello.

"So about the geese—" Roseanne says.

"Oh, please, don't remind me. One of Marco's employees called
and asked what we're doing about it. Can you imagine? Guess Marco
was too scared to call me himself." I chuckle. "I did get pretty hor-
monal on him the other night."

"He deserved it."

"Yes, he did. One Web site suggested putting visuals up to
frighten the geese. Evidently, our feathered friends don't like things
flying above their heads. They suggested putting up helium balloons,
so I thought I'd go buy some today and place them strategically
around the pond. The thing is, I can't put them there while the geese
are there. They might hurt me."

"Right. You need to be careful."

"Sometimes they leave for a while and come back. I hate to get
all those balloons and bring them back if the geese are still here."

"Gill is good friends with the guy in town who owns that party
store. I'll bet he'd give you a good rate if he knew how many you
needed and what you needed them for."

"That would be awesome. And the sooner the better. Marco's patience is wearing thin."

"Are you sure this is a good idea?" Roseanne asks as we creep up to the smattering of geese near the pond, hiding ourselves behind bouquets of helium balloons stuffed in the big boxes we're carrying. And let me just say here, I'm downright proud of Roseanne, stepping out of her comfort zone and facing these birds beak-to-beak, so to speak.

"Well, I don't see that we have much choice. It seemed a good time to do it while many of them are gone," I shoot back. "The research I read said they're scared of things waving over them like this."

She chuckles. "If any balloons could do it, these could."

"No kidding." I take a few steps to the right. A couple of geese look at me, then saunter a distance away. "Let's take them over here and start placing them several feet apart."

"It's too bad Harold was out of his other party balloons. Do you think Marco will mind that these are black and have *Over the Hill* and *Rest in Peace* stamped across them?"

"Hey, he wanted me to do something. If he wants something else, he can do it himself. At least I'm trying. I'm just thankful Harold gave me a discount."

Dropping the weighted balloons in place, I make my way around the right side while Roseanne works her way around the left until we end up together at the northern point of the pond. The black balloons wave and blow eerily in the breeze.

Stepping over goose droppings, I put my hands on my hips and survey the area. So far the geese are just standing there looking at us like *You're kidding, right?*

"There's something spooky about it all, don't you think?"

Roseanne whispers. "Black balloons waving against an evening sky, moonlight illuminating the message of *Over the Hill* and *Rest in Peace*? It's all so . . . unnatural." She shivers and hugs herself.

I give Roseanne a hard stare. "First birds, now this? Are you watching those scary shows on TV again?"

"Just *CSI*."

"Well, stop it. Last time you watched a horror film, Gill had to read you to sleep every night for a month."

Her chin hikes. "That was a long time ago. I'm not paranoid anymore, not like that anyway." Just then something slips from her coat pocket and falls to the ground. We both reach for it, and I grab it before she does.

"Mace, Roseanne? In Smoky Heights? Where the worst that can happen is getting nailed by an overhead bird?"

"This is different from being paranoid. This is called being cautious." She crumples beneath my steady gaze. "Okay, so I'm paranoid. I don't care." She snatches the mace from my hand and turns to the geese who are watching—I can only guess what they're thinking. With all the authority of an Old Testament prophet, she raises the threatening spray like Moses' walking stick, and with a sassy voice quotes Nehemiah 13:21: "I *will* lay hands on you."

Blank stares from every last one of them.

"Guess they don't know their Scriptures," I whisper.

She shrugs.

"We'll see what happens. I'm going to check on them after church tomorrow."

"Good idea."

We edge away from the geese and head back toward our cars. "You know, it's customary to face the direction in which you are walking," I say.

"And turn my back on those guys so they can peck me to death? No, thank you," she says.

Boy, am I glad I don't have feathers.

After church I stop over at the chapel to check on the geese situation. As I round the back corner, I see that they're still there, looking as though they've settled into a nice vacation spot—minus the sunglasses. But the next thing that catches my attention causes adrenaline to explode through my veins. My legs kick up dirt and vault into full motion as I chase after two young men who are stealing my balloons. Wind whirs in my ears, and my sprint turns into a full-fledged run that could take on any track star in the county.

"What do you think you're doing?" I scream after them.

They look afraid. They look very afraid.

"You put those down or they'll be lining your graveside, buddy," I say to the one I reach first.

He turns to me, eyes wide with horror, and raises his hands in total surrender. Unfortunately, he's taken the sand sacks off the balloons already, and his surrender sends an abundance of *Rest in Peace* messages into the Smoky Heights skyline.

I'm hoping no one sees it as a sign of some sort.

"What do you think you're doing on my property with my balloons?" My fists are firmly planted on my hips. Adrenaline has obviously pushed me beyond my limits, because right now, with one look at the fright in his eyes, I'm feeling pretty good about this turn of events.

"Sorry, ma'am, but Mr. Amorini told us to get rid of the balloons."

He may as well have pulled a carpet from beneath my feet. I'm trying to help with the geese problem, and this is how he repays me?

"Well, you tell Mr. Amorini I said the balloons stay," I say with utmost authority. When I glance over and see that there are only a handful of balloons left, it sort of takes the punch out of my statement.

Before I can comment further, the boys mumble their apologies and skedaddle back to the lodge. It suddenly occurs to me that I actually confronted those boys. Terrified them, actually. Which proves that I can confront people when push comes to shove! This little epiphany makes my day. I'm practically in a happy mood as I strategically place the few remaining balloons around the pond.

Brushing my hands together, I look around. Nearby, a goose glares at me and begins to head my way. As she or he—it's hard to tell, and well, we're not exactly on friendly terms—approaches me, she's looking rather inhospitable. I'm wondering if it would help to point out that I own this pond.

She's honking now. Loudly. Her webbed feet thumping against the ground with every step she takes toward me. It's like Mother Goose with PMS.

Honk. Honk.

I could probably use Roseanne's mace right about now, but the truth is this bird is honkin' me off. "Scat," I say, clapping my hands. "Shoo. Go away. Scat."

She's not backing down.

Just then a dog's deep bark cuts through the air. I turn and see Marco's boxer coming straight for the birds. His ears are back, and his expression is caught somewhere between playful and dog-on-a-mission. The feathered flock scatters and struts about until Brutus breaks in through them. His presence stirs them up, causing them to flutter, honk, and finally take off one-by-one, flying who-knows-where.

"Brutus, thank you," I say, bending down as the dog comes over to me. I scratch behind his ears. "I owe you. Or maybe this was your way of apologizing for cutting me off the other day, hmm?"

Marco steps up behind me. "Brutus, come."

I jerk around and stand up. Just as I'm about to give him a piece of my mind, Marco cuts in.

"What were you thinking, putting up all those *Rest in Peace* balloons? This is a place of business, Wendy. Do you have any idea how tacky that looked to my customers?"

"I—"

"A large senior citizen group came for lunch, and they were clearly offended by the display of balloons. They don't want to be reminded of their impending deaths. They wouldn't order dessert."

"Well, I—"

"What could you possibly have been thinking? The helium in those balloons won't last over forty-eight hours, tops. What good does that do? The geese will just come back."

"I was just trying to get rid of them. I read somewhere—"

"It obviously didn't help," he snaps.

I don't know who's honkin' me off more, the geese or Marco.

"You insisted that I do something immediately. I did what I thought might work." I take a deep breath, trying with everything in me not to explode. "You know, Marco, the birds really don't bother me. For a wedding setting, I think they look nice."

"You can't be serious. Wedding guests don't want to walk around goose droppings. Good grief, Wendy, don't you have any business sense whatsoever?"

The retort sticks right in my throat, which is exactly where it belongs. If I release it, things could get ugly. "What do I owe you for the dinner?"

He blinks. "The dinner?"

"Monday night, when I left. I owe you."

"Forget it."

"I pay my debts. And if you don't mind, I would appreciate it if you could pay your half for the balloons."

"We'll call it even," he says, nostrils flared.

Mustering up a professional voice with a teensy edge to it, I say, "Fine."

"Fine."

I turn to leave, then swivel around to face him. "By the way, since you're better at the business thing than I am, I'm sure you won't mind taking care of the geese."

Logan's right. Marco Amorini is a jerk.

thirteen

"If you'll hang up our jackets, I'll get us some iced tea," I say to Logan.

"Where's your dad?"

"He went out with some friends for pie and coffee," I call over my shoulder. "Something he likes to do on Sunday nights after church. He won't be home for a while."

I'm ashamed to say I didn't get a thing out of church tonight. All I could think about were those stupid geese and Marco snapping at me. He brings out my dark side, there's no question about it—but the thing is, I didn't know I had this side. That's kind of scary. I've always been about the bright side of things, happy and positive. But that man just knows how to push my buttons.

Come to think of it, Logan does too.

"Hey, you moved the furniture again," Logan calls out.

"Yep. Here we go." When I sail into the living room with the drinks in my hand, I am not prepared for what awaits me. There on the floor sits Logan in a sort of pretzeled position. One shoe and sock are off, and he's got his foot bottom-side up, studying it carefully.

"Did you miss the chair or something?"

"Very funny," he says, staring a hole in the pad of his foot.

Okay, here's the deal. I've been hiding something in my life about which only God knows.

I hate feet.

Can't stand to touch them, look at them, or think about them. Makes me twitch just to think about it. It's not that I feel mine are superior to others, mind you. But they are, after all, mine.

The worst part about it is it doesn't matter how many times I've read that Scripture in I Timothy 5 about widows being known for their good deeds, among which are washing the feet of the saints—I just can't do it. I don't think that will keep me from Heaven, but most likely I won't own the best cloud on the block. Hopefully, it will be a cloud where socks are required.

You've got your run-of-the-mill bunions; rough, cracked heels; and, oh yeah, nails that could rival the bark on a redwood. Something about the way they look, the big bony toes with a couple of sprouting hairs, all that, just sort of creeps me out. No doubt I have a past. Maybe one of those repressed memory things. Probably had a run-in at the beach with someone sportin' ugly toes.

But it's a problem I suffer in silence. No one has ever found out. Fortunately, the subject never came up with Dennis because his feet were always cold and he wore socks even to bed. Bless him.

So here I am, facing Logan's foot in all its glory, and twitching in places I didn't even know existed.

He glances up at me. "Maybe you can help me."

Um, no.

To my utter horror, he sticks out his foot. "Somehow, I got a splinter in my foot this morning, and it's starting to bother me," he says, as though this is my fault. "And I'm having trouble with my contacts. Could you help me out here?" He lifts a smile and a set of tweezers.

"Well, I don't know, Logan. I've been having trouble with my contact"—I only wear one—"too."

"Yeah, but can't you take it out and put on your glasses? I thought you had a big magnifying glass too."

Doggone it, he remembered.

It seems a shame to bring up this little flaw in me right now. The last thing I need is for word to get out and half the town to make fun of me. My daughter is already suspicious. She took me in for a pedicure once, and I had nightmares for a month. I had never seen so many feet and toes in one place in my life. It was wrong, that's all. Toes are toes. Neglected or slicked up with polish, they're still the same.

"I'll go take out my contact and get my glasses. Be right back." Setting the tray of drinks on the coffee table, I head for the bedroom.

Once inside, I lean against the door and try to gather my wits. I keep telling myself they're only toes. After storing my contact, I grab my magnifying glass and reluctantly rejoin Logan in the living room. His legs are so long and twisted together right now that I'm wondering if he'll ever stand again. Last thing I need is Logan and his naked foot forever memorialized in my living room.

Trying desperately not to show my age, I lower myself to the floor as gracefully as possible—meaning, minus a grunt—to sit beside him. Once I'm down and before I can blink, Logan scoots away from me and flops his foot smack dab in my lap. There, staring me full in the face is the bottom of his foot, wrinkly and littered with sock debris. The map of America is reflected in his cracked heel, which is, by the way, so rough it could snag a hole in my carpet. I won't even go into that nail thing. My left eye twitches like a band director stuck in cut time.

"Do you see it? A little sliver right around the top part of my heel."

He's kidding, right? Like I can see a little sliver with everything else he's got going on with this foot? I'm amazed he can feel anything.

"Could you lift your foot?" I ask.

"Huh? Can't you just pick it up?"

We lock eyes. "You want me to pick up your, um, foot?" My voice sounds small and vulnerable. Sort of like Little Red Riding Hood once it sinks in that Grandma has been replaced by the wolf.

"The tweezers are down there on the floor beside you," he says.

By now my left eye is flapping like a flag at a used-car lot. With a silent gulp, I lift the tweezers, face his foot, take a deep breath, and then another breath. Mentally holding my nose and closing my eyes, I scoop his heel into my palm and lift it so I can look for the splinter. My eyes crack open. The sooner I pluck that sucker out of there, the quicker I can drop his foot.

"Do you see it?"

"I'm looking," I say a bit too crossly.

I spot the sliver to the far northeast side of Minnesota and take the tweezers to it. "Logan, do you wear socks around the house, or do you go barefoot?"

"Oh, I don't bother with socks and shoes around the house. But don't worry about me. I don't usually get splinters. This is a fluke."

He lifts a broad smile, and I feel like slime. He thinks I'm worrying about him, when in fact, I'm worrying about his feet. And myself. And both of us in the same room. This puts a whole new twist on our relationship.

"Hey, take it easy there," he says, squirming his foot away from me.

"Well, if you want me to get it, you'll have to hold still."

Just then the front door shoves open. Logan and I exchange a glance. Footsteps bring the visitor into the living room. Dad takes one look at us on the floor in the living room, me holding Logan's foot in the palm of my hand, and shakes his head.

"I don't want to know," he says.

"Wasn't going to tell you." I stop the surgery for a moment and look at Dad. "Where'd you eat your pie?"

"We went over to the lodge," he says. "Marco showed up. Said his dancing commitment cancelled." Dad laughs. "Guess even Casanova has an off-night now and then."

I shouldn't have asked.

Fueled by the news, I yank the tiny sliver free, along with a piece of Canada. "Got it." I drop Logan's foot to the floor with a thump.

"Owww!" he wails.

Casanova my foot!

So what's Brooke gonna do about that baby? Dad asks when we meet in the kitchen the next morning for breakfast. The blinds are lifted, allowing squares of sunlight to hit randomly about the room.

"What do you mean 'what is she going to do'?"

"She's alone and having a baby whose daddy has no intention of raising it. She ought to consider other options, that's all."

Turning toward the stove, I scrape the sausage from the frying pan with a vengeance. Hot grease splatters onto the stovetop. Quickly, I grab a dishcloth and wipe up the grease. If only careless words could be wiped away as easily.

"There are no other options, Dad."

"She could adopt it out."

I spin around, mouth dangling. "How can you say that? Brooke is my daughter and your granddaughter. You're suggesting she give up her only child, my grandchild, your great-grandchild?"

Dad stops chewing and looks at me. "Stop being so selfish, Wendy. It doesn't matter if it is your first grandchild—Brooke can barely make enough money on her own to feed herself, let alone a child."

Anger burns my words to a crisp.

"You don't give a child away because things get tough." Is that what he wanted to do with me? Give me away because Mom wasn't there to take care of me?

"I know that. I kept you, didn't I?" His voice has a been-there-done-that-and-I'm-not-doing-it-again quality to it.

Is that what this is about? He resents me because I was there and Mom wasn't. Though I'd rather take my breakfast into another room, I set my plate of eggs and sausage at the table across from my dad and slide into my seat.

After whispering a prayer—which once again I'm wondering if God can hear, what with my bad attitude and all—I take a bite and find Dad staring at me.

"What?" I ask.

He shakes his head. "Nothing." He takes an ambitious bite of his wheat toast smothered with strawberry jelly.

I know he's waiting on me to say more about Brooke, but I don't want to argue about it.

"Are you working today?" I ask.

"No. I have the day off."

"How's that going, by the way? Your work at the lodge, I mean." I stab a piece of sausage with my fork. The spicy scent hits me before I take a bite, calming me a tad. But just a tad.

"Great." Dad scratches his chin. "Marco is a good man. Hard worker. Knows what he wants and doesn't let other people run over him. I admire that."

So many times when my dad says things, I can't help feeling he's making a comparison of me and someone else. Maybe I'm overly sensitive, but I've never lived up to his expectations. I'm going to need more sausage to spear.

Dad always wanted me to be stronger, to speak my mind. Like him. But I've seen how he alienates people with his assertions. He will not stop arguing until he convinces people to see it his way. Most of the time, they just give up and agree with him so he'll move on to another topic.

Speaking your mind hurts people.

"So what are you and your pals doing today?" I ask.

"We're going to play a little basketball this morning."

Dad stirs more milk into his coffee, causing my thoughts to swirl with his drink. The aroma of strong coffee, seeing him across the table from me this way, all remind me of days I'd sit at the table with him and Mom. It was the one time of the day when he was calm—before the busyness of his work claimed his energies and consumed his thoughts. It was the time when love sparked between them, and I needed to see that. Once work claimed Dad, he treated everyone differently.

Now that I'm older with responsibilities of my own, I understand how life can get in the way, but should we allow it to interfere with kindness toward the people we love?

Did I ever do that?

He drinks the last sip of his coffee and looks at me with a slight smile—which is about as good as it gets—traces of his earlier frustration seemingly gone. Just once I wish I could make Dad proud of me. Pretty pathetic that I'm forty-four years old and still seeking his approval.

"Where are you playing?" Should I mention the fact that he's sixty-five and should be careful playing basketball? Does he care that he causes me concern?

"One of the guys has a big driveway, I guess, so we're going over to his house."

"Be careful," I say before I can stop myself.

He waves his hand. "Oh, you're just like your mother. Always worrying over nothing."

Should I point out he's the one who thinks Brooke should give up her baby? Maybe not. I watch him as he finishes his toast. My dad has always been handsome, and even though he's showing signs of age, he still looks good. Snowy white hair falls soft across his forehead, attempting to hide the wrinkles. Age lines trail determined blue eyes. A smile that I'm sure broke a few hearts in his day rusts beneath a bushy mustache. If only he'd revive it.

"Dad, why did you never remarry?" I can't believe I just asked him that. Dad and I rarely talk about personal things—well, except for our little banter over Brooke. It's like an unspoken law between us.

"They don't come any better than your mom." His chair scrapes across the floor, and he pushes away from the table. Heavy steps carry him to the sink where he rinses off his dish and leaves the room.

That's one of the few compliments I've ever heard leave my dad's lips.

I had hoped to talk to Brooke this morning. She's been going back to her house a lot, getting it prepared for the sale. It's unimaginable to me that Kevin would leave her to do this all alone.

I hope she's not falling deeper into depression. Now she has another life depending on her. It's time to buck up.

Or maybe I'm just letting Dad's comments get to me.

A quick glance at the clock tells me I have another hour before I have to be at work. Pulling my pants and jacket from the closet, I pause at the side that once held Dennis's clothes. I've left some things there so it won't look so cold and bare, but every day I notice and remember. There in the corner hangs Dennis's favorite T-shirt.

I slip the shirt from the hanger and rub the material between my fingers. Dennis sure loved this thing. The worn fabric makes me think of the Velveteen Rabbit. My fingers trace the frayed neckline, and I smile. How many times did he wear this around the house and against my wishes stuff it back in the closet without washing it?

Now I wonder why I made such a big deal of it. After his death, this shirt was my lifeline to sanity. Night after night, I laid it beside me in bed, my hand groping for it through the pain, refusing to believe Dennis no longer filled it.

"Buck up," I told myself then. "Get over it. No amount of crying and anger will bring him back."

So, drying my tears, I forged ahead to a new life.

Without Dennis.

With a sigh, I place the shirt back on the hanger.

And now my daughter has to go through a separation—hers may be even more painful than mine. Dennis didn't choose to leave me. And my kids were nearly grown when he died. Will Brooke's baby have a relationship with Kevin? Assuming, of course, that Kevin is the baby's father.

I refuse to believe anything else. My little girl would never be unfaithful to her husband. She adored her daddy, and with his strong stand on marriage, she wouldn't do such a thing—would she? On the other hand, her daddy is gone, and anger has replaced the part of her heart that he once held.

These nagging thoughts follow me to work.

"Good morning, Sunshine," Roseanne says when I step into the office. "Bad night?"

Smiling, I take off my coat and hang it on the rack. "Just have a few things on my mind."

She pours coffee in a mug and hands it to me. "Here. Something tells me you need this. Want to talk?"

"Not now, but thanks."

"You've got a lot going on right now, Wendy. Anyone in your shoes would be overwhelmed."

"Maybe I should change shoes."

We both laugh, and the conversation segues to a shoe sale over in Pigeon Forge. Roseanne says we should go before the sale is over, but I know my life is too busy right now to think about shoes.

She notices my reluctance. "Okay, spill it."

I take a deep breath. "I know we're best friends, but Roseanne, there's something you don't know about me."

She takes a sharp breath. "Please don't tell me you've had Botox. I just couldn't handle that right now. Especially after you talked me out of it."

"No Botox." I hesitate. "Okay, I'll tell you. I can't stand the sight of feet."

She happens to be drinking from her mug when I say this, which causes her to spurt a fine mist of coffee over her desk. I jump up, grab some paper towels, and help her clean it up.

"Where in the world did that come from?" she asks.

"I don't know. All that talk about shoes, I guess. It's a repressed memory, I think."

Roseanne looks at me in a rare moment of speechlessness.

"I had to pluck a splinter from Logan's foot last night, and it nearly cost us our relationship."

"You mean to tell me that all the time I've known you, you've been secretly recoiling at the sight of my feet?"

"Of course not."

"We've gone swimming, Wendy. You saw my feet."

"I didn't notice them."

"Would it strain our friendship if you saw them and noticed the bunion on my right foot?"

I try not to wince. "It would take more than a bunion to come between us, Roseanne," I say, mentally reevaluating our friendship.

She eyes me suspiciously, then leans over, threatening to pull off her shoe. Beads of perspiration pop up on my forehead, but I hold perfectly still, making her believe I'm up for it.

Her back catches while she leans over. "Help me up, Wendy." Her hand gropes for her back.

I run over to help her and can almost hear it crack back in place as we straighten her.

"Guess I'll have to take your word for it that you could handle my toes."

"I can handle it." Some things are better left unsaid. "You okay?"

"I'm fine." Though she still tosses me a wary glance. "You know how my back catches at times. It's that getting-old thing."

Well, let's just take my bad mood farther south, shall we?

"I didn't see the geese when I came in. Do you think they're gone for good?"

"I don't know, but there was some weird light thing in the middle of the pond this morning." Roseanne clicks on her computer.

"Light thing?"

"Yeah. You might want to check it out."

"I think I will." I grab my coat. "Oh, make sure we have the photographer scheduled for the Samson wedding, two weeks from Saturday."

"Will do."

I head outside and make my way back to the pond. Sure enough, there in the middle of the pond is some sort of weird light thing. Wonder how much that cost?

"Looks like it worked," Marco says, walking up behind me.

I swivel around. "What is it?"

"It's that gadget you told me about that you saw on the Internet. I decided to try it out. Thankfully, the geese weren't here long enough to really settle in or they would have been harder to get rid of. But we'll keep that in the pond for a few weeks just to make sure."

I nod. "So how much do I owe you?"

"For what?"

"That thing, whatever it is."

"We can talk about it over coffee."

My back visibly stiffens.

Marco places his hand on my arm. "Listen, Wendy, seems I've been messing up a lot lately, and I want to apologize—again. There's no excuse for my behavior."

Okay, I have to say I admire this in a man. Maybe because I've never seen my dad apologize over anything. I believe it takes a real man to be able to admit when he's wrong.

"It's all right. I've overreacted a few times myself."

His hand is still holding my arm, and I swallow hard, but I don't pull away. Well, it would be rude.

"You never overreact about anything. I'd like to see you get stirred up good just once."

When I look up, I see a sweet teasing glint in his eyes. He smiles, and something warm swirls in my stomach.

Before I get too comfortable, his business manner returns.

"We still have this matter of the kids to deal with." He says that as though he's making an appointment with the plumber to talk about toilet problems. "I thought maybe we could discuss it over lunch or dinner?"

He's right, we do need to talk about the kids. So why am I disappointed that he's not inviting me to lunch without an agenda?

"I'll have to check my schedule." Why should I be at his beck and call?

He blinks, and I'm pretty sure I see a trace of amusement on his lips.

"When did you want to meet?" My voice is purely professional.

"Could you work it into your schedule today?" Something flickers in his eyes, but I can't stare at him long enough to figure it out without making us both uncomfortable.

I glance at my watch—the silver one that Logan bought for me last Christmas. Why can't he remember that I prefer gold? "Yeah, I guess so."

"How about lunch, since that wouldn't interfere with you and Mr. Carter."

I don't know why it bugs me that he's always bringing Logan into it. I mean, why does he point it out, and with that particular smirk on his face?

"That would be fine," I say, once again in my most professional tone.

"Why don't you meet me at the lodge, say, around one? I should be out of court, and the lunch crowd is thinning around then."

Why does that matter? Is he ashamed to be with me? Afraid that people will get the wrong idea about us?

"That's fine." Thankfully, I have some chocolate popcorn in the office to tide me over.

When he turns and walks off, my heart takes a dip. I'm not sure why. Am I struggling with pride? I've never considered myself a proud person, so why do I suddenly have this need to impress my dad and now Marco?

I should take a day off, go somewhere, anywhere, to get away from everything. Roseanne's right. I've been through a lot, and I need a break—before I'm broken.

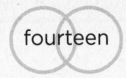

fourteen

By the time one o'clock rolls around, my stomach is tangled like the rubber bands on my desk.

"Oh, it's nice out today," Roseanne says when she comes through the office door, peeling off her jacket. "I haven't made you late, have I?"

"No, no." I grab my coat and handbag. "I'm not exactly in a hurry to get there."

"It will be fine. Though I still say he's using the kids as an excuse to see you."

I give her "the look."

She laughs. "Okay, I'll behave. You'd better get over there. Have a good lunch."

Upon entering the lodge, I hardly have time to catch my breath before a hostess walks up to me and whisks me away to the restaurant.

"Mr. Amorini will be joining you shortly," she says while ushering me over to a secluded corner table.

She hands me a menu. Right on her heels is the server who takes my drink order. These people are on the ball, I'll give them that.

Instrumental music plays softly overhead, mingling with the quiet murmuring at tables in the room. How did my life get in such a mess? One minute I'm having a wonderful life with the man of my dreams, and the next minute I'm alone, running a business by myself, seeing someone new, then housing an aging father and a pregnant, separated-from-her-husband daughter.

While sipping on my sweetened iced tea, I attempt to sort through my life. Before I know it, thirty minutes have passed with no sign of Marco. I'm a little irritated that he doesn't think my time matters too. I don't have all day to waste here at his restaurant.

"Excuse me," I call out to a nearby server.

"Yes, ma'am."

"Mr. Amorini is obviously running late, and I need to get back to the office, so I'd like to go ahead and order, please."

"Certainly. I'll send someone right over."

He disappears, and within a few minutes a young woman appears and takes my order. The longer I sit here, the more irritated I become. I'm on my second glass of iced tea. If I keep this up, I'll be too full to eat. What if Marco stands me up? Not that we have anything going on here, but—oh, what is the matter with me?

Just then Marco steps into the room, and I try to calm my jittery heart.

"Sorry I'm late," he says, sliding into his chair. "There was a backlog of cases in court this morning, so it took longer than usual." He grabs his menu.

Okay, so I overreacted.

"Bad week for couples, huh?"

He puts down his menu and looks up at me. "History tells me we'd better not go there." A twinkle touches his eyes. "Have you been waiting long?"

Only long enough for Noah to build the ark, but don't give it another thought.

"Not that long," I say. "I did just place my order, though, because I wasn't sure how long you would be, and I have to get back to work."

"I understand." He studies the menu a moment, then claps it shut, tells the server what he wants, and hands the menu back. He folds his arms on the table and leans toward me. "So, what are we going to do about the kids?"

"I know they're young, Marco, and that bothers me too. But I wonder if it's about more than that for you. I mean, if they love one another, there's nothing wrong with having someone by your side when you stretch for your dreams."

He stares at me so long I wonder if there's something embarrassing going on with my face.

"We both know that at their age it's dangerous to pick a mate. They hardly know what love is."

A twinge of something hits me when he says that. After all, I was eighteen when Dennis and I married.

"I disagree with that," I say, trying to keep my voice calm and even. "I married at a younger age than Colin, and I had a wonderful life."

"So you've told me." He flips his napkin on his lap as the server places our meals in front of us.

The irritation in his voice makes me feel bad. Maybe he thinks I'm trying to rub it in his face that I had a good marriage and he didn't.

"I'm glad for you, Wendy, but the truth is it doesn't work that way for everybody."

Smoothing my own napkin across my lap, I say, "That doesn't mean it won't work for them."

"Listen, I know you—"

"Excuse me, do you mind if I go ahead and pray? I'm running late."

"Oh, sure, go ahead."

I say a prayer for our meal, then pick up my fork to eat.

Marco waves his fork in my direction. I watch him carefully. I don't trust him with forks.

"What I started to say was I know that you run a wedding chapel. People come to you full of dreams. Then they come to me after reality sets in. I have to pick up the pieces."

He picks up the pieces, all right. Sweeps them away and pretends nothing ever happened, totally ignoring the emotional breakage he's left behind. "Do you?"

He blinks. "What do you mean by that?"

I weigh my words carefully, not wanting to make him mad. "Just wondering if you try to persuade your clients to attend marriage-counseling sessions or encourage them to make things work? Or do you simply hand over the papers to be filled out, take the retainer fee, and send them on their way?"

"Do you try to counsel them before they get married? Make sure they're really ready to take this step?"

"Well, Dennis used to do that. Now that he's not here, I have another pastor do the counseling."

He puts his fork down and looks at me. "Listen, Wendy, I'm not a marriage counselor. People have to take responsibility for their actions. If they're going to get married, they need to discuss it with someone. If they're going to get divorced, hopefully they've tried every other option before coming to me."

My foot jiggles nervously beneath the table. This little gesture somehow helps me keep my tongue clamped behind my teeth—which, right now, is a very good thing.

"We're here to discuss the kids, not my job, remember? I think I can safely say I understand fully how you feel about my job. I just want to ensure that my daughter isn't running into something she'll regret later."

"Sometimes there is no way of knowing for sure until it's too late." Why am I so argumentative today?

"I suppose that's true," he says. "But isn't that where commitment comes in? I mean, if we're not talking abuse, but just incompatibilities, things that can be worked out if the couple is willing to make the effort, shouldn't the commitment get them through it?"

"Yes." I can't help feeling we've switched from a generic conversation to discussing his life, and suddenly he's on my side.

He swirls the pasta around in his plate. "Too bad it doesn't always work that way, though," he says in barely a whisper.

His vulnerability softens me. He's not nearly as tough as he pretends. That rough exterior is just a way of protecting himself.

"Marriage isn't easy, that's for sure. Sometimes it takes more love than we're able to give."

He looks up at me and smiles. "I can see where this is going."

I smile back. "Well, it's true."

"I believe in God, just so you know."

"There's more to it than that. It's about a relationship."

"Yeah. I know all about that. It may surprise you to know we once talked on a daily basis. God and me."

I lift my sandwich. "So what happened?"

He pauses. "My wife walked out, and I stopped talking."

My mind shuffles along with my papers, as I absently toss them about. All afternoon Marco's words hang heavy on my heart. *My wife walked out, and I stopped talking.* There's no doubt she hurt him terribly. The sad thing is he not only lost his wife, he stopped communing with God. Why is it people always blame God when bad things happen? A twinge of guilt runs through me. Did I do that when Dennis died?

"I forgot to tell you, Brooke called while you were gone," Roseanne says.

"Everything all right?"

"Seemed to be. She wasn't upset or anything."

"Okay, thanks." I lift the phone receiver and punch the numbers for home. "Hi, honey. Everything okay?"

"Just wondered if you have any snacks in the house. You know, chocolate or something?"

Her appetite has returned tenfold. Without thought, I open my bottom drawer to make sure I brought in some chocolate popcorn. I'm happy to share, mind you, as long as there is some left over for me.

"I think there are chocolate cupcakes in the cupboard. Also some Neopolitan ice cream in the freezer and chocolate topping in the refrigerator."

I make myself a note to stop at the store on the way home. I know how pregnant women are. She'll work her way through those cupboards like a locust in Egypt. I'll be lucky to have a chunk of bittersweet baking chocolate left by nightfall. That's okay, though. I'd gladly—well, almost—give up my chocolate supply if it meant putting some meat—or chocolate, as the case may be—on her bones.

Cellophane wrap crackles over the wires. "Great. I found it. Thanks, Mom."

"So, is Granddad still out playing basketball?" I ask.

"I guess. He's not home," she says in between bites of the cupcake. *My* cupcake. Even though I just ate, she's making me hungry. "Oh, you have some chocolate popcorn too. Okay if I have some?"

"Sure, help yourself," I say, fighting the selfishness that crowds my heart like single women at a bridal bouquet toss. Hopefully, she'll save me some crumbs. Dennis always teased that he didn't want to be stranded on a desert island with only me and chocolate, 'cause he'd starve. I think he was right.

Our second line rings, and Roseanne answers it. She puts the party on hold and nods to me before slipping into the restroom.

"Listen, honey, I have to go," I tell Brooke. "I've got a phone call."

"Okay—oh, by the way, what's for dinner?"

"I don't know. I'll have to think about it. Bye." Like there will be anything left to cook by the time I get home.

Punching the button with the blinking light, I answer.

"How's my best girl?" Logan says.

I wish he'd quit talking that way. "Fine. Busy."

"Sorry to interrupt. I just wanted to see if you were up for dinner tonight."

"I have houseguests now, you know. They rely on food for survival."

My food. Not to mention, I need to be home to guard my chocolate stash.

"So this is how it's gonna be? I have to schedule a meeting with you?" Frustration lines his voice.

"Looks that way."

"Well, okay, throw on an extra potato for me, and I'll swing by for dinner."

Great, now I'm cooking for four?

"I don't know what we're eating yet. Could be leftovers." Hopefully, he'll get the hint.

"I don't care what we eat. It's the company I'm after."

"Just so you don't expect chocolate."

"Huh?"

"Never mind. I need to stay after work a little bit, so plan to come over around seven thirty."

"Okay, see you then."

For a moment, I consider locking myself in a closet with boxes of chocolate popcorn. With my current mental state, I'm thinking I could easily munch my way into eternity.

After Roseanne leaves, I close up shop. It's such a lovely night. A slight chill nips the air, but since there is no breeze, it gives the illusion of spring. I decide to step around to the pond before making my way home. A little calm before my busy evening can't hurt.

A few twinkling stars have sprouted in the clear evening sky. I settle on the bench, pulling my jacket closer to me as I face the pond, which is clear and smooth as baby skin. How about that . . . I'm starting to think like a grandma. I chuckle in spite of myself.

"What's so funny?"

Marco's voice startles me.

"Oh, hi."

He settles in beside me on the bench, uncomfortably close, which can't be helped—well, unless I give up my chocolate popcorn, which ain't gonna happen—because the bench is small.

"I thought you'd be home before now."

"Last-minute tweaks for Saturday's wedding."

"Do you ever have weddings during the week?"

"Once in a while, but not often."

He snatches a few long pieces of grass and breaks them apart, one by one. "It appears the geese are gone."

"I hope so. Guess that light did the trick. It's not bad to look at, either," I say, mesmerized by its glow. "Sort of a lighthouse on the pond." I laugh.

He turns to me. "You have a nice laugh."

His face is inches from mine. In fact, one deep breath and I could blow him into Florida.

"Thanks."

"Are you cold? Your face is red."

"Is it?" Instinctively, my palms reach up and cover my cheeks.

Marco leans toward me and pulls my hands away. "Don't do that. You look beautiful."

Chills tingle up my arms, then settle in my chest like a flock of hummingbirds at a birdseed convention.

"I'm sorry if I was out of line today," he says. "I don't mean to imply that Colin is a bad choice for Sophia." His dark eyes hold me perfectly still. My breath hesitates in my throat.

Second apology today. Gotta love that in a man. "I understand."

"Do you?"

"I'm trying to."

He turns away. "I'm not against marriage . . ."

I follow his gaze to the pond and try to hold my hands in my lap so he can't see them shaking. "You're not?"

He looks back to me. "No."

I feel the whispered word against my face, causing my cheeks to tingle. I turn to him.

Caught up in a sort of dreamy Doris Day moment, I mumble, "I'm glad."

"You are?"

His surprise surprises me. I snap to focus. My mouth goes perfectly dry. The way he looks at me makes my heart skip to my throat. "I mean, it's a wonderful institution and all," I fumble.

Another smile. His fingers reach up and touch my chin, and my breath refuses to circulate. He tips slightly toward me, causing my heart to patter gently in the softness of the moment. My eyelids fall as his lips brush against mine. A slight breeze stirs between us, cooling my cheeks from the warmth of his lips. His arms caress my shoulders the way a man might stroke the frame of a new car.

Before I can fully grasp what is happening, a lodge employee's voice rips through the tenderness, shouting, "Mr. Amorini, we need you in the kitchen."

I snap to attention.

He's still holding my arm. "Listen, Wendy, I—"

"I've got to go, Marco."

He nods and drops my arm. "See you around."

I turn and walk off into the night, the hammering of my heart telling me something just happened there—something so much more than a kiss.

When I stumble through the door, the house smells of barbecue beef. The rattle of pots and pans comes from the kitchen, and I walk in to see what's going on. Brooke is standing by the stove, stirring a steaming pot and wearing a blue apron over the bump in her belly.

"What's this?"

"Well, I decided since I was home, the least I could do was help with dinner preparations." There's actually a sparkle in her eyes.

"Oh, honey, you're feeling better?"

"Yeah."

"Thank you, Brooke." Her friendly smile encourages me to reach over and hug her. She stiffens, but only slightly. At least she doesn't push me away.

The doorbell rings, and I go to answer it. "Hi, Logan, come on in." He gives me a quick squeeze.

"Hey, Mom, could you check on the buns toasting in the oven?" Brooke calls out on her way to the bathroom.

"Yeah, sure." I shrug at Logan. "Hang up your jacket, and I'll be right back."

Before I can leave, the front door swings open again. This time it's Dad's friend Roy, with a worried look on his face.

"He'll tell you all about it," he says, holding the door and stepping aside for someone.

It's Dad. And he's on crutches.

fifteen

"*I just knew something like this would happen.*" I struggle to help Dad out of his jacket, and Logan reaches over to help me. Then we walk him into the living room.

"Aw, it's no big deal. Just a little sprain," he says. I hold onto his crutches while Dad sags into the chair.

Settling across the sofa from him, Logan and I turn to him. "So what happened?" I ask.

"I zigged when I should have zagged."

Oh sure, now he's lighthearted.

He clears his throat. "I turned the wrong way."

We're at a crossroads here. I can't believe he's the one being lighthearted and I'm not. Once again, he was doing what he wanted to do, giving no thought to how it might affect those around him. Maybe I'm acting like a spoiled child, but I don't need this right now. I really don't. Now, on top of everything else, I'll have to wait on him hand and foot. It isn't fair.

"Dinner is ready," Brooke announces.

Logan and I help Dad to the table, where we soon devour the

barbecue sandwiches, chips, and salad. We carry on with a little small talk, and I clean up the kitchen while Brooke, Logan, and Dad visit in the living room. A sweet smell of apples and cinnamon squeezes through the oven door.

I'm actually thankful for the time alone. I try to pull myself away from my bad attitude over Dad. Maybe I've been too hard on him. After all, things haven't been easy for him, either. I suppose he did the best he knew how, just like I'm doing. It's all we can offer. Though had he turned to God instead of drinking, I'm sure our relationship would be much different today.

I haven't had time to sort through that whole thing with Marco today. Do I dare tell anyone? Have I fallen prey to him like every other woman in town? How could I? We have very little in common—other than the fact that our kids are in love and we want to break them up. Well, and the pond. My fingers absently reach up to touch my lips.

Brooke pokes her head around the corner. "You okay?"

I blink and drop my hand. "Yeah. Yeah, I'm fine. Thanks for making dinner."

"I was glad to do it."

"Is that apple pie I smell in the oven?"

A broad smile. "Sure is."

"My favorite," I say.

"I know," she says, surprising me. "It's almost ready."

"Can't wait. So, how are things at the house?" I ask, not looking up. I scrub hard at the stubborn stains on the bottom of the meat pan.

"Um, okay."

"Is that where you've been going every day?" I try to appear more interested in the pan than in her answer.

"Where else would I go?" The tone of her voice says she knows I'm prying.

"Just wondering. You've been through a lot. You could be going anywhere to sort things out," I say softly, in hopes she'll understand that I'm just concerned.

"What's going on with Colin and Sophia?" she asks, grabbing potholders and lifting the apple pie from the oven.

"Wow, is that homemade?" I say, clearly impressed that my daughter has this domestic side that I never knew about.

"What's that?"

"Okay, obviously not."

"I got it from your freezer. I hope you don't mind."

I had forgotten that was in there. Well, I can hardly fault her for not baking it from scratch. Obviously, I'm not Betty Crocker, or Sara Lee wouldn't have been in my freezer.

"You never answered me. Colin and Sophia?" she asks, jogging my memory.

"Oh, well, I guess they're still on. I haven't talked to him much lately."

"Really? I thought you talked every day."

"Are you kidding? Boys don't talk to their moms that often."

"Yeah, but you and Colin have always been close."

She says that in a way that makes me think there's something else there. If I didn't know better, I'd say even a hint of jealousy.

"Does it bother you that there is another woman in his life now?"

Her question surprises me. What is she getting at? "Of course it doesn't bother me. I'm just concerned that he's getting married too young."

"Are you sure that's all it is?" She pulls bowls from the cupboard and begins filling them with slices of pie and scoops of ice cream.

I grab the fresh-brewed coffee and pour it into mugs. "What are you talking about, Brooke? If you're trying to make a point, I'm not getting it."

"Come on, Mom. You know you've always babied Colin. You fussed over him like crazy while he was growing up."

I stare at her. So that's what this is all about? "Brooke, your brother had childhood asthma. It was a serious illness. Thankfully, he's better now."

Lifting the tray of dessert bowls, she looks at me and shrugs. "Just thought it might be hard to let him go, that's all."

She thinks I babied Colin. Does that mean she thinks I'm overly protective? I'm a controlling mom? The very thought makes my skin crawl.

Please don't tell me I've become my father's daughter.

After Logan leaves, I find myself staring at another foot. Dad's. I go all these years without being confronted by a single toe, and now this. And let me say here that there are no words for what I'm looking at right now. Even if he is my Dad, this foot thing—well, it's just not right.

"Thanks for your help," Dad says when I wrap his ankle in a bandage.

"You need to get to the doctor in the morning and make sure it's not broken."

"Oh, it's fine," he says with a wave of the hand. "Believe me, I'd know if it were broken. It doesn't feel that bad. Just swollen."

I turn his foot a little this way and that, looking it over. "It's pretty beat up, Dad."

"Well, that's because I fell on it."

Helping him to his feet, I grab the crutches and stuff them under

174

his arms. We hobble off to his room where I lay out his pajamas before I go to my own room. Brooke's lights are already out.

By the time I slip between my cool sheets, my mind once again drifts to what happened with Marco today. He probably thinks he has me wrapped around his little finger, like all those other women who bake him goodies and hang onto his every word.

I feel utterly ridiculous. How in the world did I let myself get caught up in the moment that way?

Yes, he is good looking, but surely I'm not so shallow as to fall for a man based on his outer appearance. Thoughts of Logan flit to mind. Logan is handsome too, though his clothes leave a lot to be desired—but there is no denying my attraction to Marco is different.

But of course this could never go anywhere. Our backgrounds are so different. Marco had a faith walk at one time. But when his wife walked out, it seems his faith went with her. I had a great marriage; his failed. Sometimes I wonder if that's why he's got the reputation for being the best divorce attorney in town—working out the frustrations of his own failed marriage. Maybe he feels he's getting a little more justice every time he wins a case.

Folding my feather pillow beneath my head, I try to get comfortable. I will myself to sleep, but my jumbled thoughts refuse to quiet down. Why did life have to get so complicated? Is it too much to ask to have a normal, routine, nothing-to-get-excited-about existence? I'm one of those who actually prefers the status quo. No major upsets. Unfortunately, since Dennis's death, nothing has been status quo.

My rambling mind won't quit, so I decide to commit it all in prayer. Now, there's a thought. Why does it take me so long to get there? My daughter, our relationship, my dad, Colin, everything. After I've wandered through the entire mix, I finally drift off to a restless sleep.

Tying my sneakers in a double knot, I stand up, do a few stretches, then head off for my run through the park. As much as I love being around family, I have to say all this togetherness is getting to me.

Brooke and Dad's constant eating is putting a strain on my budget, to say nothing of the added misfortune of Dad's sprained ankle. All the loose ends at work aren't helping. My memory is just not what it used to be.

"Well, hello." The beautiful brunette from the lodge runs up beside me. "Wendy, isn't it?"

"Yes, Wendy Hartline."

"Remember me? Dora Baden."

"Yes, how are you?"

"Presently, trying to stay warm," she says between short puffs.

We have a little small talk about the weather and the park; then she turns her attention to the lodge. "So, how do you know Marco Amorini?"

"Just through the lodge. My business is next to his."

"How cozy."

Somewhere in there is a *meow*; I can feel it. "Oh, it's nothing like that."

Her perfectly arched brows lift toward her hairline. "You're not married, right?"

"Um, right."

"Then it's something like that. I've never met a woman yet who met Marco and didn't fall under his spell." She continues to run at a steady pace, and I'm tempted to trip her.

"I can assure you, I haven't fallen under anyone's spell," I say with righteous indignation, trying to forget the kiss I shared with him.

"You must be ice cold then, because you're the first woman I've met who doesn't find him handsome."

"I didn't say I don't find him handsome, just that I'm not 'under his spell.'"

She gives me a sideways glance. "I see." The smirk on her face tells me she doesn't see at all. Her little comments are giving me more of a workout than the jogging.

"I mean, not that I care about him that way, just that—"

She laughs. "I get it."

Okay, now she's making me mad. "No, I don't think you do."

"Listen, don't worry about it. He's a good-looking Italian. What's not to like?"

It's probably my aversion to feet, but the smile on her face just makes me want to stomp her toe, which makes me wonder where all this violence is coming from.

"What about you?" I say before she can get another word in. "Are you married?"

Another lift in her eyebrow for emphasis. "No. But don't worry. I'm not competition—though not from a lack of trying. Your big competition is his ex-wife."

This woman is not listening to a word I say. "I told you that I don't care about him in that way. In fact, I am dating someone else." It's hard to be emphatic when one is jogging.

"Okay, whatever you say," she says in a patronizing tone.

I've decided I don't like Dora Baden very well, and the sooner I can get away, the better. Though I have to admit her little comment about his ex-wife intrigues me a tad.

"I think he's still in love with her," she says.

"His ex-wife?"

"Uh-huh. Oh, he tries to act as though he's still mad at her for walking out, but why did he never remarry? Why doesn't he get over it all?" She shakes her head. "He's a man scorned and still deeply in love."

I don't say anything, but her comment places a heavy weight on my chest. Coming around the bend, I see my car ahead. "Well, this is where I get off," I say with a smile.

"So soon? You don't run much, do you?"

"Just now and then." I came here to run alone, but then you wouldn't know that.

"Well, thanks for the company," she says with a wave, and keeps on running.

I smile, then yank open my car door. Sliding behind the wheel, I take a moment to catch my breath. My hands are shaking. Why did Dora's comments upset me that way? Though I admit I find Marco attractive, I'm appalled to discover that I feel disappointment at the thought of him returning to his wife. That's where he belongs, patching things up. I'm the one who climbs a soapbox shouting that we should save troubled marriages.

I need to focus on my relationship with Logan and stay as far away from Marco Amorini as possible.

Wendy? Wendy Hartline, is that you? I put the head of lettuce back in the produce bin at Gommel's Grocery and turn around to see Mrs. Dawson, Emily's grandmother, coming toward me.

"Hi, Mrs. Dawson. How are you?"

"Oh, these old legs don't go as fast as they used to, I'm afraid," she says with a chuckle, inching her way toward me. We share a little small talk, and then the conversation turns to her granddaughter.

"Emily has struggled greatly with their move. She's taking the semester off from school and coming up to help me with her grand-daddy. She says it will give her time to think about what she wants to do with her future. She'll be here Friday, so I'm stocking up on some of her favorite foods."

Excitement surges through me. "She told me she might be coming. How long is she staying?"

"I don't know. We'll keep her as long as she wants."

"That will be great. Maybe we'll get a chance to see her."

"Oh, I'm sure she'll want to see you. She considers you family." She nonchalantly looks over a head of cauliflower. "So how is Colin getting along?"

Mrs. Dawson treated Colin as one of her own, filling him with cookies, buying him birthday and Christmas presents.

"Um, he's doing well. Keeping busy at school." The last thing I want to do is tell her about Sophia. It might discourage Emily from coming over.

"I felt so bad about the timing of the family's move. The future might have been different for those kids," Mrs. Dawson says with a click of her tongue.

"I'm sure it wasn't easy for either of them."

Mrs. Dawson looks up at me with a grin. "Who knows what might happen while she's here?"

I smile. "Yes, who knows?"

Guilt nudges my insides, but then I remind myself I'm not forcing Colin to choose one woman over the other. I'm simply presenting the choices.

"Well, I'd better get going. Harold will wonder what happened to me." She reaches over and gives me a hug. "So good to see you, dear."

"You too." I watch her walk away and wonder how Colin will feel when he finds out Emily is back in town.

sixteen

"Hey, Mom. Thought I'd give you the heads-up that Sophia and I are leaving in a few minutes to come home for the weekend. She wants to start planning for the wedding. So are you in on that, or do we need to get married somewhere else?"

I plop down on the sofa and swing one foot over the arm—something I never did on our last sofa. If I had tried to dangle my feet off that one, the arm would have fallen off. Dennis didn't believe in spending lots of money on material things, so we usually bought our furniture used or cheap, and we kept it until it begged to be carried off to its final resting place. Thankfully, a wealthy lady in our church was getting rid of this one and, after visiting me one day, insisted that I take it. She didn't have to insist very hard.

"Of course you can get married in my chapel, Colin. I wouldn't stop you if that's what you truly want. I merely want you to think it through, to be sure. Because you'll be stuck together 'for better or for worse, for richer, for poorer,' all that—till death, you know."

"I get it, Mom. It's what we want." His words are firm and deliberate.

I plump up a throw pillow and toss it at the opposite end of the sofa. "Listen, Colin, there's something I need to tell you."

"Mom, don't start—"

"No, it's not about you and Sophia," I cut in.

He hesitates. "Okay."

"Um, Emily is back in town."

Silence.

"I haven't actually seen her yet, but I ran into her grandmother at the grocery store, and she told me Emily was taking the semester off to come here. She's had a hard time adjusting to the new place and all."

"Look, Mom, I know you and Sophia's dad want to split us up—"

"Colin. I didn't *invite* Emily back to town. She came on her own. I just thought you'd like to know."

"Okay, so now you've told me. I'll go to Sophia's house for a while, then I'll be home."

"All right. We'll see you then." I wonder how Marco is going to handle Colin's presence at his home.

"Mom?"

"Yeah."

"Um, thanks for letting me know."

"You're welcome. Drive safely."

We click off, and my heart squeezes for my son. There has to be some emotion left in his heart for Emily.

Dressed in her usual uniform of sweats and oversized shirt, Brooke slugs into the room looking like death warmed over.

"You all right?"

She nods, sagging onto the sofa and rubbing her belly.

"You hungry? I'm fixing to start dinner pretty soon."

"Not really. Was that Colin on the phone?"

"Yep. He's coming home for the weekend again."

She raises an eyebrow. "Did you tell him about Emily?"

"Yeah."

"Well, this will certainly be a test—especially if Emily shows an interest in him. Do you think she will?"

"Who knows? Though with her return home, I can't help but wonder if she hopes to run into him."

"That's what I thought." She rests her hands on her belly in a protective manner. "It's too bad it didn't work out between them. I like her."

"Yeah, me too."

"But Sophia's a nice girl too."

I nod. "Are you sure you're all right?"

"Yeah."

The way she says it doesn't convince me. "Anything you want to talk about?" Dumb question. But I figure it can't hurt to ask.

Her face takes on a somber expression. "No."

"Are you sure?"

"I wish Dad were here," she says, as in *I could talk to him, not you.*

Let's drive the wedge further between us, shall we? Defying rejection, I settle onto the sofa beside her and touch her arm. "Brooke, why can't you talk to me?"

"Nothing personal, Mom, but you just can't understand."

"And Dad could?"

"Dad just knew me, that's all. We were close."

The more she talks, the more I hurt. Not wanting her to see the tears in my eyes, I keep my gaze on my lap. "I'd like us to be close too."

"You don't understand me the way Dad did. We spent a lot of time together."

My mind flips through her childhood years, and I wonder where she thinks I was every day.

"Who do you think walked the floors with you when you were sick? When you wanted to learn how to make spaghetti, remember the woman in the blue-and-white apron? That would be me."

She pulls a pillow onto her lap and fidgets with it.

"When you struggled with your schoolwork, your dad wasn't here. He was working on his upcoming marriage retreat or counseling with someone. But I was there, sweating through algebra with you."

She still says nothing.

"You and I had plenty of time together, Brooke," I say, softer this time. A framed family photograph on a nearby stand captures my attention. A snapshot from our trip to Disney when the kids were little.

"Not really, Mom," she says. "You were always busy with Colin."

Her comment stuns me. "You mean when he was sick?" Okay, this is the second time she's mentioned it. We have a problem.

She rolls her eyes. "Whatever." Without another word she gets up and walks back to her bedroom.

I have no idea what just happened.

Another glance at the photograph. Dennis and I are standing in the middle. Brooke is standing to Dennis's left, and Colin is in front of me, with my arms on his shoulders. Could it be that she has held it against me all this time—my concerns, prayers, fussing over Colin? In all my motherly attention to him, did I really neglect Brooke?

Rising from the sofa, I walk into the living room and rummage through the cupboards. Sometimes gut level honesty is just too hard to bear without chocolate. Right when my fingers touch the box of chocolate popcorn—

"Finding anything good?"

Dad's voice startles me, and I whip around to face him. "Oh, uh, I'm getting ready to fix something for dinner. You must be hungry."

"Not too much. Just wanted a snack," he says.

Shamelessly, I shove the popcorn box farther back into the cupboard.

"Cold chicken sounds good to me." Dad hobbles over to the cabinet, pulls out a plate, then walks over and opens the fridge. He helps himself to some chicken, along with a hefty helping of coleslaw.

That's a snack?

"You seem to be getting along all right on your foot," I say, with a slight snarl. Not that I want him to be in pain, but the thought of stomping on his toe when he walks past me does cross my mind. Okay, so I'm seeing a pattern here.

"Not bad for only a few days, huh? I'm tough."

Oh, yeah. Mr. Invincible.

"Well, the best thing you can do for me is stay out of trouble. Slow down a little. I'm not asking you to sit in a rocking chair and knit, but just take it a little easier, will ya?"

"I'll wait a few weeks before I go bungee jumping."

Just hearing him say that makes me break out in a cold sweat. If I have to face another injured foot, *I'm* moving out.

Since Brooke isn't hungry and Dad is eating a sizable snack, I decide to hold off on meal preparations. We walk into the living room, and Dad clicks on the television with the remote. Did he bother to ask if I wanted to watch TV? Why is it whenever I visited him in Florida his home was his home, but when he comes to my house, my home is his home too?

My thoughts shame me. While he concentrates on the remote, I look at his crumpled and worn body. He's suffered plenty. I need to let my issues go and learn to love him regardless of what I feel he's done to me.

"Dad, I thought I might fix beef-vegetable soup tonight. That all right with you?"

"Soup doesn't stick to my ribs, but I guess since I'm eating this chicken, it will be all right." He licks the tips of his fingers.

The doorbell rings, which is probably a good thing. When I walk over and open it, I'm surprised to see Marco standing there in all his gorgeous Italian glory.

"Did you hear that the kids are coming home tonight?" he asks.

"Yes."

He steps inside, and I move away from the door.

"What are we going to do?"

"There's nothing we can do, Marco. They're adults."

"I thought you were with me on this." He runs a hand through his hair, causing a couple of curls to coil and then spring back into place across his forehead. Instinctively, I want to reach over and tuck them back in place, but I stop myself in the nick of time.

"Look, I don't think they're ready for this, but I've come to realize there's not a whole lot we can do," I say.

"That's why we should be putting our heads together, trying to come up with something."

I sigh. "It's not as simple as that, Marco. I don't want to lose my son over this. I'm afraid if we push too hard, we could push them together that much sooner."

The doorbell rings again. And to think it wasn't all that long ago when I sat at home alone, in the quiet, just me and my clock, tick tick ticking, asking for nothing in return but an occasional winding.

When I open the door, there stands Emily on the front step.

"Emily!" I yell. "How are you?" I didn't realize how much I missed her.

A beautiful smile breaks out on her fair face, and she gives me an enormous hug. "Hi, Wendy."

Her golden curls spill across her shoulders in the most charming way. Funny, with her fair skin, blonde hair, and blue eyes she's a total contrast to Sophia's brown eyes, dark hair, and Italian skin. Maybe the pain of losing Emily caused Colin to pick a woman completely opposite in appearance. Oh, dear. Now I'm doing the Roseanne thing and thinking like Dr. Phil.

"Let me take your coat. You'll stay for dinner, right?"

She looks up to see Marco. "Oh, I'm sorry. I should have called first."

"No, no problem at all. Marco Amorini, this is Emily Dawson. Emily, Marco."

Marco gives her his hand. "Nice to meet you."

"Emily is a friend of Colin's," I say, and I immediately see Marco's eyes make the connection. His eyes spark to life. The thing is, I see Emily's face spark to life too.

"Is Colin home?" she asks.

"Well, not right now—"

"But he'll be home later, right?" Marco asks, no doubt picking up on Emily's enthusiasm.

"Well, yes."

"Do you think he would mind if I stopped over later? I mean just to say hello?" she asks, and I'm figuring Sophia will hate me for life.

"Sure, he would love to see you," Marco pipes up.

We both look at him.

"Well, I mean, just knowing Colin and all, he would enjoy seeing an old friend. What guy wouldn't—especially if that old friend was as beautiful as you?"

He lifts his heart-stopping grin, and Emily smiles. My jaw drops as I watch the master at work.

"Great." She turns to me. "If you don't mind, I'll pass on dinner and come by later tonight. What time?"

A tsunami has hit my stomach, and I'm ready to deck Marco. "I'm not really sure. He said it would be late. Maybe stop by around ten? Is that too late?"

What's the matter with me? I want him to see Emily and fall madly in love with her again, don't I?

Wait. I thought it was the idea of him getting married so young that bothered me. He'd be the same age whether with Emily or Sophia, so what gives? Do I view Emily as safe . . . just like Logan?

"No, that will be fine. I'm used to staying up late to study."

"A wonderful quality in a woman," Marco says with a little too much enthusiasm.

Why doesn't he just give her an engagement ring on Colin's behalf and be done with it?

She smiles. "Well, I guess I'll see you later." She gives me another hug, then pushes through the door.

Marco vigorously rubs his hands together. "This is perfect. An old friend shows up—"

"Wait, Marco. Colin was serious with this girl not all that long ago, so—"

He grins and rubs his hands together. "All the better! This will cause a split for sure."

I stare at him a moment. "I am not going to use Emily to bait Colin just so you can split those kids up. That's not right." Never mind that I was thinking about it myself.

"Are you kidding me? It's not using anyone. You saw the way that girl lit up at the mention of his name. She's obviously still in love with him."

"And I don't want her to get hurt."

"Maybe he's still in love with her." He paces a few steps and looks back at me, all smiles.

"And what about Sophia?"

He frowns. "She'll get over it."

"And if you succeed in splitting up Colin and Sophia—how do you think your daughter's going to feel toward you?"

"She'll never know I had anything to do with it."

"Don't you think that's a little deceitful?"

He turns a dark expression my way. "I'll do what I have to do to protect my daughter."

"Control her, don't you mean?"

"Whose side are you on anyway? I thought you wanted Colin to wait too."

"I don't want him to rush into anything, that's true. But I would feel that way with anyone." Wouldn't I? "Still, I can't stop him. He's an adult."

"But that's not to say we can't give fate a nudge in the right direction."

The sound of Dad's shoes scuffling against the floor causes us both to turn to him. He leans against the doorframe, looking a tad frail and bedraggled. He rubs his jaw with his free hand. "You'd better watch yourselves. You don't want to lose your kids."

His gaze flits to me. Something flickers in his eyes. Sadness?

I'm not sure what to say. The look on Marco's face tells me he knows he's outnumbered.

"Look, that girl is coming to see Colin. I have nothing to do with that. I'm just saying if something comes of it, I won't be upset." He grabs the doorknob. "I'll see you later, Wendy. Martin."

"Come on, Mom. Sophia wants to spend some time to get to know you. It will be fun. It's an awesome spring day. Don't you want to take advantage of it?"

"But hiking in the Smokies? This is also the first weekend I've had free in forever." The couple scheduled to get married today called it off. That always saddens me. Another love bites the dust. "It would be nice to get something done around the house."

Not to mention, it would be nice to be home and have Colin home when Emily comes over since she missed him last night. He stayed over too late at Sophia's house. Plus, I'm ready to get all this out in the open. I'm nervous enough as it is. If Colin finds out she's in town and thinks I'm trying to get them back together, well, he could hate me for life.

"You'd rather clean house than spend time with us?"

He gives me a puppy-dog look, and I know I'm a goner. If Emily comes over while we're away, she'll surely come back again, if she loves him . . . and I believe she does. Otherwise, why would she come back and ask about him? No, she won't give up so easily. And she'll be around awhile.

"Oh, all right."

He thrusts his fist into the air. "Yes! I'll call Sophia and let her know while you get dressed to hike. We'll leave in about an hour."

I think it's a little strange an hour later when Colin takes me straight to the park without picking up Sophia, but he says she was shopping and just wanted to meet us there. When he pulls his car into the parking lot and I spot Sophia, I smell a rotten egg.

"This is a setup, isn't it?" I say when I see Marco and Sophia exiting from her car.

"Well, you can call it what you want, but we thought if we could get our parents to spend some time with us and get to know each other a little better, you guys wouldn't fight us so much."

I can only imagine what Marco is thinking right about now. When he walks over to me, he rolls his eyes.

"Don't get mad at me, it wasn't my idea," I say.

He leans close to me. "Did that girl come over last night?"

"Yes, but as you know, Colin was with Sophia till midnight. Emily didn't stay that long," I whisper.

He sighs and shakes his head. "I tried to get him out the door, but they insisted on watching a movie. I stayed right in the room and watched it with them, but they still didn't get the idea."

"You didn't." I laugh.

His hand touches the small of my back while we walk together, causing an involuntary shiver to run through me.

He grins. "I sure did."

"You're pitiful."

"Don't I know it."

Colin throws me a winning smile, and I decide I want to support my son, no matter what he chooses to do. Sophia seems to be a lovely young lady—despite her father. As is Emily. Colin can't go wrong.

After trudging up a few inclines on the mountain path, I take off my jacket and tie it at my waist. Me and heat just don't mix. I take a swig from my water bottle.

"Don't tell me you're hot already," Colin says.

"Okay, I won't tell you that."

He laughs. "Listen, no offense, but you old folks are just a little too slow for our taste. We'll meet you back at the car."

Before we can protest, he grabs Sophia's hand, and they go running up the trail together.

"If your son is trying to win me over, he's going about it all wrong," Marco says with a look of resignation.

I sigh. "And he told me he wanted me to spend time with Sophia. We've been set up. You know that, don't you?"

"I'm an attorney. Of course I know that."

We walk along the rough path, crunching twigs and leaves beneath our feet. Though the mountain air is crisp with spring, the exercise takes the bite from the chill.

"Want to sit on that a moment?" Marco asks, pointing to a fallen pine log.

"Sure."

The log is a little rough, but my rump couldn't be happier. Marco sweeps his arm across his forehead. Okay, so I'm not the only warm one here.

"Wish I knew how to handle this thing with Sophia. We've always been close, and I don't want to mess that up."

To hear the gruff divorce attorney show his emotional side tugs at my heart. And I know where that gets me, so I try to keep my guard up.

"You two have a good relationship," I say, wishing I shared that with Brooke.

He looks at me. "You're close to your kids too."

I can't tell if that's a statement or a question. With a shake of my head I say, "Brooke's always been headstrong. We've never seen eye-to-eye on much, but after her dad's death, she became downright angry. Now this with Kevin—well, I shudder to think what she might do next."

Marco squeezes my hand with his own, causing my knees to

tingle. Some people wear their hearts on their sleeves. What with the way my legs sometimes give out and get goose bumpy to boot, I figure my heart is located somewhere around the middle of my kneecap.

"Maybe you'll grow closer while she's staying with you."

"She won't talk to me, not that way. Surface stuff, mainly. I'm not sure she talks to anyone, to tell you the truth. I've tried to develop that type of relationship with her, but it's never been there. I don't know what I've done wrong." I feel stupid for opening up to Marco this way. I've never really voiced this to anyone. I wanted to talk to Dennis about it, but since he had such a great relationship with Brooke, it always made me feel like a failure as a parent.

"It's not your parenting, Wendy. I've seen you with your kids. No one can predict the way a kid will turn out. Guess it's all that free-will stuff," he says, surprising me.

He's right, really. All we can do is raise them the best we can, pray for them daily, and leave the rest to the Lord. But it's scary. I want to protect Brooke—sometimes from herself.

The hoot of a screech owl grabs our attention.

"Wonder what he's doing out this time of day?" Marco says.

I laugh. "Guess he couldn't sleep."

We look at our gray-feathered friend with wide yellow eyes before his large wings carry him off to a tree with more privacy.

"So how are things going at the lodge?" I ask.

"I'm really enjoying it, but it's wearing me out to practice law and run an inn."

"Can't you get someone to help out at the lodge? Hire a manager or something?" I spot a single blue wildflower and reach down to look at it. "There's nothing better than seeing wildflowers poke through the grass."

Right after the words leave my lips, I feel embarrassed that I would talk so sappy to him. Thankfully, he doesn't laugh.

"So what's your favorite flower?" He helps me to my feet, and we start walking again.

"Daisies, bar none."

He gives me a long look. "Is that right?"

I laugh. "Why? Is that weird?"

"No. I think daisies fit you."

I feel myself blush. "How so?" I'm trying not to show that I'm winded. Winded is synonymous with old, and I refuse to go there.

"They have a simple beauty about them, a sort of innocence."

Oh, he's good. "Thank you." I pick up my pace so he can't see how red my face must surely be right now.

"Hey, wait up. What are you trying to do, kill me?"

I turn around and laugh. "What's the matter, old man, can't keep up?"

He blinks.

"Catch me if you can," I say, running ahead as fast as I can. I hear his feet hit the dirt at a rapid pace, gaining on me with every second that passes, and finally, he thrusts both arms around me in one huge leap.

"Gotcha," he says with a laugh, his face right next to mine, the familiar scent of his cologne making me heady. I laugh, breathless from the run—or his touch, I'm not sure which—and he turns me around to face him.

"Wendy, I—"

My pulse beats hard against my ribs, and my mouth feels like Tennessee clay. Marco's gaze holds me perfectly still, then slowly drifts down to my lips as he leans closer. A bird calls from a nearby birch tree. A mountain stream trickles softly in the distance, and the breeze seems to pause as he pulls me to him. His moist lips are soft and sweet, gentle, yet strong against mine, seeking answers to questions never voiced, lifting promises I dare not dream of.

We linger there until we're both breathless. Warning flags stand at attention and flap in my brain, but I push them from my mind. I haven't felt like this since—since—

Marco pulls away and looks at me. "Something's changing between us, isn't it?"

I look at him. "Uh-huh." There's no denying the flutter in my heart when he's around.

He kisses me once more, then looks at me, smiling. "Something tells me the kids won."

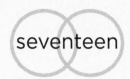

seventeen

Still reeling from sharing more kisses with Marco, I'm hardly prepared when Logan shows up at my door later that same evening. Brooke is out who-knows-where, and Dad went to Peggy Sue Hamilton's house for pie. Peggy Sue is a lady from my church who met Dad at the lodge. They've become good friends. At least, I think that's all it is.

"Wendy, we need to talk," Logan says, pushing his way through the door, coffee cups in hand. "Here, I got this for you." He shoves a cup my way.

"Thanks." Something tells me his heart isn't in the gift. "What is this?"

"Caramel latte, what else? That's what you always want," he says.

"Thanks." Peppermint mochas are becoming a fading memory.

He leads the way to the living room with an air of ownership. Sitting down, he swings his right leg over his left knee and sits back in the chair. His eyes study me over the rim of his cup. "Now, tell me why you've been avoiding me."

"I haven't been avoiding you, Logan. I've been busy." The groaning of my muscles threatens to tattle.

He keeps staring at me. "Brooke doing okay?"

"As well as can be expected, I guess." At least I think she is. She was in bed when I left for the hike, and she's been gone since I got home.

"Your dad doing better?"

"He's fine. He went over to Peggy Sue's house for pie."

Logan's eyebrows lift, causing his forehead to wrinkle. "Good for him." He gets up, walks over to the sofa, and sinks in beside me. "Are we drifting apart?"

I'm not sure how to answer that. Averting his gaze, I say, "I don't know what you mean."

Things have obviously changed between us. He wants more from this relationship than I do, but I don't know how to tell him. I don't want to hurt him.

He lifts my chin in his hand, forcing my eyes to meet his. "Are we drifting apart?"

This should be an endearing touch, but his fingers are rough, and it irritates me that he's holding my chin in place.

I pull away and take another drink from my cup. "We're great friends, Logan. We always will be."

He stiffens. "That's not enough for me anymore." He turns to me again and strokes my cheek with his finger. "I want to take us to the next level, Wendy."

"I'm not there, Logan. I'm sorry." I truly don't want to hurt him or lose his friendship.

"I can wait."

That comment suffocates me.

He clears his throat. "I drove by your house earlier today, and you were gone."

Though I refuse to look up, I can feel his eyes bore into me like a red-bellied woodpecker on a mountain maple.

"Yes, I was gone." I don't offer an explanation. He doesn't own me. Maybe it's the lift of my chin or the look in my eyes—I don't know—but he doesn't press the issue.

"Do you have any plans for tonight?"

Inward groan here. My leg muscles are screaming for a hot bath. I'm not hungry, but if I say no, I'll hurt him for sure.

"Wendy? Do you want to go to dinner?" He glances at his watch. "It's about that time. Six fifteen."

"Sure, that would be fine. Let me freshen up first."

That seems to encourage him. His face brightens, and he leans back to enjoy the rest of his drink. Meanwhile, I get up and head for the bedroom. I'll just let him know I don't want to be out long since Colin is home.

Looking in the mirror, I reapply my makeup. The lipstick has worn off, and I wonder if it came off when Marco kissed me. I think of Dora's words about his ex-wife. Could he be reconciled to her? I certainly don't want to get in the way of that. He didn't kiss me like a man in love with his ex-wife, but then maybe that's because he has such a way with women. Still, I feel myself drawn to him the way Gatlinburg draws tourists.

I take a long, hard look at myself. I'm going to be a grandma. Grandmas are old and crinkly. I may look it, but I don't feel old and crinkly. My heart tells me I'm still seventeen, giddy, and in love with Dennis. Only Dennis isn't here. Marco is—or is he?

Logan certainly is here. I've no doubt that it's the threat of Marco that has prompted Logan to want to take our relationship to a new level. He's probably no more ready for it than I am, but his ego is getting the better of him.

I am starting to act like a silly schoolgirl with a crush. It doesn't help that our kids threw us together today. What was that all about anyway? We're trying to break them up, and they're trying to get us together? Together, as in friends—or together, as in, well, together?

What makes Colin think I could fall for Marco, when he's not at all like Dennis? Marco doesn't strike me as the kind of man who ever wants to settle down with one woman again. Why would he need to when they're falling all over him, baking cakes and goodies? Besides, I'm no Ginger Rogers, and he obviously thinks he's Fred Astaire.

Maybe the kids aren't trying to throw us together in that way, but rather giving us a distraction so we won't try to split them up. Or maybe they just want us to get along enough that we won't make a scene at their wedding.

I feel foolish. What was I thinking, sharing a kiss on a mountain path? Am I going through midlife? Is that what this is? Maybe somebody should lock me up before I dye my hair pink and plaster my arms with tattoos.

"You ready?" Logan shouts down the hall.

What's his problem? I'm not one of those women who takes her sweet time dawdling with this or that.

Well, maybe I am dawdling right now. I'm having a crisis, after all. A meltdown. Okay, I'm talking to my makeup. I need help.

I do need help. I need God's help to deal with all this.

I walk down the hall, and Logan meets me with my jacket and an impatient smile. "Let's go," he says.

He leads the way, and just as he opens the door, Colin greets us on the other side. "Hi, Logan," he says with forced politeness.

For some reason, Colin has never been crazy about Logan. Says he doesn't trust him. I think both of my kids just resent him because he's the first man in my life since Dennis died.

"I hope you guys aren't leaving. I brought some company."

We step out of the way as Colin, Sophia, and Marco step inside.

Audible intake of breath here. I'm not sure if it's me or Logan. But judging by the way all the blood is leaving Logan's face, I'm thinking it was him.

"We were just going out to eat, weren't we, Wendy?" He keeps his eyes on me, and his fingers actually squeeze my arm to the point I'm uncomfortable.

"Well, I—"

"Mom, I'm not here that often. Can't you order takeout and hang around with us?"

Though I can't help feeling I'm being manipulated by both my son and Logan, the look on Colin's face makes me melt. And it's true, he isn't around that often, and I do want to be with him while I can—especially since he's talking marriage, and that means I'm being replaced as the woman in his life.

Taking a deep breath and easing my arm from Logan's grasp, I turn to him. "He has a point."

Logan turns slightly, so no one else can see his face but me. Nostrils flared, mouth pursed as though he's just eaten a persimmon. "What do you want me to get us to eat, then?"

He's struggling to control his breathing. If he opens too wide, I'm pretty sure he'll singe my eyebrows.

"Whatever everyone else wants."

"How about pizza?" Colin suggests. "We haven't eaten, either."

"Pizza sounds great," Marco says, all smiles. "Though it won't be as good as mine." He tosses me a wide grin. "I still need to make one for you."

Okay, this is awkward.

Logan's mood is taking a nosedive. Pizza doesn't agree with him. On the other hand, pizza doesn't bother me too much, if I keep the spices at a minimum. Logan pins me with his eyes, then swivels around to Colin. "Well, how about you and your girlfriend go get it."

This is not merely a suggestion, mind you.

Colin grins. "Sure, we can do that. Mom, why don't you call in the order? Then we'll go pick it up."

We make a decision about what we want—cheese pizza for Logan and me—then the kids leave while we head for the living room. I angle over to the sofa. Logan quickens his steps and pushes past Marco to slide in beside me.

Marco settles into his seat and flashes me the grin that so often melts my heart. "So, Wendy, what have you been up to?" he asks, eyes shining.

If ever I were in danger of swallowing my tongue, it would be now.

Just hiking mountain paths and kissing you?

Noticing my moment of hesitation, Logan turns to me.

"Uh, oh, not too much." By the way, thanks for asking. Is he trying to break up Logan and me? Why? So he can go on to his next conquest?

"Sure was nice out today," he says with a grin, stretching out in his chair.

"What are you doing here, Amorini?" Logan asks, stripping the room of all pretense.

Marco blinks. "Why, I'm going to have some pizza. Pepperoni, all that. Any of this ringing a bell?" He winks at me.

The knots in my stomach could rival a macramé project. "Does anyone want anything to drink?" I ask, already standing—though I hesitate briefly, wondering if it's safe to leave these two alone.

"The question is why are you having pizza here? Don't you have better things to do?"

I'm not sure I like the way Logan says that. Is he saying it's not all that appetizing to come to my house and eat?

"Actually, I can think of nothing better than good food and great company." Marco looks at me and smiles again—a smile I might enjoy if the circumstances were, well, different.

"Cut the baloney, Amorini. I want to know why you would bother to come here for dinner, to *my* girlfriend's house." The possessiveness in his voice irritates me.

"Logan, stop it. Marco is welcome here. Our children are friends—"

Marco jumps in. "Come on, Wendy, we might as well tell him—"

I'm not sure, but I think my grandfather clock momentarily stops ticking. All spit leaves my mouth, and I couldn't swallow if my life depended on it. Now, I'm no gambler, but I'd be willing to bet I'm the color of cauliflower from the neck up. Surely he isn't referring to our kiss.

Logan whips around. "Tell me what?"

I'm not sure how to answer. Not that I could. All air has left my lungs.

"Why, that our kids are serious about one another, that's what," Marco says, bringing air back into the room.

"I already knew that."

"Did you know that they're engaged?"

Logan gasps. "Engaged?" He whips around to me. "Wendy, they're engaged?"

I sigh. "So they tell us."

"Well, break it up," he bellows, standing up.

"Logan, sit down," I say, tempted to push him.

"I will not sit down. Why didn't you tell me this?"

"Can we talk about this later?" The emphasis in my voice should give him a clue that I don't mean to discuss this in front of Marco—who, by the way, is pleasantly settling back into his chair as though he has front row tickets at a Vince Gill concert.

"We will talk about it now." He starts pacing.

Hot adrenaline runs through me and works its way up my neck and face. The color is probably a good thing, considering that cauliflower deal and all. "No, we won't. I'm going to the kitchen to get us something to drink. I'll be back when you calm down." I turn on my heels and head for the kitchen.

"Wendy, you come back here."

Hot. Hot. Hot. If I go back in there, I'll scorch him to death.

Once in the kitchen, I stick my head in the freezer until I notice the ice start to melt. This would have come in handy years ago, before self-defrosting freezers.

When I've calmed down, I wash my hands and fill glasses with ice and sweetened tea for Logan and me, one unsweetened tea for Marco, then return to the living room.

With the recliner flipped out in full position, Marco reaches for the drink I extend to him. "Thanks."

"Where's Logan?" I ask, looking around.

"Your boyfriend left." He watches me while taking a drink from his glass.

"What do you mean 'he left'? Without saying anything?"

"He did. He yelled out that he was leaving. I think it was more of a threat. But when you didn't come out, he left."

"But I didn't hear him." I don't bother to add that my head was in the freezer. The timing seems off. A slight throb starts at my right temple. I put my drink on a stand and fall into the sofa.

Marco shoves the recliner closed and leans over to me, touching my hand and sending tiny pinprick shocks through me. "Listen, I'm sorry. My presence set him off, and I knew it. I provoked him, pure and simple."

And he thinks I don't know this?

I look at him. "What are you doing here?"

He shrugs. "The kids asked me to come."

"And you agreed?" Okay, not the smartest question I ever asked.

His touch grows tighter on my hand. "Seemed the thing to do." All of a sudden, he pulls his hand away and straightens. "I want to keep my relationship with Sophia intact while helping her through this."

"Right." I'm wondering how I'm going to fix this with Logan. Right now, I'm just too tired to care, and the pounding in my temple is getting worse.

"We're home!" Colin calls out from the front door. The smell of pizza wafts into the room. I get up to help in the kitchen and explain that Logan had to leave.

When we all settle back in the living room with our pizza, I see that Colin has lit the fire. Flames dance in the hearth, giving the room a cozy ambiance. He's also lit a few candles and turned on soft instrumental music.

Dennis was romantic once in a while, though not often. In a way, it was odd that he was so caught up in the chapel and weddings, since he wasn't really a romantic type of guy. There were times I wished he would surprise me with flowers, a card, something out-of-the-ordinary, but he thought those things were frivolous. Guess it's not wrong to be frugal . . .

The front door opens.

"If you're a friendly intruder and you're hungry, we're in the living room," Colin calls out.

It's Brooke, and she looks happier than I've seen her in days. "Hi, everyone."

"Hey, sis. Grab some pizza in the kitchen and come join us." Colin lifts a round pepperoni from his pizza slice and sticks it in his mouth.

"Sounds good," she says.

When she leaves the room, the rest of us share a glance. Maybe Brooke is getting her life back.

We're barely into our meal when Dad shows up. Just call us the Waltons. He greets us all, then follows his nose to the kitchen. We may have to send the kids for more pizza.

While the others talk in the living room, I go into the kitchen to see if I can help Dad. He grabs a plate from the cupboard, and I set to work filling his glass with ice and pouring some sweet tea.

He takes a slice of the pepperoni-mushroom pizza and pulls off the mushrooms. "Saw your boyfriend at the coffee shop," he says.

"Logan?"

"Unless you have another one I don't know about."

"Did you talk to him?"

"No, he was busy," he says matter-of-factly.

There's obviously more to this story. "Busy doing what?"

"He was sitting at a table talking with someone."

"Anyone I know?"

Dad shrugs. "I didn't know her." He darts a glance at me.

"He was with a woman?"

"He sure was. And seemed to be enjoying himself too."

I can't tell if Dad wants to hurt me or just wants me to dump Logan.

"He has the right," I say. "It's not as though we're engaged or anything."

"Is that why Marco is here?"

My head is pounding now. "The kids invited him." I reach into the cupboard and pull out a bottle of Advil. Pouring two in my hand, I wash them down with water.

"Well, if you ask my opinion—"

"Dad, if you don't mind, I'd rather not talk about it right now."

"Suit yourself," he says. "I reckon you'll figure it out. You always do." With that he turns and walks away.

While we're still eating pizza, the phone rings. After a few minutes of conversation, I rejoin the others.

"Something wrong?" Marco asks when I enter the room.

I blow out a sigh. "I can't believe I forgot to get the photographer for tomorrow's wedding." Sitting at the end of the sofa, I stuff my chin into the palm of my hand and try to think what to do.

"People get married on Sundays?" Colin asks, face scrunched.

"Every now and then."

"Can Roseanne take pictures?" Brooke asks.

"Only if I want a headless bride and groom. She tends to cut off body parts."

"I knew there was something sinister lurking beneath all that jewelry," Colin says with a laugh.

He turns to Sophia, and they talk a moment while I continue thinking. I just can't tell Roseanne I've messed up again.

"You know, Sophia's a great photographer," Colin says.

"She sure is. I was going to mention that." Marco tosses his daughter a wink.

"She takes all the yearbook photos on campus," Colin says. "She shot the photos for a couple of her friends' weddings too." He looks at Sophia with a *what-do-you-think* look on his face.

"I'm not the greatest, but I'd be happy to snap some photos for the wedding tomorrow, Wendy, if you want me to."

My spirits perk up. "Really? That would be wonderful."

She twirls a strand of hair between her fingers. "Shoot. I just remembered. I left my camera back at school."

"That's not a problem. We have one at the chapel for emergencies like this."

"Well, why don't you ladies go in the dining room and discuss the particulars while the rest of us watch *Mission Impossible 3*," Colin says.

"Guess they don't want us," Sophia says with a laugh, following me into the dining room.

I'm really beginning to like this kid, and not just because she's bailing me out of my dilemma. Once we settle at the dining room table, I give her the details of when and how, according to the package the wedding couple ordered. Surprising myself, I reach over and cover her hand with my own.

"I can't thank you enough for helping me out this way, Sophia. Of course, I'll pay you for your work."

She lifts a warm smile. "Don't worry about that. I'm glad to do it."

"Well, I will pay you. You have a wedding to save for, you know." The words tumble out before I can stop them. Am I actually endorsing this marriage?

One look at her face says I've offered her the moon. She throws her arms around me. "Thank you so much for your support. I can't tell you how much it means."

The warmth of her arms brings an ache to my heart for the hugs I've missed from my own daughter. It feels good. Like I matter to someone.

"You're welcome, honey."

When she pulls away, there are tears in her eyes. Though I've never seen her mother, Sophia is a feminine clone of Marco Amorini if there ever was one.

"You know, my mother left when I was thirteen. Colin told me your mother died when you were that old. So I thought maybe—" She looks down a moment and then back to me. "You might understand me better than anyone. I've really missed having her in my life. For a long time I was angry. Now I'm just sad for the years lost, you know?"

I squeeze her hand. "I sure do."

"Sometimes I want to talk about it, but Dad gets upset if I bring her up."

"Do you have any contact with her?" I ask, watching her twiddle the promise ring on her finger. Colin told me he was making payments on her engagement ring, but wouldn't give it to her until it's paid off. Seems he has his dad's good sense with money.

"Occasionally, but I feel I hardly know her. She calls when it's convenient for her."

"I'm sorry, honey."

"I'm really not sure why I miss her all that much. Guess I miss more the idea of having a mother. I had lots of babysitters when I was a kid—I always had the feeling I was in the way. She wanted to be a professional singer."

I nod. "Does your dad see her much?"

She shakes her head. "He doesn't want anything to do with her. She's been married a couple of times since she left us."

I'm not sure what to say. Dora evidently is getting the wrong information—either that, or Sophia isn't up on what her father is doing these days.

"Oh, well, at least we have our dads, right?" she says off the cuff.

I sigh. "You and your dad have a great relationship. My dad and I, not so much."

"Well, don't be fooled. Dad and I have our moments. Sometimes he tries to control me too much. You've probably noticed that since he's trying to split up Colin and me."

Well, now I feel guilty.

"What keeps you so level-headed when you could get angry with him?" I ask.

"Oh, I get angry. But he's my dad, and I love him. Which means I have to take the whole package, the good with the bad." She looks at me and shrugs. "He does the same for me."

What's not to love about this kid? I have to know, because I'm just not seeing it.

"Besides, he's just scared, that's all. I mean, he lost Mom, and he knows one day he will lose me. Well, he thinks he will. He won't ever completely lose me. He will always be my dad. Still, it will be hard on him. Fear makes people hold a little tighter than they should."

"How come you were able to figure that out and I wasn't?"

She smiles.

I'm not sure how long we sit at the dining room table while Brooke and the guys watch their movie, but by the time we rejoin them we're walking arm in arm, and I feel I've gained a daughter.

Brooke looks up at us, and something flashes across her face. She probably can't imagine anyone relating to me in this way. But then again, she probably thinks Sophia's doing it to get into the family. Who knows?

Through the laughter and fun of the evening, Sophia's words continue to ring in my ears. *Fear makes people hold a little tighter than they should.* I can't imagine that's been my dad's problem.

But what if . . .

eighteen

No sooner does my head sink into the pillow than the phone rings. My fingers fumble for the receiver.

"Wendy? I'm sorry to call so late."

Propping my pillow behind me, I sit up. "Logan, what is it?"

My voice sounds civil, which he doesn't deserve in the least, considering he left my house in a huff and went to coffee with another woman. But who am I to talk? I had a wonderful time with Marco and the kids tonight.

"Well, first off, I want to apologize for the way I acted this evening. I don't know what gets into me. The mere sight of Marco Amorini makes my jaw clench."

"Yeah, I picked up on that."

"The man's a snake."

Obviously, I don't share Logan's opinion of Marco, but this doesn't seem the time to point that out.

"Anyway, I wanted to apologize and to remind you that I'm leaving tomorrow for Chicago."

"Chicago?"

"Remember the literature conference I told you about?"

"Oh, I'd forgotten about that."

"We haven't talked about it in a while—haven't had the chance."

I can almost picture him shaking his index finger at me.

"Anyway, I'll be leaving at noon."

I yawn. "I'd like to take you to the airport, but I'm teaching a Sunday school class in the morning, and then of course I have that afternoon wedding."

"That's all right." The way he says that makes me visualize his drooping shoulders, dejected expression.

"I'm sorry." Why am I apologizing? He's the one who's been acting weird lately. Okay, maybe we both are a little off-kilter.

"Listen, Wendy, I know things have been a little strained between us. I really care about you, and I think you know that. While we're separated this week, it might be a good time for us to think about what we want out of this relationship. See where we want it to go, you know?"

Unfortunately, I think we've both already decided that—and have differing destinations in mind.

"It will be hard," he continues, "but I'm not going to call you while I'm gone. I want to give you some space. Time to think things through."

I'm not sure what to say. "So, my dad says he saw you at the coffee shop tonight."

"He did? I didn't see him."

That's all he offers.

"He says you were with someone." I'm surprised at how outspoken I'm becoming these days.

"Yeah, I ran into one of the professors from the college."

"A female someone, from what I understand." I hurry on. "Please don't think I'm jealous, Logan, because I'm not. But what bothers me is that it's okay for you to go to coffee with another woman, but you don't want me going to coffee with Marco. I'm seeing a double standard here."

"Professor Lane is hardly the same as Marco Amorini."

"Whatever. I just don't see that it's a problem to go out for coffee with another friend."

The silence over the phone wires is broken only by our frustrated breathing.

"You need to think about where you want our relationship to go," he persists.

"I'll think about it."

"Good. Stay away from Amorini. He's bad news."

My scalp bristles. I'm noticing more and more how Logan orders me around, and I don't appreciate it. In fact, it makes me feel like a rebellious kid, and I want to do the very thing he tells me not to do.

"Thanks for the warning."

"I'll be home late next Saturday night, so I'll contact you a week from tomorrow."

"Good-bye, Logan."

We click off, and the sensation that washes over me is completely unexpected. It's as though I've been lost in the woods, and I've suddenly been found. How strange. Maybe it's because of his display of jealousy lately and the pressure he's been putting on me—I don't know. All I do know is that I feel completely free.

Just then the phone rings again. What did he forget?

"Hi," I say with a yawn.

"Well, hi, yourself." Marco's voice shakes me from my lethargy.

"Marco?"

"Guilty as charged." His voice sounds mellow and low. "You're probably wondering why I'm calling."

"The thought had crossed my mind," I say.

"It's like this. I've been thinking about things, and—"

Boy, there must be something in the air to cause these guys to do so much thinking.

He clears his throat. "I shouldn't have been so smug tonight." Hesitation. "I'm not trying to cause trouble with you and your boyfriend, but when I see him, something just seems to come over me."

I hear a slight chuckle in there somewhere. "It's obvious that neither of you has an admiration society going for one another."

He coughs once. "I think that's a safe assumption."

"Must have been a hard divorce to handle," I say, plumping my pillows behind me and getting comfortable.

"It was. I can't divulge more, but just remember things aren't always as they seem."

The way he says that pricks me the wrong way. Not in a way that makes me mad at him, but in a way that tells me there's an obvious warning. The way he says it is different from Logan's warnings. Marco's words hold concern instead of jealousy. I need to think about that, but not now.

"I was wondering, do you think Logan would mind if we met for dinner Monday night? Sophia talked to me tonight about more of their plans." He pauses. "Now, before you say anything, I know you don't want to split the kids up. I just wanted to discuss what she told me."

The soothing lull of his voice—or maybe it's what he's saying—puts me in a dreamy state. "That sounds nice." I sink further into my covers, the comforter warm around my face.

"Want to meet at the lodge, or do you want to go someplace else?"

"The lodge is fine," I say, snuggling further into my covers.

"Great. I'll look forward to that."

His words are soothing, like a gentle summer rain.

"Me too," I say dreamily, my eyelids drifting lazily to a close.

"What?"

My eyelids pop open, and I shoot up in bed. "What?"

"You said *me too*." He's teasing now. "*Me too*, as in you're looking forward to meeting with me."

My hand flies to my cheek. It's warm. And growing warmer by the second. I whip off the covers. "Did I?"

"Yes, you did. You definitely did. Plain as day." Obvious amusement in his voice.

"I took some Advil—my headache—"

"I'm glad, Wendy," he says, letting me know it's all right. "See you tomorrow. Oh, one more thing."

"Yes?"

"Thanks for connecting with Sophia like you did tonight. You didn't have to do that."

"She's easy to love, Marco."

"That's what she said about you, and I couldn't agree more. Good night."

The phone slips from my hand and thumps hard against the carpet.

When Colin gets home, I wonder how I'm going to break the news to him about Emily. If only I hadn't run into her at church. What possessed me to invite her for lunch? I wouldn't hurt Sophia for the world. Something tells me it's the pastor's fault. Preaching about hospitality and reaching out to others. Gets to me every time.

Colin won't be pleased, and I just want to get through it. We'll enjoy a nice lunch together, and whatever happens, happens. I can't worry about it. I've got enough to think about with Dad hiking in the mountains with his buds today. Knowing I lost my husband in a mountain-climbing accident, you'd think Dad wouldn't put me through the worry—saying nothing of the fact he's still recovering from a sprained ankle.

"Hey, Mom, I'm home." Colin steps through the front door and walks into the kitchen. "Mmm, that smells good. I'm famished."

I stir the barbecue pork in the Crock-Pot and pull out the dishes. "You want to set the table for me?"

"Sure."

I hand him three plates.

"Oh, that's right, Granddad is going mountain climbing," he says with a chuckle, taking the plates from my hands.

"Don't say that. He's hiking." Walking over to the food pantry, I pull out the hamburger buns and set them in a warm basket.

Colin looks at me and grins. "Okay, hiking. I think it's pretty cool that Granddad does all those things, Mom. He's enjoying life."

"Right, and taking years off mine."

Colin walks over to me, bends down, and gives me a kiss on the cheek. "You worry too much. Remember when I was a kid, you ran for my inhaler every time I coughed."

"Okay, okay, so I'm a worrywart. But it's only because I care about you."

Sophia's words come back to me. Am I so different from my dad? He handles his fears with control, and I guess I have control issues of my own. I just go about it differently.

"Listen, Colin, I need to tell you something." While I search for the right words, the front doorbell rings.

Before I can say a word, Colin heads for the door. "Since when does Brooke ring the doorbell? She must have forgotten her key."

I brace myself for the wrath that's sure to come. "Actually, Brooke is out with—"

"Hi, Colin," I hear Emily's voice say.

"Emily, hi."

I peek around the corner and see her give him a hug. He looks uncomfortable.

"It's so good to see you," she says.

"Um, you too." He shoves his hands in his pockets. "We were just getting ready to eat." They stand a moment in awkward silence, and his manners prevail. "Do you want to join us?"

I breathe a sigh of relief, thankful Emily didn't tell him that I had already invited her.

"You don't mind?"

"Well, uh, no, that would be great. Just let me tell Mom."

I whip back around into the kitchen and busy myself with gathering the meal.

"Mom, Emily is here, and I've invited her to stay for lunch," he says, shrugging.

"Oh, that's fine. We have plenty," I say, throwing on more buns for emphasis as though I hadn't expected her. I feel a tad deceitful, but if he asks me, of course I'll tell him the truth.

"Colin, would you lead us in prayer?" I ask, after the table is set and we're in our seats.

"Isn't Brooke going to join us?"

"She had other plans," I say.

He shrugs and automatically reaches for our hands. When he realizes what he's done, his eyes connect with Emily's. Something flickers between them, though I'm not sure what. He leads us in prayer and quickly releases his grip.

"I was so sorry to hear about Brooke and Kevin's split. Is she doing all right?" Emily asks with true concern.

"She's had a rough go of it," Colin says.

She nods. "Marriage can be tough, I hear."

Is she trying to bait Colin? She's probably heard rumors about Colin and Sophia. Word travels fast in small towns.

He ignores her comment. "So how is school?" he asks, and soon the kids are discussing campus life, studies, all that, while I listen in. I watch the chemistry between them, and though it's tender, a special friendship between two kids, I'm not sure I see anything more. But I've been wrong before.

After dessert, Colin announces that he has to go pick up Sophia for the wedding.

I glance at the clock. "Oh, that's right. I need to get ready." I explain the situation to Emily, and she quickly helps me clear the table. When Colin returns with his duffel bag, we gather in the entryway to say our good-byes, so the kids can leave for school right from the wedding.

The doorbell rings. I answer it, and my heart plummets.

Smiling, Sophia says, "Hi, Wendy. My friend dropped me off to save Colin a trip to my house." She looks past me and obviously spots Emily, because her smile suddenly evaporates. As in, leaves. As in, not a trace of it anywhere on her face.

"Hi, Sophia." Emily turns and throws her arms around Colin in one dramatic gesture and pulls him against her before he can know what hit him. After a big hug and a kiss so quick Colin couldn't have stopped it if he wanted to, she says, "So good to see you again, Colin. Don't forget to call me."

With that she smiles at a surprised Sophia and walks out to her car, leaving all of us gaping after her.

The next morning after I finish the accounting, I put the notebook away and stare distantly out the window, thumping my pen on the desk.

"Uh-oh, you don't look so good," Roseanne says, swiping the fingernail file across the tip of her cherry red nail one last time.

"Thanks."

She gives a slight laugh. "You know what I mean. Is everything all right?"

"Nothing a little business won't cure."

She bites her red lower lip. "Are things that bad?"

"Oh, I don't know." I push away from my desk. "We did better this time last year. Maybe marriages are down this year. More people are living together than ever before."

"I suppose that's true," Roseanne says, studying me carefully.

Walking over to the window, I glance outside, then turn to her. "Who am I kidding, Roseanne? I'm not cut out for this. I love the wedding side of things, but organization is just not my forte. I messed up yesterday big-time with the photographer deal. If Sophia hadn't stepped in, I don't know what I would have done. Then I made a mess of everything with her and Colin." I explain what happened with Emily.

Roseanne gets up. "Oh, honey, don't be too hard on yourself. We all make mistakes." She pats me on the shoulder. "Sit down at the table, and I'll get you some coffee." Roseanne's answer to life's problems.

We exchange a smile. "Um, Roseanne—"

She holds up her palm. "Now, don't you argue. I'm getting the coffee."

"I was just going to tell you that you have lipstick on your teeth."

She lets out a friendly chuckle. "Oops." She walks over, grabs a tissue from her desktop, and swipes it across her teeth. "I always do that. Gill and I are too blind to see it." Walking back over to pour the coffee, she says, "Do you think I'll be an eccentric old woman some day?"

"I wouldn't touch that with a ten-foot pole."

"Smart woman." She places the coffee cup in front of me with two packets of sweetener. "You've just got too much on your mind these days, what with your dad and Brooke at your house. It's a lot of change."

"I don't know." I tear open the packets and pour the sugar substitute into my coffee.

"You're upset about the Roberts wedding canceling, aren't you?"

"They didn't just cancel. They moved the wedding elsewhere. Now why would they do that?"

"Could be lots of reasons."

"I'm afraid we're getting a reputation for being unreliable. And our cabins aren't all that special." As Marco so graciously pointed out.

"The cabins are cozy. Besides, we didn't make that much money off the cabins anyway. The lodge offers one more alternative. It's convenient. It's a plus for us, really."

"Maybe. But what will I do if this goes under, Roseanne?"

"You'll find something else to do."

"I put everything into this."

Roseanne reaches over and touches my hand. "Wendy, you could sell this place and make plenty. It's a great location. It has everything going for it. Can I be honest with you here?"

The way she says that causes me to look up at her. "Sure."

"It just seems your heart isn't into running this place. Are you sure you're doing this because it's what you want to do?"

"Why else would I do it?"

She studies her manicure a moment. "Oh, I don't know. Maybe you're doing it because it's what you think Dennis would have wanted."

"Well, sure, Dennis loved the place, but that's not why I keep it going."

Roseanne's eyebrows shoot up.

"He's not here to see what I do. Why would I do it for him?" Okay, maybe originally I wanted to keep it going for Dennis's sake, but that's not the only reason. I'm pretty sure it's not the only reason. No, it's not. I know it's not.

"Maybe you're trying to keep his memory alive?"

I stare at her, mouth gaping. "Are you going to bill me for this session?"

"It's on the house."

"Thank you, Dr. Phil."

Roseanne chuckles and shrugs. "People do a lot of things for a lot of reasons."

The phone rings. "Guess it's time to get back to work," I say, thankful for the reprieve. I walk over to my desk and pull out my hand lotion. I close my eyes as the smell of coconut permeates my area, making me think of a tropical place, away from . . . all this.

"You look great, Wendy," Marco says, pulling the chair out for me to sit down at the restaurant. My heart flips in response to his gesture—or is it his words?

"Thanks, Marco."

He hands me a menu. After we get our drinks and place our dinner orders, he looks up at me. "Sounds as though the kids had quite a day yesterday."

I sigh. "Yes. And I feel it's all my fault."

"Oh?" He studies me over the top of his iced tea.

"It's a long story," I say, not having the energy to talk about it, though I know we must. "So did you take Sophia back to school?"

She hardly talked to me at the wedding, and then it was very professional.

"Yeah." He swirls the ice in his tea. "She wouldn't have it any other way."

"I'm sure it looked bad, but truthfully, I don't think Colin has any romantic feelings toward Emily. I watched them through lunch, and he doesn't look at her the way he looks at Sophia."

Shaking his head, he stretches back into his chair and looks at me. "You women read so much into a single glance, touch of the hand, whatever."

His comment piques my interest. "And you men see?"

"We see it for what it is. A glance, a touch. We don't read all the hidden meanings."

I laugh in spite of myself. "We just have that built-in intuition thing."

"I guess." He looks sad.

"What's wrong?"

"See there. I haven't said a thing, and already you know I'm concerned about something."

"Well, that's not hard to figure out. We're both concerned about the kids."

"Sophia cried all the way back to school." He looks at his hands. "I've never seen her this way. In the past, if she had a scuffle with a boyfriend, she quickly moved on."

"Colin was pretty upset too. I was worried about him getting to school safely, and I made him call me when he got there."

"Do you think they talked today?" Marco asks, leaning forward, eyes bright.

"I'm sure Colin tried. He won't rest until she hears his side of the story."

"I finally got what I wanted, and the victory is not nearly as sweet as I thought it would be," he says.

The server brings our meals, and though I thought I was hungry, the smell of chicken and the baked potato do little to tempt me. We both pick at our food, clearly consumed with how the kids are doing.

Just then Marco's cell phone rings. "Excuse me," he says, lifting the phone to his ear.

While he's talking, I glance around the room. There's a hefty crowd for a Monday night. His business is doing well—unlike mine. Maybe I should go back to school for management skills.

Who am I kidding? That doesn't interest me in the least. But what does? My husband is gone, my kids are gone—well, they're supposed to be gone. What will I do with my life if I don't have the business? Guess I could always go to work in an office, but the thought of that makes me want to break out in a cold sweat. The thing I really love to do is decorate, but without a degree in that area, I can't really do anything about it.

Fortunately, before a cloud of doom can settle in, Marco hangs up his phone. "Sorry. Client."

"No problem." Picking up my fork, I shove some peas into my mouth.

"Would you be up to a walk through the park after dinner, or do you think Logan might see us?"

"Look, Marco, you need to understand something. Logan and I are seeing each other as friends. We're not engaged. He doesn't own me." Guess I've made up my mind about this relationship.

Marco holds up his hands.

"Sorry. I just don't want you to worry about Logan every time you mention us getting together. Logan has no say over my life. And besides that, he's out of town this week."

Good grief, why did I say that? It doesn't matter if he's out of town or not. He doesn't own me. Period.

Amusement flickers in Marco's eyes. "That's good to know."

"What? The out-of-town thing, or the he-doesn't-own-me thing?" I try to sound lighthearted and realize I'm digging myself into a deeper hole.

"Both," he says.

And I think he means it.

"Mmm, this is nice," I say as Marco and I take a stroll through the park. The night air is cool but not uncomfortable. Stars are glittering across the clear sky while a smattering of couples and families meander about the area.

"Yeah," he says. Definitely a man of few words.

It relieves my mind to know there is nothing going on between Marco and his former wife. I could never come between a man and his ex—not intentionally. Not that anything is happening here, but just in case something is happening . . .

A young couple walks by, pushing a baby in a stroller. That will be Brooke soon. Maybe even me—as a grandma, of course. We exchange greetings and move on.

"Ever notice how people are friendlier in a park than, say, a grocery store?"

I laugh. "I hadn't noticed."

"Oh, man, last week a lady almost ran me down with her cart." He looks serious, and I stifle a giggle. "What happened?"

"We were racing toward the last box of Lucky Charms."

"Who won?"

He pauses and adds sheepishly, "She did. My cart had a wobbly wheel."

We laugh together.

"I'm in a good mood tonight."

"Oh? Is that a rare thing?" I step over a crack in the sidewalk.

"Let's just say I'm a good one to have on your side." He wiggles his eyebrows.

"You know, I've heard that."

We continue on the path in comfortable silence for a little bit before he speaks. "I think I've messed up with Sophia."

"It's my fault. I never should have invited Emily to lunch. I finally told Colin the truth, and he wasn't happy with me. I'm surprised he called once he got to school. Though he didn't talk, just merely said, 'I'm back at school' and hung up."

"I can't believe I'm saying this, but I feel like we need to do something to make it up to them."

His comment surprises me, and I look at him. "Like what?"

"I don't know. But something." We walk awhile, each lost in thought. "I could send her flowers and say they're from him."

"I don't know. It might make her angrier when she finds out the truth."

"Yeah, you're right." The shuffle of our shoes sounds against the sidewalk. "Do we know how Colin truly feels? Maybe we should get to the bottom of that first before we try to get them back together."

"That's a good point. But I'll tell you, by the look on his face, I'm pretty sure I know the answer to that. Sophia has won his heart."

"Well, just to make sure, why don't you try to get in touch with him? Once we know the answer to that, we'll move forward."

"Sounds like a good idea."

We arrive back at our cars. Marco walks me over to mine and reaches for my hand. "Thanks for meeting with me tonight, Wendy. Even though we didn't solve anything, I feel better just talking about it."

He gives my hand a squeeze, and I want to float, but dinner is holding me firmly in place. I look up at him. "I appreciate the chance to talk about it too."

A slight breeze blows a curl across Marco's forehead. Without thought, I reach up and brush it away. As I lower my hand, Marco catches it with his own, and his eyes never leave mine.

He presses soft kisses across the top of my hand, then turns it palm-side-up and kisses it twice more. Giving it a final squeeze, he whispers, "Good night, Wendy."

I simply stare, goose bumpy and speechless. He walks toward his car. My fingers release the clump of keys, and they fall in a heap on the cold pavement. I bend over to pick them up, then fumble with the remote. When I finally click the button, it's the wrong one, and the horn goes off, threatening to send me straight to Jesus. I drop the keys again, pick up the remote, click off the horn, and finally click the door open. Mortified beyond belief, I keep my gaze firmly fixed forward while putting the key into the ignition.

After waiting what seems a lifetime, I dare a glance in what was Marco's direction and find him still sitting in his car next to mine, waiting on me. With a smile and a nod, he motions me to go first. An isolated cabin away from civilization—and humiliation—that's what I need.

Backing out the car, I'm careful not to touch the palm of my hand against the steering wheel. Not just yet . . .

nineteen

"*Well, it's about time you got home,*" Dad says when I step inside. He and Brooke are standing in the entryway, Brooke holding a bowl of popcorn—thankfully, it's regular popcorn—munching like nobody's business, Dad standing there looking the way he did years ago when I returned home late from a date. Not that that happened very often.

I kick off my shoes and hang up my jacket.

"You want to tell us where you've been?" Dad's tone catches me off guard. Suddenly, I'm transported to a time when my dad towered over me and my legs trembled.

I'm so tired of cowering.

Straightening the jacket in the closet, I seize the moment to catch my breath and count to ten. I turn to Dad with a smile. "I'm sorry, but you told me you were going to be gone today. I didn't think anyone would be here." I look at Brooke. "You said you were going to be out as well. Did you go?"

She nods, and the fact that her face turns red doesn't escape me.

"Okay, the truth is, we didn't know how to cover for you. Logan has been calling since the time I got home—before dinner. And he left messages on the answering machine before that," Brooke says.

"Logan?"

Dad scratches his jaw. "Remember him? That professor fellow who enjoys telling you what to do?"

Now there's the pot calling the kettle black.

"He told me he wasn't going to call this week," I say.

"He lied," Dad says. "So where were you? Shopping? Jogging in the park? Out with Marco?"

I stare at my fingers and mumble, "Yes."

"'Yes' to which one?" Dad presses.

I look up. *Don't you have some prune juice to drink or something?*

Dad's eyes study me, and he grabs a handful of Brooke's popcorn.

"So, what were you doing?" Brooke asks in a demanding tone.

Now Brooke is getting bossy. Dad is definitely not a good influence. Here I thought they'd half kill each other living under the same roof. Instead, they've joined forces against me.

"If you must know, I was talking with Marco."

Dad turns to Brooke. "I told you."

"What?"

"Granddad thinks you and Mr. Amorini are falling for each other. Says he can tell by the way you look at each other." Brooke tries to throw a kernel of popcorn into her mouth and misses. She bends over to pick it up.

"First of all, we are not 'falling' for each other." I throw Dad a dirty look. Well, not officially, anyway. "We were merely discussing Colin and Sophia."

"I don't know how you could even think of dating another man after you've been married to a perfect man like Daddy," Brooke says.

Dad raises his eyebrows.

"Brooke, we both loved your dad, but hard as it is, I have to move on with my life. So do you."

She shakes her head. "I'll never move on."

I'm not sure if she means from her dad or from Kevin.

Before I can take this conversation to a deeper level, she cuts me short.

"So what's going on with Colin and Sophia?"

I tell them what happened with Emily.

Dad whistles. "What were you thinking? That Sophia's a sweet little thing. Why don't you want her with Colin?"

"It's not that I don't want them together, Dad. I just want to make sure Colin is over Emily—that's all. I want him to know for sure before he makes a mistake."

Dad's eyes narrow. "Are you sure that's all it is?"

"Yes." Okay, plus the fact that he was in diapers only yesterday— at least it seems that way to me. "The kids are so young—just like I was when I got married. Still, they're old enough to marry, if that's what they truly want. But is their love strong enough to survive the difficulties of life? Is there any way of truly knowing that when you're so young?"

"Those are things beyond a parent's control. When the children are grown, we no longer have any say."

All right, this coming from my dad just makes me want to deck him. *I mean, come on, Dad, walk the talk.*

I cock my head and pin him with my look. "Oh? So why the thirty questions when I walked in the door tonight?"

He shrugs. "I didn't say we don't ask. Just that we have no control." He grunts. "You know as well as I do, you'll do what you want."

"Like father, like daughter." That little burst of bravery makes me feel downright proud.

Another grunt.

"By the way, how was the mountain climbing today?" Brooke asks.

"We had a good time. I'm plenty tired, though."

The phone rings. Brooke swallows her popcorn and heads for the phone.

"Mom, it's for you. It's Logan."

"*Where have you been? I've been trying to reach you all* evening and no one seemed to know where you were."

Logan's voice is cross and puts me immediately on the defensive. I start to tell him, but he cuts me off.

"Oh, never mind. Whatever your excuse, I guess I forgive you."

He forgives me?

"I thought you weren't calling this week. What happened to that?"

"Uh, yeah, well, I just couldn't help myself, I guess."

His lame attempt at making me feel better doesn't. "I think it's a good idea. To have a break, I mean." My voice sounds a little harsher than I'd intended.

"You're right. I shouldn't have called."

I rub my temples. Please, not another headache. "Look, I'm sorry, Logan. I'm just tired."

"No, you're absolutely right. I shouldn't have called." He gives me his phone number, in case I need to contact him for any reason. "I'll talk to you when I get back." With that he clicks off.

We both know that's another manipulative tool of his. The moment I show that I'm feeling guilty, he jumps on it and tries to make me feel worse. That's why he gave me his phone number.

Well, it's not going to work this time. Leaving his number by the phone, I say good night to Brooke and Dad and walk straight to my room.

"Hey, the good news is I've just scheduled a wedding to cover the one we lost," Roseanne says, purple fingernails waving against a glitzy purple blouse with sparkling silver studs.

"Oh, that's great," I say, dropping my purse on the desk and hanging my sweater on the back of my chair.

"Well, that's the good news." She opens her compact mirror and checks her teeth, smacks her lips together once, then snaps the compact back in place and stuffs it in her makeup bag.

"And the bad news?"

"It's this Saturday."

"This Saturday?" Stay calm, Wendy.

"Now before you get all worked up," she says pleasantly, "I already checked with the photographer, the singer, the baker, and the pastor. They're all available. Since the other wedding just canceled yesterday, they hadn't had the time to schedule anything else. I made sure the couple knew they would have to take the basic package, since we didn't have a whole lot of time."

My jaw dangles. "You're totally amazing, Roseanne."

She studies her fingernails, looks up, and flashes a smile. "I do what I can. There is one thing, though."

"Uh-oh. I knew there had to be."

"Not a big deal, really. They just hoped the doves were available so they could set them off at the reception."

"Where is the reception, by the way?"

"They've booked the reception room at the lodge."

"Well, we've certainly helped Marco's business."

"Actually, he's helped ours. They called us because they already had the reception room booked and they thought it would be nice to have the wedding so close."

"Great, so the reception comes first these days."

Roseanne stares at me.

"Okay, okay, so he's helping us."

"Right. So if you'll just take care of the doves, I think we're all set. But if they're not available, it's no big deal. Just let the couple know, and they'll plan for bubbles or something." Roseanne prances over in her spiked heels and places a sticky note on my desk with a name and number penned across it.

"Thanks."

"While you take care of that, I'm going to call the cleaning lady. She didn't scrub the shower in the Cinderella cabin to my satisfaction, so I'm going to make sure she takes extra care this week. You might want to take a look out there and see what you think."

"Okay, I'll check it out." Punching in the appropriate numbers, I ask for the person in charge of scheduling the doves.

While I'm waiting, I study Roseanne. She's so professional and kind, yet firm when she handles clients and our contractors. You'd never know by looking at her that she'd be such a serious business-woman. Her gaudy jewelry makes her seem a little too playful at times—and she is playful. But she also knows how to be professional. If I had spotted a soiled shower, I would have cleaned it myself and not held the housekeeper accountable. Roseanne should be running this place instead of me. Maybe I should buy more jewelry.

The person who trains the doves tells me they had a cancellation, so they're available. Perfect. Once all the details are set, my mood is on the upswing.

Roseanne and I work our way to lunchtime, and I decide to take my sack lunch out by the pond after I stop at the Cinderella cabin to check out the shower.

Shoving open the door of the cabin, I get a whiff of some sort of lemony clean smell. Everything looks nice in the living room. Furniture polished, pillows plumped, hardwood floor swept. But it's when I step into the bathroom and pull open the shower door that I get the shock of my life. There in all its scaly glory, a big, fat snake slithers around the basin of my shower. They say to stay calm in those moments, so of course, I slam the shower door closed and scream loud enough to rattle the trees in the forest.

I'm not all that familiar with snakes, but it is not a copperhead, I know that much. Barely breathing, I listen for snake noises. Not a sound in the room, which only adds to the freakiness of the moment. Cottonmouth is the other poisonous snake around here, and I'm not sure what they look like. My sharp senses simply tell me it's time to run. But doggone it, I'm tired of people and animals bossing me around.

This is Logan's fault.

Adrenaline pushes me to delirium. My eyes dart about the small room for a weapon. The best I can come up with is a toilet brush. Thankfully, we spare no expense on these babies, so it's a sturdy one. Clutching it with a grip so tight it could snap any moment, I edge my way to the shower door. With my right hand, I raise the weapon like a warrior in battle while my left hand reaches for the shower door.

With all the skill of a hawk, I swoop down upon the unsuspecting reptile before he knows what's hit him, whacking him time and again with the instrument of death like a Fuller Brush man gone postal. Heavy bristles pierce his scales, causing him to slither and coil as I chase him around the shower basin. Nothing can stop me as my warrior self morphs into Wonder Woman.

"Wendy, stop!"

Marco's stern voice brings me to my senses, and I spin around.

"That's a garter snake. He's not poisonous. You've dazed him half to death."

My gaze goes from Marco back to the snake, who has definitely seen better days. Wait. Why should I feel bad? That snake is in *my* cabin.

Marco picks up his cell phone. "Hey, Roy, we've got a snake in the Cinderella cabin next door. Not poisonous, it's a garter . . . No, I think she scared it more than anything. Anyway, get a set of tongs or something to come over here and get it out of the shower, will you? You can set it loose in the woods . . . Okay. Bye."

"You're going to set him free?" I ask with disbelief as Marco closes the shower door.

"What's he done to you? He gets lost, finds himself trapped in your shower, where you try to beat him to death, and you're not happy until there's no breath left in him. That's the way with you women. You trap a guy, then would rather kill him than set him free."

I have half a notion to scrub his face with the same brush I used on the snake.

"In case you haven't heard, snakes are protected in Tennessee. It's illegal to kill them."

I raise my toilet brush in a threatening way. "I'm not going down without a fight." What in the world has come over me?

Marco's expression shows, well, fear. Not liking the way I look through his eyes, I lower the weapon.

"Let's go outside," he says, carefully prying the toilet brush from my fingers, tossing it aside, then leading me out of the bathroom before I can do any more damage to the victim.

Just when I take charge of a situation, someone comes along and takes it away from me. With slumped shoulders I exit the cottage, wondering if I'll ever gain control of my life.

After washing my hands at the cabin, I walk out to the pond. Marco had to run back to the lodge to check on something, which is just as well. Wonder what he came over for in the first place.

The warm Tennessee sun feels wonderful against my skin as I settle into my seat to eat my lunch. An occasional ripple in the lake and the crinkle of my lunch sack when I open it are the only sounds around me. Pulling out my sandwich bag, I zip open the top, looking forward to the Virginia ham and cheese on the bun. After bowing my head for a prayer, I bite into my sandwich, then snap open the tab on my Diet Pepsi and take a drink.

The trees have buds on them. Won't be long until everything will be in full bloom. Daffodils the color of bright sunshine, violet and yellow pansies, bougainvilleas, red tulips, and an abundance of petunias and daisies will soon burst around the chapel like wildflowers on sunlit mountain ledges.

Sitting in the silence, I let the moment bask over me. I should do this more often. My life has been so hectic and much fuller than I'm used to. I think about it all and realize that though it's not easy, it's been good for me to have Dad and Brooke at my house. Even this thing with Colin and Sophia. It all keeps me on my prayer bones, as my grandma used to say.

I'll admit I have more work than usual these days. Laundry, meals, all that. When it's just me, I can get by on canned soup. Then there's the constant noise. Brooke coming in at all hours. What is she doing, anyway? I'm trying to give her space, but I'd really like to know.

And of course, Dad with his TV shows. I don't think I've watched one of my programs since he's arrived.

"Want some company?"

I turn around to see Marco walking up, grinning. My heart melts like cake frosting on a hot day. And of course, that makes me mad because he made me feel stupid with the snake thing.

I scoot over to the edge of the bench, trying to give him plenty of room. I will not have him thinking I'm drooling over him like every other woman in town.

"You've heard I'm contagious?" His chin is raised in a challenge.

"Only if you bite—or so I'm told."

"Oh, trust me, I won't bite. I've seen what you can do with a toilet brush."

I look at him, and we both laugh.

"If you could have seen yourself." More laughing. "I felt sorry for the snake."

"Hey!" I punch him playfully on the arm. "What's that supposed to mean?"

He laughs low and husky, then grabs my hand and holds it, along with my attention.

Somebody call 911—I think I've stopped breathing.

"It means I don't want to get on your bad side. I don't want you to hurt me."

Something in his eyes tells me there's more to that comment. My throat constricts. Looking into those chocolate pools, I wonder who could hurt whom. It's time to face facts. I care about Marco Amorini more than I want to. Nagging questions haunt me. Despite what Sophia said, does he still care for her mother? What about the women who bake for him? And go dancing with him? And where does he stand on his faith now?

I pull my hand away. "So, have you talked with Sophia?" I ask.

He blinks, and a shadow flickers in his eyes. Did I offend him by taking my hand away? He's probably not used to women refusing his flirtatious attempts.

Opening the carton that holds his hamburger and fries, he says, "Yeah. She says Colin has tried to call her, but she won't talk to him until she has time to think about it some more. She's afraid Colin still has feelings for Emily." He dips a French fry into some catsup, then shoves it into his mouth. "Have you talked with Colin?"

"Not yet. I've tried to reach him all day. He finally returned my call, but I didn't hear my cell phone. Hopefully, I'll get to talk to him tonight."

"I've got an idea."

"What's that?" I ask.

"I have a trial tomorrow, but how about if we take Thursday off and go see the kids on campus?"

"Together?" Part of me screams, *What, are you nuts? This is a no-brainer. You go, girl.* The other part of me says, *What are you thinking? Stay away from that man!*

"Well, it would be nice to ride together as opposed to taking two cars, don't you think?" He winks.

"Yeah, I guess so." Do I trust myself with him?

"I promise you, I will not bite."

My heart quickens. "If it's all the same to you, I'll bring the toilet brush just in case."

His head dips back, and he laughs out loud. "Point taken. Besides, we owe it to the kids to bring them together and at least explain what happened. After that, they're on their own to decide where they want to go from here."

I eye him suspiciously. "And what if they decide to stay together?"

A slow smile breaks out on his face. "I'm not going to fight it."

Now I'm really suspicious. "And why the sudden change of heart?"

"Let's just say, as much as I hate the thought of Sophia making a mistake, I can't bear to lose her. We've always been close. Right now, I feel her pulling away. I guess she'll have to make her own mistakes just like the rest of us."

My thoughts run to Brooke. "It's hard, isn't it?"

"That's an understatement." He stares out at the water. "I'd do anything to spare her what I—to spare her pain." He turns to me, and a look of vulnerability passes over him, making me want to wrap him in my arms and assure him everything will be all right.

Embarrassment heats my face. "Well, I'd better get back to work."

We quickly make arrangements for Thursday, deciding he will pick me up and we'll head to the kids' school from there.

For some reason, my heart feels light as a feather the rest of the afternoon. I know I have to be careful where Marco is concerned. I can't let my heart get tangled with him—though I know it's a little late. But I'll just go long enough to get the kids straightened out, then head back home and keep my distance. It's only one day.

What can happen?

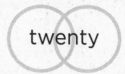

twenty

"Hi, Colin. Thanks for returning my call," I say the next morning when he calls. Grabbing my coffee mug, I sit at the kitchen table.

"Well, I thought I'd better get you before you leave for work. What do you need?"

Uh-oh, he's short with me. I guess I can't blame him. "I just want to apologize for that whole thing with Emily and see what I can do to make things right."

"No offense, Mom, but I think you've done enough already."

His words hurt, but I deserve them. I never should have meddled. "I'm very sorry, Colin."

He blows out a sigh. "Don't worry about it. It's what you've always said. If she loves me, really loves me, she'll come around."

"You really do love her, don't you, Colin?"

"That's what I've been trying to tell you." He pauses. "I know it must seem crazy, since I thought I was in love with Emily all that time. We've been friends since grade school. Guess I confused it with love. But after meeting Sophia, I knew it was different. And then when I saw Emily on Sunday, it clinched it for me. The only feeling I had for her was one of friendship. There's no doubt in my mind that I love Sophia."

"Then that's what you need to let Sophia know."

Just then Dad walks into the room. I wave and point to the pot of coffee that's ready and waiting. He nods, fills his cup, and lifts it in thanks.

"I would if she would let me talk to her."

"Not returning your calls?"

"Well, she let me talk to her once. I explained everything and she listened politely, then said we need time apart to make sure this is what we want. I've respected her wishes."

"You'd better not wait too long."

"What can I do? She thinks I don't love her, but she won't work through it with me. We have to be able to do that if we're going to get married."

"Sounds to me like you're both learning something," I say.

"I guess." His voice sounds tired and defeated.

"She just needs a little time, that's all. Her pride has been wounded. She'll come around."

"I hope you're right."

I consider telling him that Marco and I are coming to visit, but I figure he'll tell me not to, and I don't want to risk it. I'm not sure if it's because I want to help the kids or because I want to be with Marco.

"Well, I've got to get to class. I'll keep you posted. Pray for us, okay?"

"I'll pray the Lord will give you both wisdom. Love you."

"Love you too." He clicks off.

Grabbing my cup of coffee, I walk into the living room to join

Dad for a few minutes before work. "Morning, Dad. Mind if I join you?"

He nods toward the chair. That's as much of an invitation as I'm going to get.

We talk a moment about the kids, the weather, and the snake I came across in the cabin.

Finally Dad says, "I should tell you I might have found a place to stay."

My heart leaps. Maybe this is the first step toward getting my life back.

"Oh?" Keep calm. Don't act overly excited.

"Yeah. And the funniest thing happened."

I'm practically on the edge of my seat, mentally packing his bags.

"I remembered I'm not making enough money for my own place."

The words hit me like a stupid punch line at the end of a joke. For the fraction of a second, I consider going for the toilet brush.

"Still, Peggy Sue says that's okay. She says I can pay whatever I can afford, and when I find a real job, we can go from there." He slurps his coffee, lets out a manly cough, and scratches in a way that would make Bart Simpson proud.

"Peggy Sue?" My fingers grab hold of the nearby stand. Dad is going to move in with a woman, as in, live with her without being married? This sounds like a job for Focus on the Family.

"Yeah, that woman from your church. She sure is a looker."

Peggy Sue has the skin of a prune and blue hair.

"She has an apartment upstairs that's empty at the moment. She gets nervous about renting it out to people she doesn't know. All I have to do is pay utilities for now. It won't be ready for several weeks, though, because she has some kid coming over to paint a couple rooms."

Hope has zipped back into place.

"And if that doesn't work out, one of the boys has offered to let me stay at his place for a while."

"Which 'boy'?" And let me just say here that's using the term loosely. The boys to which my dad refers can't be a day under sixty-five, any of them.

"Alvin Reeder."

And that's another thing. Do I dare trust my dad to an Alvin? He's named after a Chipmunk, for crying out loud.

"Dad, you know you're welcome to stay on here, right?" Okay, so that's not entirely true, but I'm working on it. But wait. Maybe I'm getting on his nerves as much as he's getting on mine.

"I know. I just don't like telling folks I'm living with my daughter. Makes me look like a charity case."

"That's not charity, Dad. That's called love. Lots of parents live with their kids." I wonder why now, of all times, I'm getting vocal.

Dad locks eyes with me. "We both know I don't deserve this."

My heart flips as I feel a father-daughter moment coming on. At least, I think that's what this is. We've never had one before, so I'm not sure.

"Dad . . ."

"Let me say my piece, Wendy." He holds up his hand. "I've been a failure as a dad, and we both know it."

A glance at the clock tells me I need to get to work, but I'm not about to stop him from talking now. I've waited years for this.

He leans over in his chair and stares at his clasped hands. "I've never been gentle with words. I speak my mind. Always have."

Now there's a news flash.

"Sometimes I come across—"

As loveable as mountain thistle?

"—well, harsher than I mean to, that's all."

I'm not sure what to say.

"After your mom died, all I could think about were those times I could have said something to encourage her, to let her know I loved her, but I didn't." He rubs his right eye with the ball of his fist. "God help me, I didn't."

Ironically, everything is quiet in the house as Dad cracks the wall between us.

"But it's too late. Then I come here, thinking I might make things right with you, and every time I want to say something that might bridge the gap between us, I just don't know how to do it."

His words are like a cool mountain stream at the end of a long hike. Wanted, desperately needed, savored. A lump fills my throat while tears fill my eyes. "Listen, Dad—"

"Don't stop me now or I'll never finish." He clears his throat. "I know my presence here makes you nervous. To be honest, it makes me nervous too—because I know I have unfinished business. I don't know how to make things right—but I want to."

Now his eyes are filled with tears—something I've not seen since my mother died.

We stand up simultaneously. For the first time in years my dad hugs me. Truly hugs me. No pretense. No awkwardness. Just pure huggin', clear through.

When Dad pulls back from me, he looks at my face and brushes away the hair from my eyes. "I love you, Wendy girl. A man couldn't ask for a better daughter."

Now a flood of tears rolls down my cheeks. Tears for moments forever lost, tears of joy for those that are yet to be.

"I love you too, Dad."

We embrace once more, and Brooke steps into the room. She stops cold when she sees us. "Everything all right?"

We pull apart and look at her.

"Everything is fine," I say with a chuckle.

She studies us a moment. "Just wanted you to know I'll be gone most of the day."

"Should I expect you for dinner?" I ask, hoping to pull more information from her.

"No. See you later." With no consideration for our feelings whatsoever, she walks out the door.

Dad blows his nose on a handkerchief. "You're going to have to talk to that girl, you know."

Smiling inwardly, I realize it will take Dad some time to get over his bossy ways. "I know." I glance at the clock. "Oh, I've really got to go, or I'll be late for work. You working today at the lodge?"

"Yeah, but I don't have to go in until ten."

I grab his hand and give it a squeeze. "Dad?"

"Yeah?"

"Thanks."

"All set?" Marco says when I answer the door on Thursday morning. "Here, I got you a little something." He passes me a covered disposable cup.

"What's this?" I ask, flattered that he would be that thoughtful.

"I called Roseanne and asked her what you liked. She said peppermint mocha. So if that's not right, it's her fault."

I laugh. "It's exactly right."

"Ready to go?"

"Yes. Let me say good-bye to Dad. I'll be right back." I turn around, and Dad is already standing behind me with a goofy grin on his face.

"You kids have a good time," he says, stepping up to give me a hug. Another real hug. "This one's good. Better not let him slip away," Dad whispers in my ear.

Things are changing between Dad and me. Maybe there's hope for our family yet.

"Bye," I say, my eyes giving him a cold warning to behave himself. "Tell Brooke I'm sorry I missed her."

"Oh, she's not home," he says.

I stop and turn around. "Where did she go so early this morning?" I ask, though I doubt he knows.

"She didn't come home last night." Upon seeing the look on my face, he hurries on. "But she called late. You didn't hear the phone, so I picked it up. She said she was staying at her house."

"Thanks for letting me know. I'll see you later."

Marco closes the door behind us and we head for his car, but the thought of Brooke's mysterious behavior shadows my footsteps.

"The weather is perfect today," I say, staring out the window at the bright sun and the clean, blue sky.

"Yeah, it is nice," Marco says. "I was glad to get away from the office. I needed a break."

"You're doing too much. You need to take care of your health."

"Yeah, I know. I need to run more."

Over the quiet hum of the car engine, we talk about our exercise routines, and then the conversation drifts to our families.

"Did I ever tell you my parents are both gone?"

"No. I'm sorry, Marco."

"Yeah, it was hard. They died a couple of years ago in a plane crash. Dad had a pilot's license, owned a Cessna. They had engine trouble and went down."

"How awful." I can only imagine how hard it would be to lose two at the same time.

"It was pretty awful. They were a real support to me when Sophia was little."

"You've not had an easy time of it."

He turns to me. "Neither have you."

"I couldn't have gotten through without my faith in God."

Everything grows quiet.

"I'm sorry. I wasn't trying to preach. It's just that, well, it's true. In those dark days after Dennis died, it hurt to breathe. God gave me the strength to take one breath at a time."

"I used to feel that way once. Guess I've just let life get in the way. It's not that I don't believe in God—like I told you before, I used to talk to Him a lot. These days I guess I've just forgotten about Him."

"He's not forgotten you," I say, looking down at my fingers.

"I know."

For a moment we're lost in the silence.

"Hey, how about some music?" he asks.

He flips on the radio, and our conversation cuts to bare bones. Somehow I feel I've overstepped my bounds, though I didn't mean to. Everyone has to take his own journey. I just don't know how anyone does it alone.

"Are you sure she'll come?" I yell against the rumble of bowling balls rolling down lanes and blasting clusters of pins.

"Yes, she'll come." Marco picks up a ball, tries his fingers in it, then puts it down. "She'd be suspicious of a quiet, talking-type place like a restaurant or coffee shop. That's why I picked the bowling alley." He tries his thumb and fingers in another ball. "Right now, she thinks she's meeting me for a fun game of bowling." Marco keeps his eyes on the entrance door. "How about Colin? Did he say he'd come?"

"He's on his way."

"Great." He puts the ball down and rubs his hands together. "We might as well get a lane and some shoes while we wait. I haven't done this in a long time. Should be fun."

I don't say anything, but I'm hoping this whole thing works out as well as Marco intends.

We go up to the counter and let the lady know two more people will be joining us. I no sooner pick out my bowling ball and walk over to our lane when I spot Colin coming through the door.

He walks toward me with purpose, worry lines on his face. "Mom, what's up? Is something wrong?"

Fortunately, Marco is in the bathroom, so that gives me time to explain.

"Oh, honey, everything is fine. I just wanted to come up and see you. Surprise you."

He looks around the room. "I smell a rat," he says.

"See, you are learning something in college."

"What are you up to?"

I confess.

"Look, Mom, I appreciate your gesture, but I don't think it's going to work. Sophia said she'd tell me when she was ready, and she hasn't called. She's going to be mad when she sees what you and Marco are up to."

"Ready, schmeady. Sometimes a woman just needs a nudge." I

wink. "Besides, we thought it was worth a try, since we've created this whole mess."

Over Colin's shoulder, I see Marco take broad steps for the door in time to catch Sophia when she walks inside. They hug, talk a minute, and he points to us. She hesitates, then takes a deep breath and heads our way.

"Well, the rest is up to you," I say, turning Colin around.

"Hi," Sophia says quietly.

"Why don't you two go over and talk at the snack stand while we bowl a game? Then if you want to join us, we'll bowl a game together."

"Sounds good. Thanks, Mr. Amorini," Colin says.

By the time we're halfway through our game, I'm sure I hold the world's record for gutter balls. I'm not a great bowler, mind you, but I've never been this bad.

I lift my ball into position to throw it down the lane.

"Do you mind if I help?" Marco's whispered words brush against my cheek.

He places his arms around me, which is a good thing, for I'm starting to feel woozy.

"Uh—no, no, that would be great." If I turned to face him right now, my lips would run into his shoulder. Not a bad idea.

"If you hold it right about here—" He demonstrates. "And aim at those arrows—" He points to the floor. "Holding your hand this way—I think you'll knock some over."

I turn and look at him. "Thanks."

He's still holding me next to him, and my breath is locked in my chest. We might look a little weird, but it feels pretty good. I'm thinking if he tries to walk away, I'll grab his ankles and hang on for dear life.

"Are we interrupting something?"

Colin's voice cuts through the moment, startles me, and I drop the ball—on Marco's toe. He lets out a sickening groan. I scream, and everyone runs over to see what's going on.

From that point on the day is a blur of emergency room, broken big toe, bandages, orthopedic boot, and doctor's orders for Marco to stay off his foot.

"I'll have to come home and take care of you," Sophia insists.

"You can't do that. We have finals coming up," Colin says.

"This is all my fault." That seems to be my motto these days. "You'll have to stay with me," I say sheepishly.

I'm pretty sure Colin gasps. Most likely considering that call to Focus on the Family.

"Well, your granddad is there," I remind my son. "And so is Brooke. What's one more?" I turn to Marco. "Then I can see that you get your meals, help change your bandage, all that. It's the least I can do."

"No, no, I'll not have you waiting on me hand and foot."

"Pardon the pun," I say with a chuckle. "Get it? Hand and foot—oh, never mind."

"You need to take her up on it, Mr. Amorini," the doctor pipes up. "You have to stay off that foot for at least three or four days. You'll need this boot when you walk on it, but I don't want you on it for a while other than the basic essentials of walking to the bathroom, that sort of thing."

"It's settled then," I say with more assertiveness than I feel. "Colin, would you and Sophia please stop at the store and pick up a couple of pillows?" I hand him some money and turn to Marco. "We'll stick you in the backseat on the way home, and we can prop up your leg."

He doesn't look happy.

Hand in hand, the kids walk toward the exit. As much as I hate it that Marco has a broken toe, the common cause of helping him through this seems to have drawn the kids together.

The one thought that keeps nagging me is this: *How can I change his bandage when I can't stand the sight of feet?*

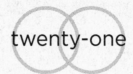

twenty-one

"*This is ridiculous. There is no reason why I shouldn't be able* to take care of myself. I'm not a wimp," Marco says before swaying a moment and sagging back onto my sofa.

I put my hands on my hips and give him "the look." "I rest my case."

Marco rubs his temples and glares at me. "That's my line."

I smile. "Where do you think I learned it?" To elevate his foot, I stuff a couple of pillows underneath, all the while trying not to stare at his toes, which, by the way, is no easy, um, feat. I hand him the remote. "You and Dad can fight over what to watch."

I'm in a take-charge mood tonight, and I have to say it feels pretty good.

"After seeing you pulverize that snake with the toilet brush, I'm not about to argue."

"Smart man."

"Have you ever seen the movie version of Stephen King's *Misery?*" he asks.

"Huh?"

"Oh, never mind."

I brew a pot of coffee and carry two mugs back to Marco. "Here you go."

"Thanks. You really don't have to be so nice, you know."

"I know," I say with a smile, "but I did, after all, drop a bowling ball on your toe."

He groans. "Don't remind me."

"The coffee is decaf, by the way. I didn't want the caffeine to work against your pain medication."

"Thanks. Sophia's mother never fussed over me this way. It's kind of nice."

He looks as surprised as I feel by his comment.

"I didn't mean anything. I mean, I—"

"It's all right, Marco. I'm glad to help."

"I think I always knew she married me to get away from home and because she knew our family had money. I tried everything to make it work, but she was restless from day one."

I'm thinking the medication is loosening his tongue, and while I'm enjoying this informative conversation, I'm not sure I should encourage it.

"Uh-huh."

"When she finally left to pursue her dream of becoming a country western singer, I wasn't all that surprised. What shocked me was that she would leave Sophia behind. How could a mother leave her child?" His eyes penetrate mine.

"I have no idea."

"I won't do anything to jeopardize my relationship with my daughter. That's why I'm stepping away from this whole deal with Colin. If that's what she wants, it's her choice. Plus, there's not much I can do about it right now." He looks at his toe, then smiles up at me.

There's something very endearing about his look.

Though I want to continue this conversation, it doesn't feel right to take advantage of a man on drugs. "I didn't tell you the latest." I settle with my coffee into a nearby chair. "Dad's thinking about moving into an apartment."

"Is that right? Wonder if he could use additional hours? It would be great to have him around more. He does good work."

"I think he would welcome it." I take a drink.

"How do you feel about him moving out?"

I think a moment. "He's a grown man. He can do what he wants."

"Is it as hard to let a parent go as it is your child?" he asks.

He doesn't know my history with my dad. Still, with things improving, it's been nice to have him around. I never would have dreamed it.

"You know the answer to that as well as I do. We've both lost parents."

"Yeah, I guess." Marco looks at his foot. "My toe looks and feels like a big, fat, red onion. Probably smells like it too."

Okay, I can't begin to describe what that little comment does to my stomach.

"I'm so sorry, Marco. Are you in terrible pain?"

"I'm fine, just trying to get comfortable." His speech is starting to slur, so I figure it's time to call it a night.

"Listen, your room is ready. Why don't you let me help you get there?" I reach down to help him, and he puts his arm around my shoulder, while I put my arm around his waist, allowing him to lean on me for support. Seems the only thing I'm good for these days.

We take a few steps, and Marco sways a bit, so I stop. "Are you okay?"

"I'm fine. Just a little dizzy. Keep going. I'll be all right."

We start walking again, and he leans his head down into my hair.

"You smell good," he says dreamily, causing my skin to flame.

I'm not about to think on that. It's not right to take advantage of a man with a broken toe. Now there's a quote that will last through the ages.

"I'm putting you in Colin's room, since he won't be home for a while."

A slight nuzzle against my hair. "Thank you, Wendy." His warm breath on my hair makes my knees wobble.

As I make my way back to the living room, I tell myself there's nothing to Marco's murmurings. It's the drugs. I pick up a new magazine that came in the mail, and Brooke stumbles in through the front door with a suitcase.

"What on earth are you doing?" I ask.

"I'm going back home."

"Right now?"

"Yeah. I'm tired and don't want to get into it all tonight, Mom. I'll tell you more later, but Kevin finally got in touch with me. I told him about the baby. He's not ready to come home, but at least we're talking. Guess he sort of flipped out for a while. Said he's been doing a lot of thinking, so we'll see what happens." She grabs the handle of her luggage and sets it on its wheels to cart down the hall.

Is that what all the disappearances have been about? Meeting with Kevin?

"Why didn't you tell me?"

"I didn't want you to get your hopes up. I'm not sure that we'll get back together. I'm not even sure I want to after what he's put me through."

"You could probably use some counseling at this point to make it work."

"I'm not sure if we want to make it work." She blows out a frustrated sigh. "At any rate, I'm headed back to work next week, and I need to use my evenings to get the house ready to sell. I'm ready to move on—whatever that may bring."

"So you're going to sell the house no matter what?"

"That's the plan for now."

So why not stay here and work over there at night? For the life of me, I can't get past the feeling there is something more.

"What?" she asks.

I dare not ask her. She wouldn't appreciate my intrusion or my advice. It would just stir up trouble. "You sure you're ready?"

"I'm ready," she says with zero emotion.

"Well, I'm here for you if you need me."

"Thanks," she says, grabbing her suitcase handle.

She walks down the hall, leaving me to guess what she's up to. Is she really moving back to her house, or is she seeing that guy Kevin told me about? I don't even know my own daughter.

Brooke suddenly reappears. "Mom, who is sleeping in Colin's bed?"

"Oh, I'm sorry, I should have told you. Did you go in there?"

"I started to. I left a sweater in there."

"Oh, I forgot to take off his boot," I say. "I'll do that in a little bit, so he can be comfortable."

"Mom, who is it?"

"Marco Amorini."

Her jaw drops like a broken nutcracker.

"It's a long story," I say, and proceed to give her a condensed version. Afterwards, she finishes her packing and comes back out to the living room to say good-bye.

"Brooke, I can't help feeling there's more you should be telling me." There I go again, prying.

"What's left? I told you everything."

My gaze does not waver from hers. "Everything?"

I try to stop myself, I really do, but I just have to make sure she's okay. She and Kevin are making such a mess of things.

"Look, Mom, you've led a sheltered life. Things aren't black-and-white anymore. Life happens. Sometimes you just refuse to see it."

"Is that what you think? That I'm clueless about life in general? That I have no idea what the real world is like?"

She grunts.

"We need to talk."

She starts to protest, and I reach for her arm. "Now." I lead her back into the living room where we settle on the sofa.

"Listen, I've not led such a sheltered life. When I was a teenager, I messed up. Really messed up." Now I have her attention. "Your dad and I had—had—well, we had to get married."

Her jaw drops again. "You're kidding."

"No. I was pregnant with you."

"Why didn't you tell me before now?" she asks.

"It's not something we were proud of, Brooke."

"Thanks a lot."

"It's not like that, and you know it. We loved you from the start."

"Yeah, whatever." She tosses her long blonde hair behind her shoulder. "Getting pregnant before you're married is nothing, Mom."

I stare at her point-blank, willing my mouth not to drop. "It doesn't matter what the world's views are on the matter, Brooke. It was wrong, pure and simple. We messed up."

"Is that why you've always favored Colin?" she whispers. "Because I brought you shame, and he didn't?

"Brooke, you can't think that."

"And why not? When we were kids it was always 'Colin this' and 'Colin that.' When I wanted to go to the zoo, it was always, 'We can't. The heat is too much. It could trigger Colin's asthma.'" She stands up and paces across the floor. "'Can we go to the pool then?' 'No, honey, you know how the chlorine bothers Colin.' It was always about Colin."

I get up and reach for her, but she steps back. "Brooke, you know it was only because I was worried about him."

"But did you ever worry about me?"

"Of course I did. What do you mean?"

"I've always shamed you, haven't I, Mom? Colin always got the good grades, had the good manners, all that. I've always been one to speak my mind, never really excelled at anything. I'm just me. A constant reminder that you messed up, is that it?"

"I don't love you based on what you do. I love you because you're my daughter."

"I've got to go."

"Brooke, don't leave like this."

She marches to the door, grabs her bag, and walks into the night, leaving an ache in my heart almost as deep as the one Dennis left me.

After many tears, I wash my face and settle on my bed, trying to pray, though the words refuse to come. Would Brooke have taken the news better had I told her when she was younger? Were we wrong to keep it hidden?

We'd hurt our parents enough by our elopement. I couldn't bear to tell them about the baby. Then when she came late, we were able to convince people she was a honeymoon baby. Though I'm not sure we ever fully convinced my parents. Yes, it was deceitful, but we were trying to spare our families additional pain.

With her comment about my perfect life, I thought it might help her to know I can relate to her more than she thinks. Obviously, I was wrong.

I hear Dad coming in, and after deciding I look presentable again, I walk out to greet him.

"Is that Marco's car outside?" Dad asks.

"Yeah, it is. We've had quite a busy day. Let's go in the living room, and I'll tell you about it." I'm beginning to think I should record this story and just push the play button on the recorder when needed.

I fill Dad in, and after a long pause, he rubs his jaw and grins. "They say the Lord works in mysterious ways."

"Now, Dad, don't you start."

He holds up his hands. "I'm not saying another word."

"Listen, I need to take Marco's boot off so he can rest better. Would you mind doing that for me? I feel kind of funny going into his bedroom without his knowledge," I say.

"I don't know how to take it off. I'd probably hurt him," Dad says with a slight panic in his voice.

"Well, how about you make sure he's decent, then I'll come in with you and you can be there for moral support?"

Dad scratches the five o'clock shadow—or should I say ten o'clock shadow—on his jaw and reluctantly agrees.

Tapping lightly on Marco's door, we hear no sound, so Dad slips inside. Then he comes back to the door and whispers, "The coast is clear. Come on in."

I step inside and grope my way in the dark, trying to get a sense of the room with the hint of moonlight filtering in through the blinds.

"Help me out here, Dad," I whisper. "I'll undo the Velcro straps, and then you help me lift his leg so I can slip off the boot, okay?"

Slowly, I pull away the Velcro, trying to keep things quiet. After the second strap is off, I whisper, "Okay, help me lift his leg."

Dad edges over and on the count of three lifts his leg, and I strip off the boot. After placing the boot on a nearby chair, we head for the door.

"Wendy," Marco whispers into the night air.

The way he says it makes my heart pause midbeat. I turn around and take a step, the floorboard creaking beneath my feet. "Yes?"

His breathing returns to a quiet hum.

"Marco?"

Nothing.

Dad and I continue to edge out of his room, closing the door softly behind us. He turns to me. "I reckon you've slipped into the man's dreams." He grunts. "That's just like a woman."

After shrugging on my pajamas, I place my robe on a nearby chair in case I need to get something for Marco in the night. Stepping into the bathroom, I wash my face and pull the night cream from the medicine cabinet. Just before applying the cream, I take a good long look in the mirror. Tiny lines bunch near my eyes like a tangled vine.

I'm going to be a grandma. It's been so long since we've had a little one around the house. A disturbing thought slams into me. What if Brooke doesn't let me see my grandchild?

My heart kicks into gear. No, no, I can't worry about that now. Everything will turn out all right.

Plunging my fingers into the cream, I work it into my skin with a vengeance. I slather so much grease on my face that I'll probably slide off my pillow and break my neck. Once my nightly ritual is over, I slip in between the covers and turn out the lights. It's been quite a day, and I'm very tired.

So many things to think about, but not now. I need to sleep. My beauty depends on it. In fact, if my face is any indication, I should stay in bed for the next fifty years.

I'm just about to slip into a dreamy state when the phone rings and makes me nearly jump out of my skin.

"Hello?"

"Hi, Mrs. Hartline, this is Jennifer Lancaster, Brooke's friend from work." Her voice is a bit shaky, uncertain. "Um, she wanted me to call you and let you know she's in the hospital."

Fully awake now, I reach over and turn on the light. "Hospital?"

"She's having contractions." Hesitation. "She asked that you pray. She's afraid she's going to lose the baby."

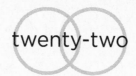

twenty-two

"Where you going?" Marco's groggy voice calls behind me.

"Oh, you startled me," I say.

His curls are tousled against his forehead; his eyes droop with fatigue. The rugged shadow of a beard covers his lower jaw. He's leaning against the doorframe, sore toe hiked a bit. One glance at him and my heart flops about in my chest with all the energy of lake trout, but I refuse to dwell on it. I have other things on my mind. I pull on my jacket.

"Are you all right?" I ask.

"I'm fine. But what about you? You look upset."

"I have to go to the hospital. Brooke's in labor. It's way too soon. She could lose the baby."

Marco's face shows genuine concern. "I'm sorry, Wendy."

"Just pray. If I'm not back in the morning, let Dad know where I went, okay?"

"Will do." He reaches out, putting his hand on my shoulder, then looks at me through kind, caring eyes. "It's late. Take care of yourself."

His concern touches deep to the core of me. "Thanks, Marco. See you later."

When I arrive at the doorway of Brooke's room, I see her in the bed, red blotches forming patchwork on her pale skin. Swollen eyes show the pain she's going through. Given our last conversation, I'm not sure what she'll say when she sees me. I step into her room slowly, with hesitation.

"Mom," she cries out in the voice of my five-year-old baby girl—at least to my ears—and I rush to her, lean down into her shoulder, and hold her as tight as I dare. We cry together.

"What if I lose the baby, Mom? I already love him—and he may be the only thread that holds Kevin and me together."

"He?"

She nods. "I didn't tell you when they did the ultrasound. It's a boy."

A pain shoots through me. Why didn't she share that with me? I force a smile. "A boy. How wonderful."

"But what if we lose him, Mom?"

Just the other day I had thought if only Brooke wasn't pregnant, things might be a little easier for her. Now hot grief works through my stomach with the force of a mountain storm for this grandchild that I can't bear to lose.

I hand her a tissue. "Don't borrow trouble, Brooke. What do you think started the contractions?"

"Like an idiot, I moved some furniture around when I got home."

I gasp, which, by the look on her face, I see was definitely the wrong thing to do. Mental note. When daughter confides, don't gasp.

She frowns at me, but thankfully, continues. "Not real heavy stuff. Just scooted a chair or two. I know it was a stupid thing to do." She wipes her face with the tissue. "I'll never forgive myself if I lose this baby."

"Are you still having contractions?"

"They gave me meds to stop them. I haven't had any in about half an hour."

My breathing comes easier. "Well, you see there. You're going to be fine."

"Why do people always say that?'" She straightens the sheets around her with frustrated yanks. "Things aren't fine, and we don't know that they will be."

"I'm sorry, honey. I didn't mean to minimize what you're going through."

She looks up at me with such sad eyes it breaks my heart. Her hands stop moving, and in a whisper she says, "I'm sorry, Mom. You of all people know how it feels to lose the man you love."

For some reason, hearing her say "the man you love" makes me feel better. Not that I believed for a moment that she was having an affair—still it's encouraging to hear her say she loves Kevin.

"Yes, but I didn't have this on top of everything else," I say, making a sweeping gesture of the room with my hand.

She hesitates. "Mom, do you think God is holding it against me—all the things I've done wrong, I mean? I'm not the greatest wife." Her worried eyes search deep into mine for any shred of hope she might find there.

"Oh, honey, you know He doesn't work that way." My fingers brush a strand of hair from her face.

She turns a sorrowful gaze toward the window. "I don't know. I've messed up in so many ways. I don't want my baby to suffer because of me."

I reach for her hand. "Brooke, we're caught up in a sinful world. Things happen. Certainly, your choices can affect your baby, but God isn't waiting to zap you because of your sin. He loves you— enough to set you free—to offer you hope in the midst of sorrow. The Bible says, 'There is no one who does good, not even one.' Apart from Him, we're all the same. Pretty much slime." I smile.

Blowing her nose, she gives a good honk. Her muffled words sneak past the tissue. "This coming from Pollyanna."

All these years, and I never knew her to be a honker.

"Why do you make it sound so easy? Life isn't like that, Mom."

Why does everyone keep telling me that? Scooting my chair over to her bedside, I sit down. "Brooke, you know we had hard times in our family. There were lean years. Times when people hurt us. It wasn't easy. I never said it was easy. Still, God was and is faithful."

"Then answer me this."

"What, honey?"

"If God is so faithful, why are our husbands gone?"

"I don't know. It's life—and sometimes life stinks. All I know is, in those dark days after your dad died, I would never have made it without God in my life. In the good days and, yes, even in the bad days, I want Him by my side. I may not have all the answers, Brooke, but God does, and I trust Him completely."

In the quiet she looks up at me. "Keep praying for me. Maybe one day I'll get there."

I stick around the hospital long enough for Brooke to get settled into a regular room. They want to keep her overnight to make sure the contractions don't start up again. When I'm ready to leave, I turn and see Kevin standing in the doorway.

"Hi, Mom."

"Kevin." I walk over and hug him. It's a little awkward at first, but he finally gives in to the hug.

"Are you all right?" he asks Brooke.

"We're fine," she says, letting him know the baby is going to make it. Obvious relief washes over him.

"I'll see you tomorrow, Brooke," I say, wanting to leave them alone. "Good to see you, Kevin. We've missed you."

All the way home, I pray for Brooke, Kevin, and the baby, praying that their little family will heal and come together once again.

By the time I stumble back onto my front walk, birds are squawking in their nests—no doubt wondering if that stinkin' worm is really worth the effort—and sunlight is crawling over the mountaintops.

With a yawn, I shove through the front door and step into a quiet house. Marco will need me in a little while, and coffee isn't igniting the tiniest spark of energy in this body right now. An hour or two of sleep is better than nothing, so I finally settle back between the sheets.

In a little while the phone rings, jarring me from a distant place. I fumble to answer it. "Hello?" Don't people sleep anymore? Have we changed time zones? What?

"Hey, sleepyhead, don't you have to work today?"

"Huh?"

"I just couldn't wait any longer to call you. I miss you terribly. Please say you miss me too."

Okay, the voice sounds familiar, but it's just not coming to me. "Logan?"

"Well, that can't be good. You're not sure who I am?"

"It's been a long night." I explain what happened with Brooke.

"I'm sorry you're going through that. Want me to come home early and stay with you?"

Just pull a wool blanket over my head and tighten all the ends so not a smidgen of air gets through. That's pretty much how his words make me feel.

"No, thanks. We'll be fine. You just enjoy yourself."

"All right, if you're sure. I've decided to skip the last session and take an early flight home. I'll be home tomorrow afternoon. You don't need to pick me up at the airport, my car is there."

"Oh, okay." No need to tell him the thought had never entered my brain.

"I'll pick you up around six o'clock for dinner. Can't wait to see you. Hey, I've got to go. The session is about to start." He clicks off.

No *Do you want to go out for dinner?* or *Will you be busy with your daughter?* Just, "I'll pick you up at six." That's what irritates me about Logan. He never gives me a choice. Reluctantly, I lift off the covers and crawl out of bed. My feet barely touch the floor when it hits me. Marco! I didn't tell Logan about Marco, and Logan will be here tomorrow night.

Can my life get any worse?

I can think of other ways I'd rather spend a Friday night, but I've put this off long enough. It's time to face Marco's toes head-on.

Dad and Marco are sitting in the living room talking over sports when I come in with a roll of bandages. Now, I'm no Mother Teresa, but the fact I'm working with someone's foot should earn me some kind of award—or at the very least a basket of chocolates. Most definitely a bag of chocolate popcorn. Maybe I'll mention it while I'm working with his sore toe. I'll have him right where I want him then.

Taking a deep breath, I square my shoulders and prepare to come at this like a pioneer woman—with sheer grit and determination. I've seen enough shows with women cutting out bullets, saving children from hungry bears, and fighting wildfires. And yes, I do believe caring for toes belongs in the same category.

For dramatic effect, I roll up my sleeves—okay, so they're not all that long, but it seems the thing to do before a medical procedure— and I settle down in front of Marco's foot.

"All right, Marco, we need to take a look at this toe." Just saying that makes my stomach roll. "And replace the bandage."

"Good luck," Dad says. "Wendy has a thing against toes, but then you already know that." Dad laughs at his own joke.

Marco's eyes take on the look of a duck that's spotted a hunter.

So my secret wasn't so well hidden. How did Dad know that? "Don't listen to him," I say, trying to sound lighthearted. "We'll be fine."

Well, *you* will. I might need some smelling salts.

Slowly, I unwind the wrap, revealing a smattering of hair across the top of his foot and a bruise with colors that could rival an angry sky. I gulp. Further unwinding reveals long, slender toes, also bruised. And his big toe? Well, let's just say that baby puts me in mind of a battered Humpty Dumpty. I'm tempted to put a smiley face on it, but then that would just be mean. I swallow. Hard. Several times. But the truth is Marco's foot isn't bothering me nearly as much as the pain I've obviously caused him. I glance at Dad for moral support, but he's holding his breath. Why is he doing that?

"Oh, come on, guys. This is no big deal," I say, praying St. Peter won't hold it against me when I stand before the pearly gates. Carefully, I peel away the medical tape from the big toe that's buddy-taped to its neighbor with a gauze padding in between. Glancing up at Marco, I see him wince. This is awful to admit, but I'm feeling a bit Florence Nightingale-ish. A strength I didn't know I possessed overtakes me, and I whip off the old tape, apply new, and finish everything off with an Ace bandage. By the time I'm done, I think I'll check into the nursing program at our local college.

It's not until Marco's toes are safely tucked away that Marco and Dad dare to breathe and settle back into their seats. I walk away from them lifting my gun fingers and blow away the smoke from the imaginary barrel. "You're good, Wendy Hartline." With a smile I make my way to the bathroom, and that's when it hits me. I actually touched Marco Amorini's foot and lived to tell about it. Is it possible—I mean, could it be?

For some women, true love is revealed when they hear wedding bells, their toes curl, or a leg lifts in response to a kiss. The fact I was able to hold Marco's foot in the palm of my hand and actually touch his toes? Well, this could be serious, that's all.

The next morning, Roseanne and I pull off the wedding without a hitch. The sky is a canopy of clear blue, while sunlight glitters off snow-capped mountaintops. The weather is surprisingly warm for mid-March, for which the bride, I'm sure, is thankful. The doves are an instant success—though I notice that Roseanne is nowhere in sight when they are set free. In a beautiful white-winged display, the birds flap their way out of their wicker cage and fly toward a distant home, leaving guests to ooh and aah at the spectacle. Even a couple of lodge guests who happen out on the parking lot look up with pleasure.

"Hey, Dad," I say into my cell phone when I finally climb into my car after the wedding. "Did Jennifer bring Brooke home yet?"

"Yeah, they just got here," he says.

"Okay, I'm stopping by the store to grab some things for dinner. Then I'll be home."

We hang up, and I start wondering how I'm going to explain Marco's presence to Logan. Not that I owe him an explanation, but Logan always makes me feel as though I do. He'll just have to understand that we need to eat at home tonight. Not only for Marco, but Dr. Gross—I can only imagine what he endured as a child with that name—said Brooke has to stay in bed for a few weeks to make sure she doesn't go into labor again. She and Kevin are taking things slow and discussing the possibility of counseling. Baby steps.

Once the chicken and noodles are prepared, I am just ready to call everyone to the table when the doorbell rings. Six o'clock sharp. Could I expect any less from Logan?

He greets me with a dozen red roses and grazes my lips with a kiss. "How's my girl?"

"I'm fine. Glad to see you made it safely home," I say. "Listen, there's something I need to tell you."

"It smells good in here," he says, already stepping toward the kitchen to investigate.

"We can still go out if you want, but I needed to make dinner for—" I'm practically out of breath trying to keep up with him.

His footsteps come to a stop when he walks into the dining room. Dad, Brooke, and Marco are all seated at the table. I walk up behind him.

"What are you doing here?" Logan says to Marco.

Marco ladles a clump of noodles onto his plate and looks at Logan. "I live here now. Didn't Wendy tell you?"

There is an absolute gleam in Marco's eyes. I blink, thinking I've imagined it, but sure enough it's there. Bright enough to rival the blinding light on Paul's road to Damascus.

"Um, I haven't had a chance to—"

"Nice flowers. But you really shouldn't have," Marco says, causing Logan's ears to turn blood red.

"Hi, Logan. Good to see you," Dad says.

"How about I just go get my jacket, and I can tell you all about it over dinner. First, I'll put these in water," I say, giving Marco a dirty look before I go. I had planned to eat at home, but I can see right now it won't work to have Marco and Logan in the same room.

"Okay, ready," I say, forcing a grin and putting a little snap in my walk as I head for the coat closet, hoping to persuade Logan to follow. "We'll be home later," I call out.

Logan follows hesitantly. The color on his face puts me in mind of Marco's bruised foot, and something tells me I'll be eating Rolaids for dessert.

"What is he doing here?" Logan opens the door to the car, and I quickly get in before he has a chance to shove me inside.

"Well?"

The driver's seat protests as Logan climbs in and starts the engine.

"It's a long story." I'm really not in the mood for this.

"I have the time, and I have a right to know." The car squeals out of the driveway and heads toward who-knows-where. By the sound of Logan's voice and the look on his face, I figure I'll end up in a dumpster somewhere.

"Stop right there," I say. "I don't owe you an explanation." With the anger boiling inside me right now, I think I can take him.

Logan's throat makes a squeak, and then he turns his stony expression to the road. "So that's how it is? We're dating, I come home to find another man staying at your house, and suddenly you don't owe me an explanation? What has come over you, Wendy? You're not the woman I thought I knew."

"The truth is, Logan, I can never be myself around you, so how could you possibly know what kind of woman I am? You want me to be your version of me. I'm not going to do it anymore. For anyone. I am who I am. If that's not enough for you, then it's just not enough."

"What are you saying?" Logan pulls the car into the parking lot of a fast food restaurant a couple of miles from my house, puts the engine in park, and turns to me.

"I'm saying I'm tired of living for everyone else. I'm tired of trying to be who everyone thinks I should be."

"No one is trying to make you—"

"Logan, I have to go." I open my door.

"If you leave, Wendy, you're closing the door on our relationship," he snaps.

Without hesitation my shoes hit the pavement. I bend over and look in at a stunned ex-boyfriend. "By the way, I prefer peppermint mochas, not caramel lattes, and daisies instead of roses. If you truly knew me, you would have known that. Good-bye, Logan." Closing the door with a slam, I walk away and I don't look back.

Not even once.

Blisters have formed on my heels by the time I step into the house and pull off my shoes. Still, the walk helped. Gave me time to calm down and actually feel good about my decision to call it off with Logan. The house is quiet, and I spot a note with my name on it perched on the hallway stand.

As much as I enjoyed the little tussle with Logan, you've been too kind to me for me to stay and cause more problems. Thank you for your hospitality. I'm sure I'll be fine from this point on.

Disappointment drops in the pit of my stomach with a thud. It's too soon for Marco to go home. Why didn't somebody stop him? It's only been two days. The doctor said around four days, didn't he? Maybe I should take him dinner tomorrow. That's what I'll do. At least he won't have to worry about his meals. I'll ask him if I can do anything to help at the lodge. I absently bite my lower lip, wondering if I'm being too pushy. No, this isn't about being pushy. This is about me wanting to be with Marco.

I read further:

One more thing. I've been praying for Brooke, Kevin, and the baby. Got a few things of my own straightened out while praying. Thanks.
Marco

A sliver of hope shimmers through me. Marco's cologne lingers in the hallway. I lean against the wall and take a deep breath, shamelessly allowing the scent to make me heady. It's time to face the facts. I'm not in love with Logan. I'm in love with Marco. The question is, how does he feel about me?

Heading for the kitchen, I do what I always do when life gets too hard to figure out—grab a bowl and fill it to the brim with chocolate popcorn.

twenty-three

When I walk into Brooke's room to gather her lunch tray, Jennifer is sitting at the foot of Brooke's four-poster bed and Randy Feldon, another coworker, is sitting on a nearby oak rocker.

"So, Brooke, my roommate moved out, and you are more than welcome to stay with me. What do you say?" Jennifer has one hand holding onto an end post, while her other hand smooths out a wrinkle on the bed cover.

"Kevin isn't coming to your house to help?" I ask.

"He offered, Mom, but I don't want him to come home for the wrong reasons. Now is not the time."

"If you're at Jennifer's house, what will you do if you get into trouble during the day while she's at work?"

The unwritten words on Brooke's face say I'm being overprotective.

"The same thing I would do here when you and Granddad are at work. I have a cell phone. I can use it. Besides, her office is closer to her house than your office is to me here. She could get to me faster."

That makes me feel a little better, though I can't deny I had

271

hoped Brooke and I would have more meaningful talks. We can't very well do that if she leaves.

Gathering her lunch dishes, I keep my mouth shut. She's left half her food, and I want to comment, but there's that overprotective thing again. At least she's eating something.

"I don't mean to get in the way of things." Jennifer stands.

"No, no, it's fine, honey," I say. "Brooke can stay where she wants." I try desperately to keep the motherly longing out of my voice.

"Mom, no offense, but I want to go to Jennifer's house."

Dip in my heart here.

"You have enough with Granddad hanging around."

There's no use telling her that my dad is leaving too. I won't manipulate her with guilt.

I adjust the tray in my hands. "You do what you need to do."

I finally worked though the empty nest, and here I am taking everything back, trying to bring my chicks back into the fold, protecting and guarding them.

My gaze scoots to Randy, who has his nose stuck in a business magazine.

"I'm going to have to get going," Jennifer says, slipping the Bluetooth around her ear and shrugging the strap of her handbag onto her shoulder. "I'll come by and pick you and your things up later. See you guys." With a wave, she's out the door.

With the full lunch tray in hand, I spy a dirty glass on Brooke's nightstand and make a mental note to come back for it. After rinsing out the dishes in the kitchen and stacking them into the dishwasher, I head back to Brooke's room.

"You've got to believe me. I don't know what came over me," Randy is saying as I step closer to Brooke's room.

"Shh, I don't want Mom to hear you."

I step back and shamelessly eavesdrop.

"I hadn't planned to kiss you. Please, believe me. But the talks, the lunches, the coffee stops. I just thought—"

"Well, you thought wrong. I was sharing with you as a friend. I don't want to talk about it, Randy."

His footsteps sound against the carpet, and I step away, but still within earshot.

"Listen, I'm sorry that Kevin saw us kiss. If I could undo it, I would. But I can't. It won't happen again."

I swallow hard. Obviously, Brooke and Kevin have some things to work through.

"See you later, Brooke."

I dash from the hallway and slip back into the kitchen, catching my breath and trying to assimilate all that just transpired.

Thankfully, things aren't as bad as my worst-case scenario, but I can't help wondering what's in store for my strong-willed daughter and her equally stubborn husband.

"Wendy, we need to talk." Marco's voice doesn't sound all that friendly, but it is Monday morning and, well, I did smash his big toe.

"Good morning, Marco." I tiptoe around the how-are-you business. Now just doesn't seem the time to ask.

"Can you come over to the lodge?"

"What in the world are you doing there? I thought you were going to stay down for a few days."

"I don't have the time. Besides, I can rest on one of the lodge beds if I need to."

"When do you want me to come over?"

"Now."

"Uh-oh, could be dangerous. I haven't had my first cup of coffee," I say in an attempt to keep things lighthearted.

"I'll get you coffee here. I'll be waiting in the restaurant."

Click.

"Give the man food and lodging, and this is the thanks I get?" Pulling out my hand lotion, I rub it in with a vengeance.

"What's wrong?" Roseanne asks.

I tell her about Marco's call.

"You probably should give him a break—oh, wait, you did that." She giggles.

I try not to laugh, but I can't help myself. "That's awful, Roseanne. Funny, but awful." Once I reach the door, I turn to her. "I shouldn't be too long."

"Just stay away from bowling balls."

"Ha ha." I attempt to dramatically jerk open the door, but the lotion on my hands causes my fingers to slide right off the knob.

Roseanne is still laughing. "Don't you hate it when that happens? Let me help you." Putting her jeweled hand on the knob, she turns to me and gives an ornery grin before twisting the knob, causing her charm bracelet to chime on her wrist.

I study her a minute. "What's gotten into you today?"

She shrugs. "I guess I'm still swooning from a great weekend with Gill." She winks and heads back to her desk.

"Okay, I think I'll just leave that one alone. Be back in a jiff."

Tromping across the sidewalk over to Marco's parking lot, I think about Roseanne's statement and wonder what it would be like to be married again. Someone who is always there to hang out with. Though I don't know why I'm thinking about that. I've certainly had plenty of company lately.

Sunlight shimmers on puddles caused by the early morning rain.

As I round the corner, a passing car gets too close to the curb and splashes cold, dirty water on my legs. Pulling a handkerchief from my pocketbook, I reach down and angrily rub at the offending spots on my pants.

I step inside and see Marco at a corner table, waving his arm. Coffee mugs are already on the table with a pot perched between them. "What happened to you?" he asks, pointing to the obvious spots on my pants.

"A careless driver." I shrug.

"They just brought out the coffee, so it's plenty hot," he says, pouring us each a cup.

"Thanks." I grab a couple of packets of sweetener, tear open the tops, and pour them into my mug. "How's your foot?"

"Well, I'm not exactly ready to go dancing, but I'll survive."

No doubt his entourage of women will be sorry to hear that.

He lifts his mug and takes a drink. "Did you patch things up with Logan?"

I shake my head. "It's over between us."

"Oh, I'm sorry."

"Just one of those things."

"I hope my being at your house—"

"It's not your fault." *Well, other than that little fact that you came into my life, and I fell in love with you. That's all.*

He nods, but says nothing, and I'm slightly disappointed. What's my problem? Just because I've figured out that I'm in love with him doesn't mean Twinkle Toes is waiting on the sidelines for me. Besides, I broke the man's toe. Put him out of commission. He could be a little bitter.

"Listen," he says, steepling his fingers together in front of him. "We have a problem."

Just as I thought. Bitter. I curl my fingers around my chair for support. "I'm listening."

"You had a wedding on Saturday, and I hear you released birds?"

The stern set of his jaw, the glare of his eyes, the way his fingers are pressed together give him the look of a school principal. I can almost see him peering over the rim of dark-framed glasses and saying in a deep voice, "It has come to my attention—"

"Wendy?"

"Oh, yes. Yes, that's true."

He shakes his head. "Won't work. Those birds evidently flew over my parking lot and deposited some gifts on a couple of my guests."

I try not to laugh.

His eyes grow darker. It wouldn't surprise me if his lip coiled into a snarl, baring his teeth. I consider squashing his other big toe. All right, I admit it. I need counseling.

"My guests weren't laughing."

"What would you suggest, diapers?"

His expression grows darker still. Suddenly, I'm not feeling so charitable. Maybe it's all the years of striving to please others. Maybe it's the car that splashed me with rainwater. Maybe it's Logan, Brooke, Dad, Colin, Marco. I don't know, but suddenly everything comes rushing in like a tardy bride.

"You know what, Marco. It is what it is. That couple wanted birds. I provided them. We have no contract that says I can't release doves. And frankly, I'm tired of people telling me how to run my business and my life. I'm sorry, but if you don't like it, find a good attorney." With that, I plunk money on the table for my coffee and storm out of the restaurant.

Instead of going straight back to the chapel office, I take a walk. What has gotten into me? It was a simple request. Not an unreasonable one at that. I could move the birds to the other end of the lake before I release them and see if that helps. I just feel pulled in so many directions. Maybe I'm disappointed that Marco didn't seem happier at the news of my ended relationship with Logan. The cash flow isn't there for my business, and frankly, I don't enjoy it anymore. In fact, I never did.

Roseanne's right. I kept this business going for all the wrong reasons. Namely, for one reason. Dennis. Something I've tried to push to the back of my mind comes to the forefront. A conversation Dennis and I had one night. He told me if anything ever happened to him, I needed to keep the chapel going. "It's a ministry," he had said, heaping on the guilt.

Funny, I haven't thought about that in so long. I never liked it when he pushed me into things. With all my romantic fantasizing, I'd brushed aside the problems we had. Dennis was my husband, and I accepted him, the bad with the good, just the way he accepted me.

But the truth is, we had our problems. I've been dwelling on all the good and blown it up until our marriage became perfect in my mind. But it wasn't perfect. No one's is. With love and strong faith, it still takes hard work to make a marriage last. But the benefits are well worth the effort.

It also takes a lot of hard work and organization to pull off a fairy-tale wedding, and honestly, that's just not my gift. Maybe I'm the one who is bitter. Is there any such thing as a fairy-tale wedding? I thought so once upon a time. Now I just don't know.

Weeds poke through the sidewalk cracks the way problems keep poking through my peaceful world. Will things ever be normal again?

"*I don't know what's come over me, Roseanne,*" *I say,* tears spilling onto my face, my earlier confidence now a mere memory.

"Oh, honey, it's all right." She hugs me tight. "Let's sit at the table."

Roseanne listens to my tale of woe and hesitates only a moment. "Wendy, do you really want to run this place?"

I look at her. "No. My heart isn't in it. I don't know why, but it isn't. Anyway, what would you do if I didn't own the chapel?"

She waves her hand. "Don't you worry about me. Gill's been wanting me to spend more time at home, so I may just do that." She winks. "Now you go take a break before you have to go home. I'll take care of things here. You need to take some time for yourself."

"I did that this morning already."

"You need more. Decide what you want to do with your life without everyone else telling you what to do."

"You don't mind handling things here?"

Roseanne's bright red lips part in a caring smile. Her world is full of color. Mine has dulled to a mere black and white. She pats my hand. "Not at all. You go."

"I owe you, Roseanne. Thank you." When I close the door behind me, I decide to visit a nearby coffee shop. Part of me feels that's so selfish, but Dad's working, and Brooke is moving in with Jennifer. No one needs me now.

I'm never satisfied. It seems when I'm alone, I want people around, and when people are around, I want to be alone.

twenty-four

"I can't believe I let you talk me into coming here," I say to Roseanne when we step into the lodge. "But I guess I owed you since you gave me some time off."

She shrugs. "Restaurants are so crowded on Friday nights, but this place is still making a name for itself, so it's easy to get in. Plus, it's close to the office." She changes the subject. "When was the last time you talked to Marco?"

"Not since he bawled me out over the birds."

"Oh, it wasn't that bad."

"Whatever. I think you two are in cahoots."

"Well, it's true I don't like birds," she says. "But I had nothing to do with his bawling you out."

I sigh.

"I appreciate you coming with me, Wendy. If I hadn't gotten out of the house tonight, I might have hurt Gill. His home repair is making me crazy."

I smile. "Glad I could spare a life."

On the way to our table in the restaurant, we pass Marco. One glance at him and my stomach feels as though the fairy godmother has set loose a thousand twinkling stars.

"Hey, Wendy," he says, standing. He gently grabs my arm. "I've been wanting to talk to you, but I've been busy here."

Obviously. A dark-haired beauty is sitting across the table from him. Probably one of his dancing partners.

"No problem," I squeak, feeling stupid that my voice falters at a time like this. But my legs are stable, so that's good.

"Hello, Roseanne," he says.

"Hi." Roseanne tugs on my arm, no doubt sensing my discomfort.

"Oh, Wendy, this is Sharon Houston with the newspaper. She's writing an article on the lodge," he says.

Okay, so she's a business acquaintance. Still, she's eyeballing him as though he's a slice of six-layer chocolate cake.

"Marco tells me he's buying your property so he can make this entire area a resort. It will be fabulous." Admiration sparkles in her eyes.

The twinkling stars come to a crashing halt and fall into a heap in the pit of my stomach.

"Whoa. That was off-the-record," Marco says to her. "Besides, I said *maybe* one day Wendy would be interested in selling."

Is that why he kissed me and pretended to be interested? I'm so stupid. All this time he was trying to get on my good side so he could buy my property. My hands feel clammy, and my knees start to buckle.

Marco grabs my hand. "Wendy, I'm sorry. I never meant—"

"I have to go. Nice to meet you." Jerking my hand from his grasp, I practically run to my seat before my legs can fold.

"That low life, I want to give him a piece of my mind."

Roseanne turns back around, and I grab her by the arm. With her in the throes of menopause, I don't doubt for a moment that she could take him.

"Please, Roseanne, sit down. He's not worth it."

With a sigh, she slumps onto her chair and drops her purse on the floor beside her.

Tears clutter my eyes but refuse to spill. I will not give Marco the satisfaction. Taking a deep breath, I gather my reserve, determined to make it through yet another crisis.

"You all right?"

"I'm fine." I hide my shaky hands on my lap under the table before they can give me away.

"I'm sorry, Wendy. This wasn't such a great idea."

"It's all right. Besides, Marco and I have nothing going on."

"Maybe it doesn't look like it right now, but I still say he has something for you. Though after all that, I'm not sure I want you to go there." She turns his way and frowns. "Although—" She turns back to me with a lightbulb moment. "On the other hand, Wendy, this could be the very thing that could get you out of the business, if you want to get out."

"So on the one hand, the guy is a jerk for using me to get to my property, but on the other hand, he could be my hero?"

"Honey, I've seen the way he looks at you. It ain't the chapel he's after."

Her words startle me.

"If he started out with that goal in mind, somewhere along the line, it changed." She fidgets with her bracelet, totally oblivious to how her words zing my heart.

If only I could believe it was more than that. But I've been fooling myself. A guy like Marco could never fall for me that way. What was I thinking? I do live with my head in the clouds—always looking for the happy ever after.

Those things only happen to Disney characters.

"Thanks for bringing me to the park, Mom. I really needed this," Brooke says as we sit together on a bench.

Though I've been busy keeping up with work and avoiding Marco this week, it's been hard not to pester her, but I'm trying to respect her need for space.

"You're sure it's not too much for you?" She's doing much better, but we've still got a ways to go to see baby safely into his mother's arms.

"I was going stir-crazy in Jennifer's apartment. I had to get out into the fresh air."

"How are things going with Kevin?"

"Slow. I'm not ready for him to move back yet, and I'm not sure he's ready either. Now, don't get your hopes up, but he has agreed to counseling. We'll see what happens."

Despite her warning, hope rushes clear through me. I know it's too early to tell how things will go for them, but at least I know it's not over yet.

"It's hard to believe it's the last day of March already. Baby will be here before we know it," I say, realizing how quickly these few months will pass.

"I know."

"I'm so glad you're feeling better."

"Yeah, I still have to watch it, but at least I can get out for an hour or two a day. I just make sure I lie down and prop my feet once I get home." Brooke grows pensive, watching a goldfinch skittering about in a nearby birch tree. "Mom, I know I haven't treated you the greatest, but now that I'm about to become a mother, I'm starting to see things a little differently."

I start to comment, but decide it's better to listen.

"I was jealous of the relationship Colin had with you. Seemed you always favored him. The other night I was thinking about how I would feel if I had a child with asthma, and how I might respond if there were two children. I understand a little better."

"Being a parent isn't easy. I certainly didn't do everything right. All we can do is pray and do the best we can."

"Well, God and I aren't exactly on speaking terms." She picks at something on the weatherworn bench.

I think I've heard that line from someone else. My heart constricts. "It doesn't have to be that way, Brooke."

"It does for now. I'm not trying to be stubborn, Mom. I just need to work through some things on my own."

"I understand that. But hold steady. Don't do things you'll regret later. Give yourself time to heal."

"The best thing you can do for me is pray. I can't be all that you want me to be, Mom. Maybe I never will be. It has to be my decision. Can you understand that?" She isn't using a snotty tone, just a determined one.

I can't find the words to respond.

"In other words, I can't love God just because You do. I have to fall in love with Him myself."

I nod, but still don't trust myself to speak. Tears sting my eyes, but I hold them back for fear she will stop talking if she sees the hurt.

All my life I've been afraid to speak my mind for fear of offending others. But panic rushes through me, threatening to strangle the breath from my lungs. As the prophet Jeremiah said, "His word is in my heart like a fire, a fire shut up in my bones. I am weary of holding it in; indeed, I cannot." Sometimes we just have to speak. Speak the truth in love.

My hand reaches for hers. "No matter what, I will never stop praying for you, Brooke. Just remember this: it will take *your* prayer to make the difference for eternity."

"So what's going on with Colin these days?" she asks abruptly, the way she always does when the conversation gets too heavy. But that's okay. I've said what I felt I needed to say.

"He and Sophia are still determined to get married, but they've decided to wait until next summer. That will give her more time to plan the wedding of her dreams, and Colin can save some money for their future. It also makes Marco and me feel better, because they'll have time to think it through—though he's still not happy they want to marry before they finish school."

A family of five settles nearby at a picnic table, the children giggling, legs swinging with childhood energy.

"That's parents for you. I remember Dad going through the same thing over Kevin and me."

I chuckle. "Yeah, he did."

"So what about you and Marco?"

I shrug. "He called me last week, and I haven't returned his call yet."

"Why not?"

"He wants me to sell the chapel, and I'm not ready to do that." Saying nothing of the fact I love him and all he did was use me in hopes of getting my property.

"So tell him."

If I could face him, I would. "Yeah, I will."

"There's a reason you're putting it off, Mom. What is it?"

"Now who's being nosy?" I ask with a laugh.

She smiles. "You win." A hesitation. "Did I tell you we finally listed the house?"

"That's great," I say, disappointed that it's come to this. One look at her face, and I reach over and touch her hand. "I'm so sorry for what you're going through. But don't give up hope. You and Kevin may be able to start fresh one day."

A tear trails down her cheek. "I don't know. Sometimes I just want to move on. That's what I was doing, you know."

"What?"

"When I was staying with you those first few weeks. When I would go off for the day or night, I was at the house, reliving those moments, crying myself to sleep, trying to work through it all to the point I could say good-bye."

"I understand, honey."

She looks at me. "I believe you do understand, Mom." We hug, something that's getting easier all the time with her and my dad.

We talk a little while longer, and finally I pull up to Jennifer's apartment and drop Brooke off. "Tell Jennifer hello for me," I say as Brooke climbs out of the car.

"Will do. And Mom?"

"Yeah."

"Thanks for giving me my space. You've come a long way."

"I'm trying," I say with a smile and a wave.

Besides, I'm not about to jeopardize getting to spend time with my grandson . . .

Taking a long way home, I drive aimlessly down country roads lined with wildflowers and mossy tree trunks. Forgotten corncribs, weatherworn barns, and cabins dot the hilly landscape, along with redbuds and flowering dogwoods. There's nothing like Smoky Heights, Tennessee, this time of year. Trailing arbutus forms a leafy ground cover in open meadows, causing a carpet of delicate pink flowers to sway in the afternoon breeze.

Rolling down my window, I take a whiff of the sweet country air. How I need this. Maybe Roseanne is right. Maybe I should do something else. Dennis will always be a part of my heart. But once again, I see now that since his death I've somehow conjured up this "perfect marriage" image. By keeping the chapel going, I could keep him with me. The chapel was Dennis's ministry, not mine. Maybe it's time to move on—to let him go.

Marco wants the chapel, and I don't. Why keep it? Doing so would be out of spite, and that's not how I want to live. But what will I do? I have no other job—other than a few window treatments on the side. That's me. The decorated window. Carefully hiding my wounds, the real me, behind a decorative smile. I'm not even sure I know who I am. It's time I threw open the drapes and discovered just who's lurking beneath.

My decision comes to me right then. Once I've settled the matter in my heart, nothing can stop me. I turn the car around and head for home.

I have to leave in twenty minutes for my appointment. With a last-minute look in the mirror, I decide if I'm going to make a change in my life, it's now or never. Someone comes through the front door, and I step into the hallway to see who it is.

"Hi, Dad."

"Do you have that bag ready that you wanted me to take to Goodwill?" he asks.

"Yeah, I'll go get it for you."

"You need help?"

"No, thanks."

"Okay, I'll wait in the car."

Stepping into my closet, I grab the bag to take to Dad when I spot Dennis's shirt. I hesitate. My pulse hammers against my chest. Lifting the shirt carefully off the hanger, I embrace it once more, lingering in the scent, the memories.

But it's empty. Mere material. I swallow hard.

"I'll never forget you, Dennis." Tears crowd my eyes. "But I have to let you go."

Once more I hold it next to my face. Nubs from the worn cloth rub against my cheek. I'm not sure how long I stand there, holding the shirt. Finally, I fold it and gently place it in the bag with my other clothes. Hauling the bag to Dad's car, I wave as he drives away.

Seems I'm back where I started three years ago. Alone.

With no time to think about it, I head over to my attorney's office, thankful that they have Saturday hours. My schedule has been too hectic to get in otherwise. Nerves bunch in my stomach like black-eyed Susans as I climb the steps to the firm. The paperwork is ready. The price is more than fair, so I'm sure Marco will be quite pleased with how everything has turned out. He can go on his merry way, and I'll start over—again. The sooner I can move past this, the better.

Once inside Greg Winningham's office, pleasantries out of the way, he opens my file, pauses, and looks at me.

"You're sure this is what you want to do, Wendy?"

"I'm sure." The mahogany leather squeaks as I shift in my seat.

"The price is way too low. I'm sure you could get more." His swift fingers dance across a nearby calculator.

I shake my head. "It's not about the money, Greg. It's about moving on. If I put the place up for sale, it could take months to find another buyer. Might as well sell it while someone wants it."

He taps the pencil nervously against his hand. "I'm just saying you ought to think about it."

The receptionist's voice blares into the intercom. "Mr. Winningham, Mr. Amorini is here to see you."

Greg gives me one more chance. "You're sure?"

"I'm sure."

"Send him in, Patricia."

My heart kicks into Indianapolis 500 mode. I take a deep breath and brace myself for Marco's entrance. Since I haven't seen him in a while, I'm not sure how I'll feel when he steps into the room. His footsteps approach, and my stomach clenches. My pulse drums hard against my ears, drowning out the shuffling of feet and extra noises in the room.

"Mr. Amorini, I'm Greg Winningham. Nice to meet you. Please take a seat over there beside Wendy."

I dare a glance at Marco. He's dressed in a navy suit, complete with tie.

"Hi, Wendy."

Two words. Just "Hi, Wendy," and I want to melt into a puddle at his feet. Guess we're right back to where we started.

Compassionate eyes search mine. Or is it pity? Horror sears through me. Does he pity me? Does he take me for a fool that I'm letting my chapel go to him? *Stop it, Wendy. You know he's not like that.*

"You okay?"

I nod, afraid to speak.

Greg explains why we're here, and Marco starts reading the

paperwork, his eyes growing wide. "Wendy, your place is worth more than that."

I gulp. Funny that he would say that. I would think he would sign the contract and run.

"I know."

"Then why are you doing this? Why are you selling at a price lower than we both know you can get?"

"Why does everyone keep asking me that? Do you want the chapel or don't you?"

"I just don't know why you're doing this. You didn't seem at all interested in selling before."

"I've changed my mind."

His gaze probes clear to my soul. "Why?"

Greg clears his throat. "I'll just step out a moment—"

"No, don't do that," Marco says, snapping open the briefcase on his lap. "I have some paperwork of my own I'd like you to look over." He passes it to Greg. "You might scan it before I give it to Wendy, then the two of you can discuss it when I leave."

Oh, I should have known he'd draw up his own contract. He never trusts anyone. It hurts me that he thinks I would cheat him. But, hey, he's an attorney.

Greg scratches his chin, and I'm almost sure I see a twinkle light his eyes. His brows arch, and he hands the contract to me. "This is something you two obviously need some time to discuss. I have a matter to attend to. How about I come back in about twenty minutes?"

"Thanks," Marco says.

I can't figure out what all the nonverbal communication is about, so I glance down at the paperwork and see that Marco has drawn up a contract of his own. Only it's not for the chapel. It's for the lodge. He's offering to sell me the lodge at a ridiculously low price. A price that offers dignity but dips very little into my bank account.

I look up at him, confused.

He shrugs. "I didn't want you to think I was interested in you just to build my dream resort," he says. "Selling the lodge is the only way I know to show you that you mean more to me than any piece of property. The lodge is yours, Wendy. If you don't want it, I'll sell it to someone else." Looking at the closed door, he reaches for my hands. "I don't need the lodge. I need you."

I'm afraid to breathe.

"If you don't feel the same, tell me now, and I won't bother you again. You can have the lodge, and I'll go back to law. No questions asked. But before you answer, I want you to know that I love you. I have loved you since the day the rain caught us at Craggy Park, and we ran under the shelter, remember?"

I nod and smile. Joy begins to shimmer in my heart, but it's not a mirage. This is real. Can a heart hold this much happiness? Tears pool in my eyes and plop onto my cheeks. "I love you too, Marco."

We both stand and he pulls me tight against his chest, burying his face against my hair, planting tiny kisses all over my tingling scalp. My tears wet his shoulders as I lean into him, laughing and crying at the same time, when all at once it hits me.

"Wait," I say between sniffles. "What about all those women you take dancing—the ones who bake for you?"

He chuckles, and his eyes flash with amusement. "The moment of truth has come."

I brace myself.

"My neighbor and her friends. All edging seventy-five. Their husbands made some remark about them getting old, so those gals decided to take dance lessons. They heard somewhere that I knew a few steps and asked me to teach them. They pay me with baked goods."

We laugh together, and my heart melts at the thought of this gruff attorney taking the time from his busy schedule to do something so sweet for a group of seniors.

"Marco Amorini, you are not at all what I first thought." Though I did think his legs were great, but I don't think I'll mention that just yet.

His eyebrows lift. "Nor you, Ms. Hartline."

"How so?" I asked, surprised.

"When I saw how you whacked that garter in the cabin, I knew then and there I didn't want to cross you."

With a lift of my chin, I say, "I can hold my own, thank you," then I laugh.

"Indeed you can."

Another epiphany. I think I truly am coming into my skin. For I've learned it's okay to speak the truth in love. It's all in the motive for what I have to share with others. Am I forcing my opinion on them because I want them to be like me, or am I truly trying to help them in some way? Something to think about.

Marco looks into my eyes and cups my face in his strong hands. His lips brush over my cheeks, my nose, my eyelids, my mouth, and with all the passion of a man in love he kisses me with a depth and intensity that leaves us both breathless. When he pulls away, his eyes widen. "Wait here. I'll be right back."

Dazed from what's happening, I merely nod and watch him rush out the door. He returns seconds later with a bouquet of daisies in his hands. He clears his throat. "Look, this isn't exactly how I planned things, because I was afraid I had lost you forever.

But before you can change your mind—" He slips down on one knee, lifts the flowers to me, and says, "Wendy Hartline, will you marry me?"

Tears have washed my face clean. I blot my cheeks with a tissue and nod.

He looks me square in the eyes. "You're sure?"

"For better or for worse."

Marco releases a heart-stopping grin and pulls me into his arms once more. "We'll shop for your ring together," he whispers into my ear, cradling my head in his hand, brushing kisses along my jaw, my cheek, my temple.

In my dreamy state I manage to say, "I never imagined it could all end this way."

Marco pulls me back and looks at my face. When he sees my smile, he kisses my nose once more. "You know there's only one way this could end for you."

His words fall over me like a morning mist. "And what way is that?" I whisper.

He lifts my chin so that his gaze penetrates the soul of me. My breath holds perfectly still.

"Happily ever after, Wendy Hartline." He nuzzles into my hair. "Happily ever after."

acknowledgments

To my family who has loved me through the "For Better or For Worse" times of life, through book deadlines, chocolate binges, and brain lapses—when I slip away from conversations into my imaginary world.

Jeremy and Holly Hunt, whose beautiful wedding at the chapel sparked my imagination for this story.

Brainstorming buddies Kristin Billerbeck, Colleen Coble, and Denise Hunter for pushing me to write conflict no matter how much I kick and scream.

My amazing agent and friend, Karen Solem, aka Moses, who "stands in the gap" for me through every project.

To my dear friend and editor, Ami McConnell, whose gracious spirit and support never cease to amaze me. Also my new friend and editor, LB Norton, whose sharp eyes for needless words have whittled

acknowledgments

this book from the size of a twenty-five pound family Bible to its current format. My readers and I thank you!

To the creative Thomas Nelson team who breathe life into my stories: Allen Arnold, Lisa Young, Jennifer Deshler, Natalie Hanemann, Mark Ross, the copyeditors, and the sales reps. Thank you for allowing me to partner with you on this project!

To those of you who share your time to travel through these pages with me, I hope you find joy in the journey!

Can't wait till next time! Until then, God bless you all!

reading group guide

1. Wendy thought she was running the wedding chapel because it was what *she* wanted to do. She later realized she was merely attempting to keep her husband's ministry alive. Are you following God's plan for your life, or are you living out someone else's plan?

2. Control seemed to be a problem for everyone else, or so Wendy thought. After a time of reflection and prayer, she began to see it was her problem as well. Do you have someone or something that you are struggling to release control of? What can you do about that?

3. Marco and Wendy interfered with their kids' relationship and made things worse for a while. They realized that some people just have to make their own mistakes. Though it's hard to stand by and watch it happen, prayer, love, and support will go a long way in helping others work through their wrong decisions. Are you taking your concerns to God in prayer?

4. While Wendy struggled with control, she also struggled with "being controlled." She realized it was time to stand on her own two feet and face her problems—with God's help. Have you ever asked God to help you overcome problems in your personality; to help save you from yourself?

5. Sometimes when we see someone we love making bad choices, we say things we shouldn't or we keep silent when we need to say the hard thing. Wendy learned that the important thing to do is to check her motive. When you face difficult confrontations, do you pray for God's guidance?

6. Wendy knew if Marco didn't get his heart right with God, she had to let him go. Is there anyone in your life that you need to surrender to God's sovereignty? Have you ever walked away from someone who couldn't get his relationship with God in order? Was it the right decision?

7. Good advice from godly people can get us through the tough times, but there are those decisions that, with God's help, only we can make. Logan was a good man, and so was Marco. But only one could have Wendy's heart. Have you asked God to help you with a decision you're facing?

8. Wendy had a wonderful marriage—though not perfect—the first time around. She found it hard to find true love the second time around, though she did. She knew true love commanded a commitment that defied divorce papers and life's challenges. Are you struggling with your marriage? Are you actively trying to make it better?

9. When life gets hard, it's easy to retreat into ourselves and withdraw from others. At the beginning of the book, Wendy lived alone, but things soon changed and she found herself caring for an elderly father and troubled daughter. While reaching out to others presented many challenges, her life was richer for the journey. Are you reaching out?

10. Life can bring changes that only God can get us through. Are you facing a hard situation with no hope in sight? Philippians 4:13 says, "I can do everything through him who gives me strength." Will you let Him be your strength today?

11. Roseanne was a friend who stood by Wendy through the good and bad times of her life. Do you have a "Roseanne" in your life? Are *you* a Roseanne to someone else?

12. Some relationships don't blossom as easily as others. Wendy wanted a close relationship with her daughter, but there were walls between them. She was finally able to break through the walls, which began the healing between them. Do you need to heal from some relationships in your life?

13. Matt and Sophia were committed to each other, despite their parents' concerns. Do you think Wendy and Marco handled things the right way? Would you have handled it differently? If so, how?

14. Marco had been hurt and was afraid to trust again. He found that only by taking a risk could he ever know love again. Are

you holding back in a relationship for fear of being hurt? Is it time to reconsider?

15. Martin, Wendy's dad, was sixty-five, but he didn't let that stop him from living. He enjoyed life to the fullest. Do you thank God every day for all He gives? Do you live life fully as a gift back to Him? If not, why not start today?

Until next time, remember to love others "For Better or For Worse"—it just may make all the difference in your journey!

Life's A Journey
Midlife's An Adventure

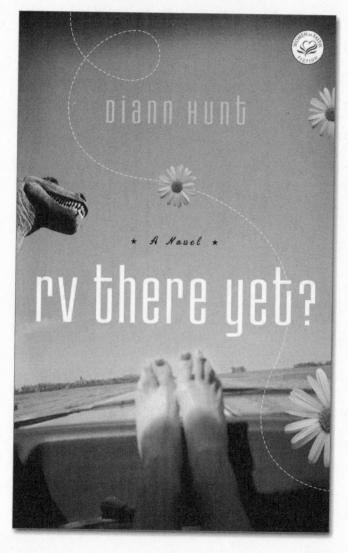

AVAILABLE AT BOOKSTORES EVERYWHERE

Same mom. Same dad.

Everything else . . . Different.

Who's to say which sister has it sweeter?

AVAILABLE AT BOOKSTORES EVERYWHERE